I0693983

MOONSTRUCK
BOOKS

Moonstruck Books
Portland, Oregon
moonstruck-books.com

ISBN (paperback) 979-8-9888154-3-3
ISBN (eBook) 979-8-9888154-8-8

Cover design and interior formatting by F.Z. Boda
Cover art by Nicholas Kahn
Interior illustration by Don Smith

"O horror, horror, horror!
Tongue nor heart cannot
conceive nor name thee!"

TABLE OF CONTENTS

A NOTE TO THE READER

Be aware that some of the stories included in this book contain graphic descriptions of violence, including sexual assault, animal death, child abduction, domestic abuse, and other potentially triggering subjects. If you need help living, coping with trauma or harm, or staying sober, these resources offer support at no cost. Please reach out for help.

Suicide and Crisis Lifeline

988

The Rape, Abuse & Incest National Network (RAINN)

1-800-656-HOPE

Adult Survivors of Child Abuse (ASCA)

415-937-1854

The Trevor Project

1-866-488-7386

Alcoholics Anonymous

aa-intergroup.org/get-help-now

introduction
f.z.boda

What is the worst dream you've ever had? Was it too real to be disbelieved on waking? Was it so bizarre that it shook you out of sleep, gasping for breath? Did your nightmare cling to you for hours, even days, after it mangled your precious sleep? Can you remember it now? Can you remember how it felt?

The word "nightmare" is a compound noun that alludes to its own pagan origins. A night-mare was a kind of succubus that visited after dark. Coined in the 1300s, this word describes "an evil spirit affecting men (or horses) in their sleep with a feeling of suffocation."

"Mare," a Middle English word for "woman," meant this night-ghast was female. The gender of the night-mare added a horrifying layer. In waking life, women were relegated to strict social roles that were defined by their relationship to men: mother, daughter, whore, lover, wife. But the night-mare could be voraciously sensual; her invasion of the sleeper's mind was an inversion of sexual dynamics. During the witching hour, a night-mare's power was such that she could slip into someone's bedroom and suffocate him, lying on his chest and face and penetrating his body and sleeping mind with terrible, perverse visions. In sleep, even the most morally upright church-goer was vulnerable to the night-mare.

Like the demon Lilith, the night-mare defied the "natural" ways of femininity embodied by Eve. The night-mare was greedy, she was wicked, she was insatiable, she was toxic. She climbed into bed to grasp and choke and wrest all she wanted from her sleeping prey. In our own time, women (especially transgender and gender non-conforming women, and even more so when they are also Black women or women of color) are still perceived as monstrous, powerful, and perverse; female desire of all types is still taboo. The idea of women taking what they want, when they want it, fuels patriarchy's nightmare; desire without consequence, in particular, is at the root of many of this oppressive system's fears.

With female desire being such a powerful cultural force, it's not surprising that the night-mare's influence was squashed over time, culturally and linguistically, through connotation and denotation. Early night-mares rode men and horses, the two domesticated pillars of agrarian society. Then, after a while, she victimized only men; horses can't testify against the women who excite them. Over the years, the night-mare evaporated altogether. Halfway through the 1600s, the meaning of her name waned and shifted from the corporeal spirit herself to her effect on the sleeper, describing the sense of breathlessness or gasping. Two centuries later, "nightmare" came to mean a bad dream or, as of 1831, a "very distressing experience." Lexical studies, such as Thomas Wright's 1884 glossary Anglo-Saxon and Old English Vocabularies says merely that the "night-mare tormented people in bed." What an understatement.

Ironically, the embodied evil of the night-mare was suffocated by time—choked out by industrialization, a process that caused Western culture to lose respect for the darkness and its inhabitants. How many magical traditions and beliefs were erased by the invention of the light switch? This was a nightmare of its own: technology fooled humans into believing they could control the night, with the power to illuminate and invade any darkness. The night-mare was banished to common use, diminished from a demon to a mere idiom. *Nightmare Diaries* attempts to resurrect her powers.

The stories in *Nightmare Diaries* deal with suffocation that manifests in many ways. Erin Brown's flash fiction "Salt of My Brother" and Kayli Scholz's story "The Intruder Theory" are both about the claustrophobia of sharing space with a familiar-looking abuser. Keith LaFountaine's story "Flu Season" is about the horror of being trapped with the outcome of an anti-vaxxer's decision. And many of the other superlative stories included here are about the unexpected twist in an all-too-ordinary life. Jeremy Horwich's story "Wrong Rabbit" shifts the perspective from victim to beast, while Kate Gorton's eerie piece "Daylight in the Swamp" tells about the terror and satisfaction of taking justice into your own hands. Claire Rudy Foster's ultra-violent story "Sophia" explores how male silence becomes tacit sanction in a culture of sexual violence.

Like the night-mare, these stories are not about women cowed by power. There is violation and then there is the rage, and the revenge that follows female fury. Many of these stories describe satisfaction taken with clawed hands, the certain feeling that *this motherfucker had it coming*. In "Forever" by Joey R. Poole, a bloodthirsty streetwalker gets an opportunity for revenge. "In The Pit of a Thousand Hags" describes the mayhem of releasing an ancient curse during a violent coup. From the buried baby discovered in a kitchen garden to the sickening curve in the road ahead, *Nightmare Diaries* is pure horror—gorgeously written, soaked in gore, and grinning with glinting teeth.

As luck would have it, the cover art for the anthology arrived like a night-mare herself, lovely and horrifying. When I first encountered Selesnick & Kahn's collaborative artwork, I felt the rusty tip of Cupid's arrow jab between my ribs. This was exactly what I was looking for.

Nicholas Kahn and Richard Selesnick have worked together since the early 1980s and specialize in fictitious histories set in the past or future. They are wildly inventive, using media of all types, textures, and proportions, including costume, sculpture, bread and fur, panoramic photographs, massive doodles, and more. Together, they created a tarot deck named "The Carnival at the End of the World," which included an interpretive guide titled *Madame Lulu's Book of Fate*. This deck captivated me at first glance. Beneath the mystical, dream-like images, this beautiful tarot deck addressed the real horrors of climate collapse, civil unrest, and unending pandemics. A bat-faced doctor in a hairy moleskin coat raised his pointed ears in a silent scream; a golem whose body is stacked from strata of city apartments staggered into claustrophobic life, animated by a storm.

Artist Nicholas Kahn painted the cover art for this anthology on goatskin vellum; he prefers to work in this medium, he told me, because vellum "closely mimics the texture of human skin." The central figure—an inverted, dreaming woman whose flame-golden hair reaches out like branched coral or lightning—is Goody Maude, a character in Keith Rosson's story, "Animals, Convincing." From the story's first paragraph:

WAKING FROM A DREAM IN WHICH SHE HUNG UPSIDE DOWN, HER HAIR TRACING STRANGE GLYPHS IN GRAVEYARD DIRT,

GOODY MAUDE PEERED OUT HER WINDOW TO SEE WITCHES, SOME HUNDRED OR MORE, FLOATING ABOUT THE AIR. IT WAS THIS WEEK PAST IT HAD HAPPENED, AND THEY HAD DANCED UPON BROOMS, SHE SAID, CAVORTING IN FORMED PATTERNS AND SPINNING ABOUT THE EYE OF THE MOON, FREE OF CLOTHING OR MODESTY BOTH. THEY HAD THEN LANDED IN JOHN BENTON'S PASTURES ALL IN A SINGLE LINE WITHOUT A SOUND BEING MADE AND BEGAN THEIR FORNICATIONS, PALE BODIES WRITHING ON THE LOAM, GOODY SAID, WITH THE DEVIL IN THE DISTANCE PRANCING ABOUT WITH A BOOK IN HIS HAND. UPON SUMMATION OF THEIR UNHOLY ACTS THE DEVIL HAD EACH OF THE BEWITCHED SIGN THEIR NAME IN THE BOOK, A THING WITH COVERS BOUND IN LEATHER RED AS BLOOD.

Kahn was drawn to this story in particular, and the imagery in Rosson's story is amplified by images from Kahn's own study of American witchcraft, the history of the Salem heresy trials, and the magical practices from that time. Broken crosses, berserk celebrants, and airborne witches appear in the background of the work. Goody Maude's hair, animated by her unconscious visions, traces burning sigils into the pasture she floats over.

Sensual and unsettling, with the vellum's texture still visible under Kahn's vivid, petite brushstrokes, this painting is the perfect representation of my vision for *Nightmare Diaries*. Every element of this diverse, freakish anthology is a tribute to the sickening feeling of a bad dream half-dissipated. Each of the stories honors the horror of the everyday, the discovery of the knotted worms writhing just below the skin.

Awakening from terrible visions into an unending darkness is its own kind of hell. Nightmares are not sanitized; they are unsafe. They want what we cannot or will not give. *Nightmare*

Diaries explores the fragile barrier between light and dark, safety and danger, the known and unknown, the monster and the mistress.

The no-fee open call for *Nightmare Diaries* garnered 3,641 submissions. Writers sent their best from around the world, including stories from the United States, Nigeria, Greece, China, Japan, Denmark, Canada, Australia, Wales, India, Iran, New Zealand, England, France, and more. The press also received a substantial number of stories from emerging or formerly unpublished authors; it's always an honor to be considered for someone's first publishing credit.

Finding stories that not only stand as independent pieces but also coalesce as a collection, with each story speaking to its neighbors (tonally, thematically, and in terms of craft) is a difficult task; my final selections were made based on a number of factors that should become apparent as you read them.

Editing this collection was a joy—and, I am not ashamed to admit, gave me the worst dreams of my life. Hopefully, you'll experience the same thrills I did when I encountered these stories, and stay up past your bedtime collecting nightmare fuel for the moment that your eyelids sag and you fall, unprotected, into sleep.

i don't think the medication is working

tiffany meuret

ONE: I WAS BORN THIS WAY

The awning of the patio casts boxy shadows across the yard where my mother waits, perched atop a very large rock. She fumbles with an egg, cracks it over a skillet, and begins to cook with nothing but the ambient heat of the wind. I remember grass, long-yellowed.

A grasshopper spark jumps the skillet and a fire consumes my mother with fantastic speed. She remains at her perch, ever fiddling with her silly little egg as flames lick the boulder, as I feel the heat on my skin, as I sprint inside this strange, dreamy house to find my father.

And I do find him with a bag in one hand, knocking and knocking on the structural column that supports the entire house. The column is coated in tacky pink stucco, and my father behaves like it is a door, and I'm begging him to come away, to help my mother, and he puts his hand down, smiles in the way he only does when he is embarrassed, but never sees me.

I return to the patio just in time to see the fire take my mother completely. My father appears at my side, transfixed. Neither of us move. Mother never makes a sound.

AND THEN

I remember a witch. At least, I call her a witch—the witch of an old west shanty town, her brown boots swinging in the wind where her body hangs limp from a noose, but she is not dead. It is my job to kill her. The adults have vanished, leaving me and one other faceless person behind to manage the task. Kill the witch before she kills us, I know this is the job, but the words blur on the pages of the book in my hands. The killing incantations are right in front of me but I can't read them, and this witch boils with a potent distillation of fury, and if I wasn't so frightened of her, I might let her go because I understand her rage. A sense of injustice passes fleetingly through my body before withering under the ferociousness of her hatred. She must die, I must kill her, this must end.

Panic stalls my progression. She claws at her ropes, she spits curses, she does what witches do, and I am outmatched. I can't win and I know it. My faceless companion knows it. I am certain we are both doomed until I remember my home, my bed, my little brother. I remember my mother, and I must get to them now, quickly, before this witch follows me. The book in my hands drops to dirt, pale dust clings to my shins. Wake up.

I close my eyes. Wake up.

Wake up—I ball my fists—WAKE UP WAKE—

AFTER THAT

I squish into a round capsule only big enough to fit one person. The countdown begins, ten to lift off, and the capsule launches into the heavens. The upward momentum rattles the metal walls, the floor, I can feel it in my teeth until it's abruptly over. Just like that. Seconds, not even a minute. The capsule doors slide open to a stark white elevator lobby, so white it makes me squint, where every measure of creature passes through, exiting here, entering there, switching elevators with the hurried pace of an airport terminal. *Ding*, going up! *Ding*, going down! Off-on, off-on, tall colorful monsters with their eyes in weird places, short insect things with limbs in weird places. Language dribbles from creature to creature, alien to alien. Nothing is sharp enough to break the surface.

Besides myself, only one other creature remains motionless—the lanky humanoid with delicate fingers and smooth, sleek features. No mouth, gray orbs for eyes, this humanoid stands still and nude and completely sexless, skin milky, almost pearlescent. Their orbs focus on me, beckon me toward them. They hold a clipboard in one hand and telepathically ask me to count to the thrix number. They speak like they work at the DMV, alien fingers tapping impatiently on the rim of the clipboard. The thrix number, please.

So, I count, one to five, then thrix replacing six. The alien, this creature, sags their shoulders as if I've annoyed them, perhaps there is paperwork to be filled out, and despite their placid demeanor I sense that they think I am extremely stupid. The door behind them swings open to reveal a lush garden, rows upon rows of manicured topiaries.

They wave me through. *Go on now, stop wasting my time, you dull human.* They do not say it aloud because they don't have to. The hustle and bustle of the elevators dies with the whoosh of the door slamming shut behind me.

Passing the threshold mutates my limbs into paws, gravity pushes my nose the grass, and I now sport a scruffy coat of fur. They've turned me into a dog, a dog! But there is no time to react because the farmer comes, and he stomps through the bushes with a shotgun in his hands. Here you are. Here you are, you goddamn dog.

He shoots without hesitation, and I sprint away, darting between the topiaries as buckshot dapples their intricate designs, leaves and sticks burrow into my fur in the wake of his unrelenting blasts. I am quick, but so is he, and he already knows the shortcuts.

At every corner he is there, shirtless in his overalls, straw hat glued to his bald scalp. I can't dart or weave quick enough; he is always ahead of me. Always. I run for a long time only just avoiding death by the dozens until I am just too tired to bother. He never stops, will never cease, and I have finally stopped caring. I can't take this kind of pressure forever. Living isn't worth the price, not anymore.

So, I bare myself to him, jump directly into his line of sight. He smirks and fires, the shot pummeling my chest, and I clutch at the wound with my hands because I am changing again, changing back. The fur on my fingers recedes to skin just as my body hits the ground and I wake up.

JUST

To fall asleep in a medical lab room. I share a bed with my mother. The room is dark, save for a dull light emanating from the space on the other side of the glass. I am safe here, safe from the green cloud of gas that presses against the divider, faceless because it is nothing more than a cloud, yet it watches me. I feel it watching me. My mother sleeps, snoring softly and I pull the covers over my head, but the cloud watches, trapped in the other room on the other side, it watches through the glass and I feel its attention on my skin like a swarm of ants. I can't sleep, can't sleep, and I want to sleep. I need to sleep.

But then I hear the hiss, a cartoonish sound of something slithering between too-small seams, this green gaseous thing pushing its wispy bulk between man-made cracks in the glass. I draw a face in the gas as it oozes above me, two pinprick eyes and a jack o' lantern smile, and I shake and shout at my mother to wake her, but she sleeps and sleeps and I have no choice but leave her and run, run, run before this entity oozes into and ossifies inside my body because I know, instinctively, like every girl knows, that this is all it wants.

I bolt, I'm outside, I'm running, kicking up dirt and papery leaves in the autumnal night, so cold in my pajamas and nothing else. Wishing my mother had woken in time to save me, hoping she is still whole now that I've left her behind.

I run like I've run in so many nightmares before and after, through the forest, in the night, through a dark house. I glimpse only traces of my attacker, who has the long limbs of many unknowable creatures briefly seen down long hallways. In the daylight far away, a man with a gun who smiles when he shoots. Sometimes, I run so fiercely my legs spin me into the air and I fly, sinking as my body succumbs to exhaustion.

I run and run and run until my heart stops completely.

TWO: AFTERSHOCKS OF *JAWS*

I am in the water which means there is a shark. This is an ironclad law. A bright sun hangs overhead, shining a spotlight on the undulating shadows beneath my stupid, land-faring body. I will the shark to appear because I fear it, because I would rather see it, rather it swallow me than spend another second steeped in this dread, and sometimes it does—I swim like a lobster escaping a boil but the shark is just behind me, mouth agape like a wreath of jagged death, and I awake in its belly to a town made of bones (sharks do not have bones) and I think to myself, "Well, fuck! I guess I live here now."

Sometimes, I breathe in the murky water. A rotting city surrounds me, composed of the same flat-roofed complexes that surround my real-life neighborhood. The shark, a great white (always a great white), erupts through the drowning walls of the city like a runaway locomotive (*Jaws III* and *IV*, look it up, baby). I am puny and I swim but this shark is massive, an absolute unit with knives for teeth and a voracious appetite for kids who refuse to let their legs dangle over the edge of the couch.

Once, I'm on a movie set, an Olympic-sized pool littered with fake, floating icebergs that bob like beach balls at the slightest touch. A crowd observes safely from behind glass. The shark is a machine, and it abides human instruction, but my mother wades out on the farthest buoy. This shark is dumb and slow, but my mother is slower because even a slow shark can outswim a human. I call for her to hurry, to *swim, Mom, please.* And she does, but casually. Very blasé, you know, this being a movie set. She does not see the flesh swinging from the machine shark's teeth, does not notice the audience beyond the glass, does not see the warp of our fishbowl. I command the shark to stop, and it obeys, but then so does my mother. She freezes as the shark does, and when I tell her to swim they both abide as instructed. Each interval of stopping and swimming shrinks as my panic mounts, and it becomes clear that I can't stop this shark from getting my mother—I can only pause the inevitable, and I'm not sure if it's worse to see my mother devoured, or to eternally freeze her in her final moment of terror. So, I beg her to swim, to try, for then she has a chance however slim, and of course she fails.

The set goes white, and all that remains of my mother are her orange flip-flops. Behind the glass, no one moves. No one says a thing. I am on the beach, so I am safe—WRONG! The biggest goddamn shark you've ever seen leaps out of the two-foot surf, bringing the ocean with it, and I drown while the shark watches.

Our ship has sunk and all I see are fins. This always happens, probably because I want it to. Teeth and black eyes flipped to white, slicing through a menacing blue just to end me. And I want them to. I do. What a dazzling sight.

THREE: THE BEST YEARS OF MY LIFE

It's the tried-and-true locker combination nightmare. A rite of passage, some might say. I'm almost forty and high school still stings, a pebble in my heel, probably because, even taking two different antidepressants, I am the most neurotic person I know. This is why my dreams revert to high school so often, where the lobby of my old school mutates with every entry (there's a cafe and a gift shop now!), where I am often an adult carrying the baggage of a teenager through the Escher-like halls that never seem to end where they should.

I know I am failing, I mean, I must obviously be failing, and the sweaty dread of failure soaks through my socks so that it's difficult to walk. Sometimes I come to my senses, realize I have a job and kids and who gives a shit if I drop out of school (just don't tell my mom), but most of the time I am still a small thing, terrified for the future. If I break through all these barriers and make it to class (Calculus, always Calculus because I, a seventeen-year-old English nerd, thought to myself, "Calculus? How hard can it be?"), I've inevitably arrived months late, missed a test, didn't study, and the weight of my neglect shames me right out of the room.

The high school nightmares often serve as a springboard into new dreams. They are as fluid and brief as their counterparts in reality, and sometimes I wander the halls collecting things—people, a child (who is sometimes my own), boxes of curious and unknowable items, criticisms. I heft them onto my lap, taking notes in the small spaces still allowed to me, and I think, "Everything will be so much better once I've grown up."

FOUR: LUST AND OTHER HONEY TRAPS

A single stripe of burning asphalt slits the desert's belly. The sun is beating but the air feels comfortable, as I and my lover await a white bus, which takes mere moments to arrive, and we squeeze each other's hands as if we know what it means. I am not sure why I am here or where this bus will take us, just that I must board if allowed. There is no question that we both must board this bus.

Climbing over the horizon in silence, the bus floats to a stop—no squeal of tires, no whine of aged hinges as the door folds into itself to welcome us. The faceless driver nods for me to come along now and not dawdle but raises a stern palm when my lover tries to follow.

"No, no," the driver says. "Only her. Only the girl."

Terror grips my stupid, silly bones; it knocks my teeth loose. I cannot leave without my other half. The pain of separation pulls on the individual bones of my ribcage like a powerful magnet and without hesitation I deboard, despite my lover's pleas to continue, that he will catch up to me further down the line, at the next stop perhaps, but please, please stay on the bus.

But I don't and I won't, and soon a soft plume of exhaust signals the bus's farewell, and we are alone on the side of an empty road. We are alone but together, despite the seed of unease blooming in the far reaches of my lizard brain as if I've missed something important, we are together, and I am content.

We are careless on this road, confident in our desolation and meandering hand in hand onto the blacktop, which is when the next oncoming vehicle torpedoes into my lover, appearing in a blink, then disappearing in my peripherals. My lover's mangled body lands in a nest of bones and blood. I cradle his cheeks in my palms and beg him to wake up, which is when the bus tumbles over the horizon once more, traveling in the same direction as before yet somehow behind us still (again?).

The driver folds open the door and tells my lover it is time to board, and he rises, uninjured, clothes shining a medicinal white, beaming, and he boards, and I am so grateful, so relieved, and I follow him. But this time, the driver raises his hand to me. "You've missed your chance." The driver speaks like the fine print I forgot to read. There is no argument. The realization of these cold facts ices me to the asphalt as my lover watches the door close between us, as he pins his face to the window, as the bus drives away again and leaves me in the desert, alone.

BUT AFTERWARD

The living room is lit only by the ambient light of the kitchen. I sit across from my lover in the tender dark. My lover's expression is blank, empty, as if he doesn't realize I am there. Another person walks into the room, and he glances toward them, but when I speak he says nothing back.

This new person, someone I've never met, plops into the empty chair beside him (my lover) and drips over the armchair. They whisper something I can't hear, and when I ask what was said, they ignore me. There is a devious sparkle in this strange person's eyes, a gleam that cuts through my good sense like soft cheese. I dislike them on sight, and I want to warn my lover, but he remains disinterested by my presence.

The strange visitor produces a metal stake, something my imagination might call a railroad tie, although it is too long and far too sharp to be of use for anything besides injury. I am yelling now, *just what the fuck is going on around here? What the fuck is going on?* And my love tilts his head, bird-like, as if I am an insect, an irritant, as if I am completely fucking up the vibe. His stare is his only acknowledgement of me so far, he must want me to see what he is about to do, so I watch while he snatches the stake and plunges it deep into the soft flesh of his own neck. The stranger is thrilled, this shit is an absolute knee-slapper, what a party trick! And black sludge cascades from the wound, splattering all over the floor, and my lover stares at me still, just stares, before turning to smile at the stranger.

I can't stand to see one more second of this, so I grab my purse and stomp for the front door, somehow expecting my lover to catch me by the wrist and pull me close, but he doesn't, he smiles at the stranger instead and runs his fingers through the long ropes of evil tar pouring out of his neck.

The grass outside is cool to the touch and I collapse there, remaining conscious long enough to see my lover bolt from the house and jump into the back seat of a convertible. He looks healthy, and I am so fucking pissed and heartsick that I might stab him myself the next time I see him.

How about this one: I'm married, and I've just bombed my Lincoln Log house building class. My new husband is so repulsed he leaves me all alone in New York City, fleeing from me on a Vespa driven by his father. That nightmare is my personal favorite.

FIVE: THE REST OF MY LIFE

I've forgotten to shop. I had one job, and it was to get punch for the party. One job and I did not do it. This grocery store is magnificent, wide enough to accommodate the bulk of my son's wheelchair, spacious as a theme park. My son loves aquariums, which, as luck would have it, happens to be the centerpiece of this building. So, I leave him there to marvel at the animals while I collect my few, paltry items (so simple—why did I wait?). So simple-simple-simple, until I return to the aquarium and my child is gone.

Immediately, I scream. I call his name over and over again, but sometimes my voice cracks and is too quiet to hear, not even the other patrons can hear me. I'm screaming for my child, and no one seems to care, but then I turn around, panicked, vision blurry with worry, and I spot my son. He is walking and in different clothes, and I spot him again holding the hand of a toddler, and again checking out groceries in line, and again and again and again, all these strangers are my son, my son is everyone, but not one of the people is him.

A mother knows. *I know.*

These strangers are not him but his face haunts me and I break into a run. I am running and screaming, my voice erupting like a gunshot, powerful, it echoes beyond the son-impersonators, beyond this fantastical, nightmarish store, toward the outside.

Empty. This outside is desolate and lined with the skeletal remains of civilization. There is no one, my voice bounces back to me empty and untouched. The name of my child whistles through abandoned scaffolding, though rotted drywall, until my motherly intuition feels a heartbeat ahead. My son. My child. He is here.

There is no one else as I career through debris toward him, as I rocket up a three-story staircase, as I bulldoze through a crumbling door into an empty apartment. There is nothing but a deep sense of mortal dread as I push through the living room and into a closet (a laundry room? A pantry?) and see the melt of the ceiling dripping onto the floor in front of me. A face populates my mind's eye, a memory I've forgotten about, a thing coming to eat me, doll-dull eyes and teeth, it could be a clown or a teddy bear, I really don't know. The walls ooze fleshy sludge, they weep with it, and I look up. Just out of reach rest pale, limp legs—the legs of my child. I find him just before he is ripped away into the dark.

ONLY TO DISCOVER

Some thugs are robbing my all-white house—why is everything white when I have toddlers?—but they are in the middle of taking everything when I stumble through the front door.

"Don't mind us, ma'am, we'll be out of here in no time," one thief says. Or I think this is what he says because his posture and behavior, even in the midst of stealing my shit, is surprisingly disarming. My tiny son squeezes my hand and asks about his trains.

We run through an all-white hallway to my son's all-white playroom and there stands one of these despicable men putting my son's toy trains into a burlap sack and *ohhhhh-honey* do I snap. My poor sweet son is sobbing. A switch flips in my brain and I go feral—I'm clutching the back of this man and whaling on his head. I am screaming and biting, assured in my rage and these motherfuckers will have to kill me to take my baby's trains.

The robber concedes to my fury. A toddler's snotty train toys aren't worth the frustration, I guess. My son and I clutch each other as the man backs out of the room. We slow our breathing against each other's chests while the strange men empty the rest of the house. But they do not take the trains.

Someone has hurt my child, who cries, bleeding, in the bathtub. I remember snatching a kitchen knife, and I remember the resistance of the assaulter's body as I plunged the blade between their ribcage over and over again.

My baby is still a baby. I hear noises over the video monitor, and when I look there is a static man, a shadow thing, reaching arms over the edge of the crib, long smoky fingers gripping my fidgety infant around the torso. I awake in the sitting position, screaming like the possessed—the only time in my life I've ever done so. My child is dead, but I search for him in a surging crowd despite the person next to me reminding me repeatedly that I will never find him. We are eating dinner while the bombs drop on top of us. I can never keep both of my children in my line of sight at the same time. I am a spinning top of dread.

The doors are never locked, the windows are always open, and there is always someone watching from the bushes outside.

FINALLY, SOMETIMES

My bed is a respite, the place my eyes close to the waking world. There is no excuse for my stupidity in the waking world, which is unfortunate because I tend to be very stupid. Or mean. Cruel. Cold. I've been called all these things, by others, by myself. I try to embrace the accusations, make sense of them, try to fold them into my psyche as if they belong, and some do—I am an animal after all—but then again some of them poke like a popcorn kernel in the gums, they irritate, stab the nerves at the slightest accidental brush.

Waking is an active clench that won't abate, and I am so tired. I'm so exhausted that opening my eyes puts me right back to sleep, where my kids are alone, and I am alone, and all I can do is scream.

I'm alone on a ship tossed by waves. There are cats everywhere, all bouncing like balls in a pinball machine against the walls. Water leaks through the hold while I reach for the nearest animal, clutching it to my breast and losing it again as the ship sways and jerks. Like herding cats, quite literally.

Even in a space bursting with cats, I can't manage to grasp even one of them for more than a few seconds. They wriggle and bite and scratch, and I just keep on trying, bruised and bleeding, until the entire ship and every breathing thing inside it sinks to the bottom of the ocean, our lungs ballooned with water, staring towards a watery sun we will never reach.

animals, convincing

keith rosson

Waking from a dream in which she hung upside down, her hair tracing strange glyphs in graveyard dirt, Goody Maude peered out her window to see witches, some hundred or more, floating about the air. It was this week past it had happened, and they had danced upon brooms, she said, cavorting in formed patterns and spinning about the eye of the moon, free of clothing or modesty both. They had then landed in John Benton's pastures all in a single line without a sound being made and began their fornications, pale bodies writhing on the loam, Goody said, with the Devil in the distance prancing about with a book in his hand.

Upon summation of their unholy acts the Devil had each of the bewitched sign their name in the book, a thing with covers bound in leather red as blood. When she tried to cry out from her window, Goody Maude said, a black cat leapt upon her chest and she found herself wordless, unable to breathe. Her husband snoring beside her, the fool sleeping through the whole gruesome affair.

Word spread of Goody Maude's vision, of course. Ours is a village full of wagging tongues, and witches had been cavorting in defiance of God in Mills County, Massachusetts for some time now. I heard Goody Maude's tale from Mary Hathorn as she called on us a few days back, and this morning I woke in the early hours to feed Eli, dawn only barely bluing the night sky beyond the trees, and saw that the baby had the witch's milk at his breast. Milk that came from his own teats, a portent of a pure dark. Sure as if the Devil himself had knocked and begged entrance.

Daily life has its cadence—prayer and fealties, chores and milking, breakfast upon the table for the girls and I. They are good girls, Betty and Martha, and at ten and twelve years seem primed for the Devil's attentions, which worries me so. For the thousandth time, I curse myself a fool, that I would so jeopardize their souls for my own foul desires. It's this weakness in me. For the thousandth time, I tell myself I will pray, petition, beg. That the Lord might be my salve.

I bring Jonathan his breakfast in the loft while the girls go about the rest of their chores. Jonathan has soiled himself in the night and I set about changing his underthings and the sheet, still with Goody Maude's story in my mind, as it has been since I heard it. Jonathan lays still and motionless. One might be able to drink from the indentation in his forehead, such is its depth.

Stop it, I tell myself. Stop it now.

After cleaning him, I feed him his breakfast. "We're blessed with syrup at this time, Jon," I coo, scooping the porridge into his mouth. Inane words that clang around the room uselessly. With each bite he lifts his head a bit, chews, and sets his head back down. Amenable enough, but doing nothing more. Blinking and breathing and chewing. The dent in his skull has long stopped being a troublesome sight to my eyes. He is my husband, after all, diminished as he is.

And I am his sinning wife. His witch-bringer.

"Mama," Betty cries from beneath us. "There's something wrong with the baby. There's milk—"

My eyes cut to Jonathan's. The doctor has said that there is nothing left of him in there, just a vessel waiting for the soul to return, but I don't believe it.

"Hush now," I call out. "All's well." "But—"

"Hush, I said."

The ceaselessness of daily life. Prayer, cleaning, washing and folding, Eli squalling throughout it, demanding. The girls wanting to speak about the witch's milk as we go about our work, but I cut them withering glances whenever they open their mouths. Shame and fear bringing bright coins of color upon my cheeks.

"I'm cold," Betty says, and I snap at her to bundle herself. Outside, snow begins to fall again, fresh snow upon the hard rime of ice we already have, and I throw an extra log in the stove as an apology to her. Eyeing the woodpile, knowing we are lucky to have even as much as we do.

Wash the floors, peel the turnips and potatoes. There is a break in the fencing that needs mending, and Eli must be nursed— he is still a baby, innocent enough even with the evidence of my own sinning heart put upon him—and so the morning moves past us, God's disappointment like a nattering in my ear, when there is a knock on the door.

It's Mary Hathorn once more, snow in her hair.

"Magistrate's called a town meeting," she says brightly. "Everyone must come." "Today?"

"Not only that, but now," Mary says. "We're to gather to discuss Goody Maude's witches."

I feel slow in my blood. "Witches?" I say stupidly.

Mary squints her eyes at me, good naturedly. "Beatrice, what's wrong with you? Were you sleeping?" Childless and widowed, the wealthiest woman in the village, she's long been allowed her eccentricities and forwardness.

I almost want to laugh. As if I might sleep, Mary. As if I might rest, with Jonathan made a half-wit upstairs, and my own sins and desires bedeviling me in my waking hours. Witches landing on the hard ground not two miles from here.

"We'll be there," I say. "What time?"

"Three hours and a half from now," she says.

"At the church?"

"Of course."

We'll be walking through the dark to the town village, then, the children and I. And through a darkness where any number of things might befall us. But to not appear at a witch-naming implies its own guilt.

"We'll see you there," I say, and Mary bids us goodbye.

I spend the rest of the day in a kind of haze, grateful for the distractions of endless work. The girls are quiet, hushed after I've snapped at them. I feed Jonathan his lunch and marvel again at what kind of man he is now. The light winnowed out of him. I roll him in bed to avoid the sores, and he gasps like a man twice his age. He's soiled himself again and hot tears slide down my cheeks as I clean the mess.

"I'm sorry," I whisper, as Jonathan's eyes rove the darkened room.

We put roasted potatoes in our pockets for warmth. I bundle Eli close to me and we set out the two miles to the village proper. No moonlight, but after a while the world becomes planed in simple white or black. Pale snow or dark night.

The girls are so strong, trudging beside me. Stronger than me when I was a child. Eli cries, this small writhing bundle. I cup his head, press it to my chest. Betty walks beside me and

I smile down at her. I look for Martha and can't find her. I look behind me; the road is dark, snow-lashed. I wheel about wildly on the path, my voice thin and small, swallowed by the woods. I see a flash of her dress behind the trunk of a tree, and I shriek her name, something in my throat threatening to rend loose. She steps from behind the tree, her eyes wide. She holds up a sprig of holly, the berries red in the gloom. I yank her arm forward, her eyes widening in surprise.

"You must stay on the path," I say, my voice harsh and unkind. I give her arm a shake, the fear wild in me. "You must, you understand?"

"Yes, Mama."

"You understand me?"

"Yes, Mama."

I imagine her wandering off the road, getting lost. It's easy enough. Imagine finding her gray and stiff, ice in her hair, eyes unseeing. I think of Goody Maude's witches, of a hooved man cavorting behind the tree line, calling out for her salaciously. All seems possible here in the winding dark.

Eli begins wailing and thrashing against me, and I bid the girls hold me tight while I stand there amid the howling wind and let him feed. Better that, I think, then his cries pricking the ears of all the unholy things out here.

We arrive late, full dark and storming now, and the meetinghouse is full of villagers. Thankfully the children and I slip in with few noting our tardiness. The booths and chairs are all occupied, ladies and older folks occupying them while the men and children stand. Eliza Corey offers me a chair, but I wave her off. The room is battened down against the storm and full of the bright light of the lamps. It would be a comforting sight, if not for the matter at hand.

The town has already sentenced a witch to hang. Last year, during the early freeze. Margaret Wuthers, recent widow of John Wuthers, had taken to weeping and wailing during services, beset by grief. Such a thing was somewhat to be expected, but it kept on, weeks and weeks of it. She could be seen walking around the village, tearing at her hair. Soon it was said—quietly, in the manner of such things—that she'd allowed the Devil to comfort her. Villagers claimed to have seen her outside her family plot, petitioning the cloven Prince for the unburying of her husband, that the dark one might bring him back to some semblance of unholy life.

Word, as it does, moved like water through the countryside, and eventually fell upon the ears of Sheriff Cheever, arm of the county law. When he questioned her about it, there was no denial. She had, in fact, been boastful.

"That I may," she'd been heard said, "end my grieving, I sought solace from the Prince. I did. I signed his dark book and he bid me a promise." She'd been hanged to death there in the bitter cold of Andover Hill, all of us relieved to have the darkness rooted out from us.

And yet, here we are. Goody Maude seeing witches in the night now, dreaming that she may hang upside down, her hair tracing graveyard dirt. In the darkness of winter, all of us stilled in our homes against the misery of the weather, evil chooses to play and cavort about.

Cheever is up there now, at the front of the room, before the roaring fire. Severe and striking in his linen shirt and breeches. Veins pulsing at the neck not hidden by his gray-threaded beard. He is a man of fair appearance, it's true. "And we do have cause, as you claim, Goody Maude, to be concerned. That witchcraft has returned to the township and county is of due note. It is a grave concern, believe me, not one I take lightly."

A man in the front row barks out, "This is what happens when those among us aren't duly petitioning the Lord," and is roundly met with boos and hisses of contempt. The man turns—Henry Proctor, hardly the most pious among us—and says, "It's true! I know a fair lot of you that can hardly be bothered to darken the pews once a week, much less twice."

We are less than pleased to be judged as such:

"A pox on you, Henry Proctor!"

"One to talk!"

"Proctor loves his beer first, the Lord second!"

The girls are titillated, eyes wide. They are rarely privy to adults talking like this. Eli lets out a squall and I hush him, rock him in his sling. Mary Hathorn, up near the front, turns and smiles at me, gives a little wave of her fingers. I nod.

"Mister Proctor has a point," Sheriff Cheever says. "It troubles me that attendance at our church has been infrequent of late. That so many of you feel that church days are ones that might better be spent at home, in torpor and laziness." His eyes rove about the room. They settle on mine and I cut my eyes to the floor, flushed.

"To be clear," he goes on, "there are interlopers in our midst. Even now, the Dark One watches and waits. Those of you who claim the Lord's fealty would do well to act as such."

"Exactly right," crows Henry Proctor.

"Now that we are gathered here," says the Sheriff, "is as good a time as not for Minister Osborn to lead us in a prayer, that we might lean closer to the Lord and beat the Devil back whence he came."

Osborn, pompous and brash, loathed by nearly all of the county for his contempt, his inability or unwillingness to aid us in our disputes, steps forth and takes Sheriff Cheever's place. I feel the room bristle toward him, and think, *No wonder dark* forces move in tandem against us. Our very minister makes us seethe like poison. Those seated grudgingly stand.

After the service—with Goody Maude commanding a crowd with the telling and retelling of her visions, her husband at her side—I am attempting to corral the girls when Mary Hathorn corners me near the doorway. The room is bright with conversation now that Osborn is done; much like with poor Mistress Wuthers, we seem as a whole excited at the notion of witchery.

"Hello, girls," says Mary. Our closest neighbor in the village, she frequently travels the mile between our homesteads for gossip and furtive cups of tea. She is, I suppose, my friend, and a kind one at that, given Jonathan's predicament and our financial restraints. Though I would no more tell her of my secrets than I would shout it in church. (To do one, I know, would be to essentially do the other, considering Mary and her loose tongue.)

"Hello, mistress," the girls said by rote.

"Goodness," Mary says to me, smiling, "it's quite the set of events, isn't it?"

"It certainly is," I manage.

"Will you be walking home? I have the carriage."

I think of the woods, the dark road. "Yes, thank you. That would be kind."

At night the wind howls about the house, blusters down the chimney, moans through chinks in the stonework. Candleflames tremble and throw our shadows dancing about the walls. The girls are good girls, pious and good-hearted. They clean their faces and get into their bedclothes after doing their chores and securing the animals. This pit of guilt sits inside me, even as my husband rattles and coughs upstairs. I know what it is I'm to do.

I soothe my husband's sores and feed him, give him sips of water, clean his soiled clothes. I pray with him. I see the dented cup of his skull reflected in the candle light. I bid him goodnight and retire to my own bed downstairs with Eli.

And then, hours later, with a wicked heart inside me both thrilled and sick with it all, I bundle up the baby. I cannot leave him in our home, after all. I open the door, which gives way with a creak; Martha stirs.

"Mama?"

"Hush," I say, "good dreams."

She settles, and I slip out into the night's bitter, howling wind.

The windows glow bejeweled. Against the night sky, a lighter thread of smoke climbs from the chimney. The barn nearby is a sturdy one; no stones fall from the dividing walls of this property, no fences are torn and leaning. An oasis, this place, a break in the unending storm of my life: Fealty, prayer, work, faith, subservience. For a moment, here, I might shuck these anchors from my body.

With a hand grown frozen as a rock, I raise it to the door. Eli looks up at me with the bluest of eyes. I tell myself I am not damning him further by bringing him with me—what else is there to do? Telling Martha to watch him throughout the night would be tantamount to a confession. In spite of everything, I am no fool.

I knock, and moments later, George Cheever—sheriff, widow, adulterer—opens the door to me. I am ushered in and spend some time laying Eli upon a pile of clothes that George has thoughtfully made into a kind of bassinet for the boy. My heart going endlessly. For months now we have met like this and the feelings—fear, lust, joy, a strident shame—still commingle within me.

"You made it safely," George says.

"Of course," I say, fussing with the child.

His hand on my shoulder. He turns me. I allow him to turn me. We kiss, this man who is not my husband.

Blood all through me, deafening. Loud enough at least to void the clamor of sin, enough to be enveloped by it. The world is firelight and this man's touch, his hands in my hair, our two griefs bound to each other. It is not love, what we have, but perhaps proximity. A willingness.

It is said that witches have bound themselves to the dark prince, that once they've done so, they live a life of faithless decadence.

I say let me live unbound, if only for a moment, from my small and constricted life. I say let the soul rejoice now, and hand me misery later.

This alone will damn me. I know it. Moor me forever to the fiery pits. And yet.

And yet I kiss George harder, pull him close.

Later, the fire is down to its embers and George puts another length of wood in the stove. We are past modesty, he and I, and I watch his ass as he crouches before the fire, his body a pale, lean thing against the brickwork. For this moment all of my fears are gone. My fatigue, my emptiness. It is simply this man and I in this home, the lashing wind outside, the snow. He pads back to bed and I feel the heat of his leg against mine. There is my son before us, flailing his arms and cooing. But for a twist of fate, I think, I might be this man's wife.

Yes, I think sourly, and the Lord might well bend down and pluck me a flower too. George sees my mouth twist, senses my distance.

"What is it?"

"Nothing," I say. "Thinking about things that matter not."

"No?" says George, turning towards me, a fey smile on his lips. Pressing himself against me. "What matters then?"

He buries himself in my neck, and I laugh, pushing him away. He takes my hand and playfully gnaws at my palm, then holds it, tracing the lines writ there. The blunt fingers, the callouses, the marks of toil. I put my head on George's shoulder, think of my poor frightened daughters should they wake in the night and find me gone. With only their poor, stunted father there for solace and company.

"Am I doomed?" I say, though to the Lord or George or even the night itself I cannot be sure.

"We're all doomed, Beatrice," George says, smiling. "Every last one of us."

"You seem unbothered by such."

"Not unbothered. Grateful."

"How so?"

"Death comes for us all, and the reckoning after. Until then, there is the body, and the body's glories."

I cannot help but smile. "You sound as if the Devil himself perches on your shoulder."

"It is no sin to love life, Beatrice."

"And what of me?"

"What of you?" says George.

"Do you love me?"

He leans back and smiles, hands cradling his head. "I love the notion of you."

"Bastardly," I say.

"I love our time together."

"Worse yet."

George's eyes rove the ceiling. "I love that you come here, clandestinely and in the dark of night. I love that you are not my wife, but still lay with me. I love that our eyes pass over each other throughout a day's work and none are the wiser. It's like a small treasure handed me."

"I believe your heart is as dark as mine, George Cheever." This earns me a smile.

"It may be so," he says.

We sleep, briefly, and as I drift off, I wonder if we are but animals without some guiding force—animals, convincing ourselves otherwise. That we do what we want, and come up with reasons for it later.

Back down the winding road then. The occasional home a hulking shape against the gloom, the white glow of snow against the trees. If I saw the Devil with his book, I would sign, I decide, and then scramble my mind to right itself, to petition God's mercy for a thought such as that one. I walk the dark, counting my blessings. My children, my home and health. That Jonathan is still, to some measure, alive. That his business affairs overseas are such that for now we are provided for. What else? Am I blessed with George's presence? With the acts that we commit? Is it not the gravest sin to call what we do a blessing? That I find some measure of solace in his arms? My wickedness seems boundless. I am tired.

A sound behind me, a snapping twig. I whirl—prepared to see a phalanx of witches with their whirling hair, aloft their brooms, breasts revealed to the cold, or the Prince himself, legs bent like a goat's, prick steaming in the night. But there is nothing there.

And still I feel eyes upon me.

I turn back, my feet seeking the road, and walk faster still.

Hours later, we're awoken to a loud banging upon the door. Eli begins howling immediately. I am sleep-numb, pulled from a dream, having only been asleep a few hours. The girls rise in their beds, eyes blinking, hair wild. The banging comes again and Jonathan moans up in the loft. Dawn's thin light in the room.

I gather my nightclothes about me and open the door. A pair of men stand before me, snow dusting their shoulders. A bluster of wind knifes through into the house like some errant spirit. Each man is bearded, bundled against the cold, scowling. I feel young Martha behind my leg.

"Yes?" I say.

"John Powell, mistress. This is Jacob Hatch. We're the magistrates of Mills County." "Goodness, I know you both, Mister Powell. What is it?"

He blushes. "We've been sent to gather you."

My hand rises to my throat. "Gather me?"

"You're to be under arrest and brought before the court, mistress. Posthaste."

I can't breathe. And yet, isn't there a part of me that has been waiting for this? "For what?" I manage.

Powell's eyes cut to Martha, and further behind me where I imagine Betty stands. Eli cries on and on.

"Best not to say with the children here," he says.

"Go ahead," I say, lifting my chin. "That they may know what foul thing their mother has been accused of."

Powell shifts his boots in the muddied snow at my doorstep and says, "You've been accused of adultery, mistress. That you've lain with a man not your husband."

He reaches for me, and in my surprise, I let him.

The cart clatters along. A rain falls upon us as we go through the village; John Powell tells me we're to travel to the courthouse in Salem for the hearing. A two, three-hour ride. My greatcoat is sodden; rain pools at my feet. My hair is a stringed curtain that I view the world behind. Shackles about my wrists and ankles, heavy rusted chains between them. Morning now, and those villagers about do certainly stare.

Hatch is sitting on the buckboard beside Powell, casting furtive, loathing glances at me. This utter contempt scrawled upon him. As if I were every woman that ever wronged him. I lift my chin and sneer, show these teeth.

He spits. "A dark-gutted devil, aren't you?" he says.

"I am that, and more," I say.

The Town House in Salem is a three-story affair, the largest building in the village. On the second floor, up the galley steps I am brought. Then to a courtroom and paraded before a judge, who appears as if he's just awakened himself. His wig is slightly askew and a dour countenance rests upon him, lines carved about his cheeks.

I'm stood before him, the rattle of my chains on the floor, and then I crane my head at the clatter of the opening courtroom door behind me, where George Cheever is brought in, himself in chains. He has been resistant to arrest, apparently, and a gash marks his face, a blackened eye that centers upon the judge with a fury.

"A baseless claim," thunders George, and a magistrate yanks him by the collar to seize him up. The judge pounds his gavel, and the door opens once again, and with yet a third court officer, Mary Hathorn is brought forth, wailing and forlorn.

There is much talk among the officers, of a nature I can't discern. The judge consults Powell and the other magistrates on matters of the law as I cast glances at George, who won't look at me. Mary Hathorn, meanwhile, beseeches me with her own glances, and it's her eyes I cannot meet. This dance of ours, the three of us. It pauses me to question, why is Mary here?

"And so it was," crows the magistrate beside George, "your Honor, that Mistress Bucke was seen to have lain with Mister Cheever and then in the darkened hours gone back to her own home so as not to awaken her family. She did this in the dark of night and with scandalous intent."

The judge casts his eyes upon me. "This is a statement of fact, Mistress Bucke?"

"It's not, your Honor," I manage.

"I seen her!" cries Mary. "I come to tell the Sheriff what I seen outside my own home, how I saw out the window a black cat dancing in the snow, and a devil jumping above it, and I ran there to the Sheriff's house, when I came upon those two in congress with one another through the window there."

Wearily, George says, "Shut up, you damned fool."

"Enough," the judge booms, pounding his gavel again. To Mary, he bids she go on.

"And I followed her down once she left the Sheriff's home, and it was her—Mistress Bucke, I mean—and she had her baby with her, and she went inside her own home once more."

This seems to cause the judge some shock, a pause—that I might bring Eli with me to a tryst such as that one, carnal in nature as it was.

The judge eyes a magistrate. "What says the woman's husband? Has he been informed?"

"We've been told he's infirm, your honor. A horse's kick to the head some while back."

"Very well." The judge is pensive, thoughtful. That harsh, planed face. The crooked wig. "So it is that for you, Mistress Bucke, given your adulterous nature, and a seductress courting a man not wed to you, you're hereby sentenced to be lashed behind the cart both here in Salem town and upon healing, again in your own village as well. Henceforth after that, you're to wear a mark. A red 'A' upon you, pinned to your clothing as long as you choose to reside in Mills County, to be worn both in public and private."

And so it is—to be bound by the hands and stripped to the waist, pulled along by a horse-drawn cart and paraded before my neighbors as I'm whipped raw. Not once but twice. And then the red letter put upon me.

The judge settles his gaze upon George. "And you, sir, have had relations with a woman not your wife. One wed in the eyes of the court and, more importantly, the Lord. Fornication is a sin in and of itself, Mr. Cheever. Do you understand?"

George dips his head to his breastbone and blubbers. Where is the foolhardy man I know? Casual and brimming with mirth? What has become of the man that loves the notion of me?

"Mr. Cheever, for the sin of fornication, you shall lose title and house, as both are paid to you by the county, and your stipend ended. Beyond that, the court sentences you to be whipped once in your own town square, and thus will close the ma—"

"Witchery!" George cries, cords leaping at his neck. He lurches forward, and the magistrate puts a calming hand at his elbow. "She is a devilment, your Honor! She bewitched me!"

The judge looks between us and then turns again to George. "Go on."

George licks his lips and shakes his arm free of the magistrate's grasp. He strides up to the judge's desk, eyes bright, his chains hobbling his walk into that like an old man.

"The bewitchment," he says, "lent me immobile. I found myself unable to move in my bed. All about me danced my possessions. Books open and shut themselves. Cutlery shivered in the air. My chimney bloomed with fire though no wood lay there." He cuts his eyes to me and there is no love there, no grand feeling save for a cold calculation. How poorly I have misjudged this man, and Mary Hathorn. How poorly I have misjudged everyone.

He says, "She lay upon me, your Judgeship, and performed her carnal ministrations upon me, a prone, defenseless man. 'Twas her powers that made it so, and when she finished her terrible work, a black cat fell down the chimney, flames and smoke bursting from its tail, and it slalomed about my house, laughing in the tongue of the Devil."

The judge sucks at his teeth. He asks me if it is so, what he has just heard.

"I am cursed," I say, "with dark and unlovely thoughts, your honor. But I am no more a witch than you."

"Exactly what a witch would say," says George.

Fury strides through me. "Would a witch know thy prick bent to the left, George? Would a witch know the wine stain that was put there at birth on your wretched, lying balls?"

"Enough!" booms the judge, pounding his gavel yet again. To John Powell at my arm: "Put her in the stocks, that the holy order might interview her for witchcraft. Let the Devil try and find her there."

And thus it was. A month in the stockade among the rats and the damp. I caught the cough while the bishops held up tongs and threatened to tear off my breasts to get at the witch's heart inside, demanding I recant. They threatened to throw Eli down a well, drowned for a witch's child, that I might recant. They told me Mary Hathorn was raising my children as her own, that I might recant. They told me Jonathan had improved and spoke now and disavowed me as a wife, that I might recant.

It was when they brought Betty and Martha before me, faces red and weeping, saying that it was better to have a mother disavowing the Devil and absolved in death than to have an un-repentant witch for a mother that I became lost. It was clearly prompted by the holy ones, this speech of theirs, but it was then I understood they would never let me go. Men such as George, who handle love with a looseness that never interferes with the saving of their own skin, would always win.

George, I learned, suffered not. Kept his silver badge and home and money. I heard told he was viewed as a man who had escaped the Devil's clutches.

While I, meanwhile, was hung from the gallows in Andover Hill on a rain-lashed October morning. All of the township, my neighbors and friends, brought forth to jeer at me and throw stones.

When asked if I had words before they opened the door beneath me, I laughed between tears. "If the Devil leaps in me," I said, "the Devil leaps about in all of us."

salt of my brother

erin brown

Can we talk?

Ignoring my brother's voice, I let my fingers drift across the bit of hallway wallpaper that isn't the same color as the rest. It's bright and new. Family portraits of Mom and me hang on the wall, unbalanced. Maybe I just got used to seeing my brother in them with us. I used to search these pictures, his smiling face, for some indication of mercy. I used to beg.

Please?

At school, at home, everyone seems so relieved and happy now, although they can't really pinpoint why. They sense something is gone; something horrible, brutal, bloodstaining.

But no one remembers my brother, since I bound him in salt. Not even Mom remembers him. I hate her less, now that I know why she never protected me from his cruelty. Or I think I know why. She's never said anything about the pictures he used to be in. She never pauses at that bright wallpaper spot. And she asks me to sweep up the stray salt every time she comes upstairs, but she never does it herself.

YOU CAN'T MAKE ME STAY HERE!

I walk home alone, free, not fleeing from anything, not hiding. I'm not limping. All my scabs and bruises have faded, and my hair is growing back. I don't throw up everything I eat, and haven't been poisoned lately. I sleep well these days; I don't shake all the time. I had no nightmares since I trapped him in the salt circle and the wallpaper door swung shut on his screams, his rage. I had peace for a while, but lately his voice—

I'M NOT GOING TO LET YOU IGNORE ME, YOU PIG! I WILL GET OUT!

—won't go away. For years he terrorized me into numbness, and now I'm free, but I'm also feeling again. Old wounds, old fear. I don't want it.

There's a handful of salt in my fist as I open the door that isn't there to the room that isn't there to see my brother, sitting in the middle of the dirty floor, eyes red-rimmed and deranged with fury. The salt border slinks along the walls, thick and white. I feel the healed bones he has broken in me, feel the teeth he's knocked out of me. I look down at the thick line of salt at my feet, making an impermanent but binding border across the entrance to the wallpaper doorway. I wonder if there's a banishing spell.

That would be a waste.

I'll make you a deal.

I look at the salt in my hand, and I smile as I drop some crystals into the sealing line. My brother curses at me, voice like sobs. I know how he feels. I flick salt at him and laugh. He's changing shapes, menacing, roaring. It's like a song. Flick. Flick. He thrashes. Howls.

I close the wallpaper door and he goes quiet. I'll be back tomorrow. I glance at the family pictures he's left unbalanced. I find no mercy.

mother's work

a.m. muffaz

The irises were budding when Elaine found the baby in the ground. It was the tail end of winter and the weather had just turned bright. The sky was a perfectly opaque blue. The wattles beyond Elaine's fence sat sugared with pollen; kingfishers laughed deep by the rushes, waiting where the water had just begun to fade. This close to a creek, wild creatures grew as thick as the grass. There were ravens throughout the woods, fighting with the magpies over neighboring plots. Sour fruit, green vegetables and the occasional sandwich through an open window were all fair game. Only the kingfishers managed to frighten both, yet even they only came when food could be found.

Elaine knelt between the irises and the orange tree, a stretch peppered with sheep pellets and black potting mix. A foot down, the soil looked like a drought, the coarse grains giving way to desert sand—a rusty, ruddy layer that ran deeper than the ocean as Elaine knew how to perceive it—right into the crust upon which the continent itself lay. It was salt and iron. It was salt on top as well, rushing in with every breeze. One day, there would be nothing left to grow except pillars of salt. Until then, gardeners would fight this climatic change, rail against a God, if they had one, for it was the way of men to make things grow.

Sand was water resistant. Mulch broke it. Manure fed it. Underneath, the tiny body curled into the soil like a sleeping seed.

The head came first, cracked where the shovel edged the earth. Old mud crusted its jaw as it lay, neck exposed to the sun. Then came a hand, its fingers curled around a rock. Elaine's fingers traced out the eight carpals, fragile as the bones of a chicken's wing. An arm bone jutted into the ground at an angle, so she pinched it out with two fingers and laid it alongside the other bones on her kneeling pad.

"You poor little thing," Elaine said, brushing dirt out of a small eye socket. "You should be out here in the light." Carefully feeling with the edge of her hand spade, she located other bones along the little girl's side. She knew in her heart it was a girl; she would call her Christine.

When Elaine had picked the ground clean of its treasure, she unwrapped the kerchief around her hair and covered the bones with that. The simple cotton blanket would do for now.

Picking up the kneeling pad covered in cloth, she gingerly carried it into the garage. First, she placed the baby in a basin with enough water to cover and gingerly poured out the mud that came off. It took her three successive rinses to remove all the clotted earth. For the last rinse, she added a squirt of dish detergent. Using hand towels, she began wiping each piece down until the nooks and crannies between each finger and toe were absolutely clean. As she worked, she sang children's nursery rhymes she remembered in bits and snatches:

"Kookaburra sits in the old gum tree... how I wonder what you are!"

Elaine grabbed the bottle of hydrogen peroxide from the first aid kit and poured the whole bottle into a clean basin of warm water. Christine quietly settled into the bottom, leaving threads of fine bubbles in her wake. Her little girl finally settled, Elaine fixed herself some toast and crashed.

• •

The baby and planting season both arrived sooner than Elaine could blink. By the time of the infant's ripening, all the beds were cleared and bare, but the drip irrigation still needed testing. Vegetable seeds saved from last year were busy poking out their first adult leaves in old egg cartons. Virtually all the flowers would return on their own come spring.

The large rectangular plot within sight of the kitchen window was a new bed, its mound dark from being freshly turned. She knew exactly what she wanted there: Lycoris radiata, the red spider lily. In Japanese mythology, *Lycoris* was also known as the corpse flower. When you saw someone you were destined to never meet again, these flowers would bloom along your path. Elaine knew that the perfect hole for establishing a healthy *Lycoris* would be lined with kitchen scraps, at least a shovel head's length down. Today's mulch-to-be was chicken bones, the remnant of a celebratory meal. (Roast chicken was difficult to get wrong. It was Greg's favorite before a long rotation.) The ravens and the magpies could dig, but the depth annoyed them, leaving whatever Elaine buried safe to ferment and put down roots without disturbance.

• •

It was noon when she woke up. She jumped out of bed, excited like a small child and quickly made for the garage. The water in Christine's soak lay still and cloudy. Elaine tipped the basin carefully, letting the water flow in a slow stream. When nearly all the water had been poured out, she got out the rubber gloves she used for cleaning, laid out a fresh tea towel and picked out each bone.

These she left to air dry on a counter while she made some tea and set about doing the day's laundry, including the small pile of browned towels she used from the night before. A little OxiClean and everything would be sparkling white again.

The garage was their laundry room and food pantry. Floor-to-ceiling shelves held dried beans and lentils in plastic buckets close to the ground, and gradually led to rows of glass jars further up. When the sun shone on the jars, the colors inside rivaled the noodle packets at the store. Orange marmalades, berry jams and yellow curd. Red marinara sauce, green pesto and peppers preserved in brine. From the rafters hung thick bunches of lavender, basil and mint. There was a shelf for leathering apples and sheltered boxes of potatoes, onions and pumpkins. All the best the garden offered, distilled, dried and pickled, were suspended in a state of still life, ready to weather them through any hardship.

While the washing machine ran, Elaine perused her sewing pattern books for nice infant dresses. There was some bright yellow fabric she had, with a pretty flocked pattern of flowers and butterflies. A simple cross-backed frock was what she needed. She might even have material left over for a matching hat and bloomers.

By the time she'd chalked out the pattern and cut it from her cloth, the laundry was done. She checked on the bones before carrying her clothes basket outside. They were still ever so slightly damp. She tickled one of the toe bones and cooed, "Soon, we'll get you nice and pretty."

Sounds of morning joined the creak of the rotary clothesline. Hens clucked from the chicken run on the other side of the house. Magpies sang their distracted, searching melodies. The ravens cried like angry, inhuman children protesting over a toy being taken away.

It would be the last load of laundry with Greg's clothes in a while. Already, she missed him. She knew every line of his body in every shirt, the way he moved and the way he carried himself when still. Could've saved at least a shirt to lay by her pillow, especially now that Christine was here. Surely, she thought, the baby would like her Daddy's smell nearby. Elaine rather regretted taking time for the laundry. She shook off her daydreams, hurrying because she longed to be close to Christine again.

The first thing she did once back indoors was remember to drink some water. Then, gathering up the bones in a dry tea towel, she carried the bundle into her sewing room and laid it on her workbench.

"Wait here a while, dear," she said. "I need to fetch some tools."

When they'd first bought their house, Elaine had wanted a room for her projects. Greg very sweetly wanted his own space as well, but also wanted to be near her while she worked. They'd decided to place their workspaces next to each other. While he originally suggested they add a connecting door between the rooms, at the time, she convinced him it was better to have privacy should he need it.

As a compromise, they'd built a closet between their rooms, which she offered up as extra storage for his tools. She never did open the closet herself before. Whenever she'd needed anything, she would ask Greg and he would get the item for her.

For a moment, remembering his presence overwhelmed her. The sight of his carefully stacked plastic bins and drawers, the way the light came on and shone on his tool belt hanging from a peg. The faint whiff of paint and turpentine raised the hairs on the back of her neck. It made her feel at once engulfed in a sacred space and caught in the middle of doing something naughty.

Elaine knew where her husband stored the case for his drill and bits. She dragged out the heavy case and shut the closet gently. Popping open the hard plastic shell, she attached the drill to the battery to test its charge. The head spun with a pleasant whirr. Selecting the smallest and thinnest bit, she carefully folded the case closed and set it neatly against the closet door.

When she returned to her sewing room, Elaine set about making holes in each bone, one on each end she needed to connect. The Christmas before, she had torn a necklace, so she'd ordered a spool of silver wire to re-strand it. Now she cut individual lengths of the thin but sturdy wire. She tested the first joint she put together—an elbow—and loved the way the fine lines of metal shone against beige bone. Her girl would be both functional and beautiful.

About halfway through, she needed to switch on the light in the room. This was all she remembered stopping for.

It was a raven's mocking laugh that broke her concentration. The bird's call was answered by its flock, a cacophony of wings outside her window.

"Hear that, Christine? That means the sun is going to bed." She turned over the little skeleton, tying the last knot into the back of the baby's knee. It was too late to work on the dress and she was getting hungry.

"Do you need to go to bed soon too?" she asked the bones. Wrapping Christine back in the tea towel, she carried her to the dining table and set her down on a chair. "Wait here a little bit. Mummy needs to get some food."

Elaine walked into the kitchen and opened the refrigerator. She didn't feel like a sandwich and was in no mood to fix something complex. So she poured herself some milk and drank it cold.

When she tucked Christine down beside her in bed, the small bundle felt blessedly cool to the touch. She couldn't stop nuzzling the small thing. Tomorrow, a dress for the baby.

••

Breakfast was toast with a bit of jam. Rather belatedly, she remembered yesterday's laundry. She swaddled Christine up and tied her to her back, put on her hat and trudged outside. The morning air felt good to be in, what little cool the day would have concentrated in those few hours. Overnight, the clothes had baked into stiff skins. They hung deathly still and forlorn on the line, not so much judging her housekeeping skills than taking an accusatory tone. Greg would be appalled if he knew. She was lucky he wasn't around to notice. By the time he returned, the clothes would have long been softened by folding, any unsightly lines ironed away.

Her most important task was Christine's dress. The cloth was cut, it just needed putting together on her sewing machine. A well-made set of clothes, sewn at home with all the love of its maker, was always the most beautiful garment a person could wear.

Elaine got everything ready by late afternoon. The *piece de resistance* had to be the matching frilly cap—as she predicted, she had enough leftover material. And Christine looked fabulous in her new outfit.

"You look so cute!" Elaine exclaimed, lifting her girl high in the air. "Daddy will be so pleased when he sees you."

Even though there was nothing she would have liked more than to take a breather, she knew she couldn't.

"Mummy's work is never done," she told Christine. "But now at least, you're dressed to impress. Now, we ought to get you a pram.

••

Spring planting was a hectic affair. Seedlings for fruiting plants went in first, taking the longest to grow. All the relatives of the nightshade family, reunited as children, went their separate ways to mature. Potatoes went into the bottom of their raised planter box. Tomatoes were set inside tall, cylindrical cages. Eggplants got their own patch, each broad-leafed seedling given its own stake. A raised bed of peppers and chillies would eventually fruit in a spectacular array of sharp colors and knobbly shapes.

The fruit trees were thinned and put out soft, cream buds. Each twig reminded Elaine of little paintbrushes, ready to open into the watercolor shades so beloved of eastern ink paintings.

The *Lycoris* arrived in the mail and Elaine carefully laid the bulbs in their bed. She spared no effort to give them a roaring start. She dug their bed six feet deep, richly improved the soil all the way to the top, and blanketed the spot in a thick layer of mulch. As a final precaution, she fenced the bed all around with chicken wire.

Christine accompanied her by riding on her back. Her little yellow hat protected her head, but also reassured Elaine when she reached back and brushed her fingers against its frill that the baby was safe.

She liked to take her gloves off to plant the wide, flat bowls of herbs. That way, after feathering down the soil around each plant, she could sniff the sweet basil, the refreshing mints and gentle fragrance of thyme. It was actually her favorite part of planting, setting freshly potted herbs to soak in the light. The aroma was soothing. Getting her fingers dirty reminded her that everything returned to the earth—rotted, decayed, even putrescent, everything could hope to become something better and more beautiful. Christine proved this every morning when she greeted Elaine with her wide staring eyes and every night when she lay beside her, a special creature that was all Elaine's own.

Elaine told Christine stories about how Mummy met Daddy, but each night the concept seemed more abstract.

When she told Christine that Daddy would one day come home, she sensed that this empty repetition was not a story for the baby. It was really to reassure herself.

• •

High summer drove the sun's merciless rays onto everything, sending up glare off the pavestones and turning the grass into sharp, dry blades. Only the toughest plants lived through an Australian summer, the kinds of plants that burned in bushfires and rose like phoenixes when the ashes settled.

These days, Elaine liked to bring out the pram onto their covered porch if she was in the backyard, just to keep Christine in her sights. Her girl's wardrobe now grew to include little frocks in pink, baby blue and apple green. Each was made from cloth she'd saved after making her own dresses, the more so she could look just like Mummy.

Elaine tried to broaden Christine's horizons by pointing out the myriad things one could find in their backyard. Snails under flower pots. A regal kingfisher on a tree branch. Laughing with the ravens.

Like her little girl, her garden was a testament to phoenixes. The beds, well fed and nurtured over the course of spring, were nourished all the way down into the roots.

Out sprouted mounds of daisies, their joyously pink and yellow heads resembling a child's drawing of the sun. Pots of salvias reached for the sky with their purple tongues and lobes. The orange tree was peppered with sweet white blossoms that bees loved and she came out to sniff every day. Beneath the far reaches of its canopy, the irises had worked hard all spring and summer to push out crumples of violet petals.

Today though, something was wrong. As she rounded the path to the vegetable patch, she saw that the earth had erupted into chaos. What was not tied down and staked looked like an animal had trampled and tossed them willy-nilly, making more than one test excavation. Kale and spinach lay on their sides, some totally upside down with leaves buried under loose hillocks of soil. All the salad greens, from the rockets to the pale green rosettes of lettuces, were outright munched down to nubs where they weren't yanked out. Ripening melons and pumpkins along with their trailing vines had also been eaten alive. Naked stems snaked out of broken embankments. The distinct cloven hoof-prints of wild hogs tracked over vegetable beds and made messy circles around the entire patch.

One place stood unmolested—the fenced bed of *Lycoris*. The small bulbs sprouted individual green stalks, each ending in a bud that spread into clusters of long red umbels. They faced the sun like bloody grasping hands. Seeing them gave Elaine a raw burst of strength.

First, she ran down to the front gate, which was shut and locked. Whatever came through hadn't come in civilly. As she ran back up to the house, she realized it was still possible she wasn't alone, so she grabbed the pitchfork from the garage. She crossed the property with her senses pricked, searching for the invaders.

At last, the only place left unaccounted for was Greg's field of oaks, and she went to it slowly. She reassured herself that her pace reflected an abundance of caution, not fear. It was a lie. The oak saplings kept their erect vigil, protecting nothing. Too young to produce acorns, too young to even survive without artificial watering, they were as helpless as Christine. From the edge of the trees, she could see the door to her husband's shed lay agape. Elaine padded softly between the row of oaks, pitchfork held with the head at waist level before her. The whipping shed was windowless, but she knew exactly where everything lay inside. The bench that sat perpendicular to the length of the shed. Sacks of fertilizer and soil, hunched over in silent repose along the wall. Spades and heavy hand tools hanging off hooks. Spare rolls of wire for the perimeter fence. On the far wall, all on its own, a cat o' nine tails on a peg.

She heard only her breathing—heavy—and the hard beating of her heart. Elaine lunged forward with the pitchfork through the open doorway. No reply. She peered in.

The sacks and tools were all there, nothing stolen. The cat o' nine tails was gone, not on the floor, not under the bench, not hidden in one of the sacks.

In a panic, she ran back out. It was then she noticed that the barbed wire fence running behind the shed seemed to be sagging. When she walked to the part of the fence that the shed blocked from view, it was clear someone had cut through each strand of wire on that section. Shoe prints going in and out were overlaid with layers of hog tracks. On a barb close to the ground, a bit of brown polyester fabric had ripped out of what she knew was a matching pants leg.

Boys would be pigs would be boys. Bastards, all of them.

Her afternoon was spent fixing the fence. Greg might have marched down to the school, gave their principal an earful. She wrapped extra barb wire around the entire back fence. Over the season, she would have to send for more.

Afterward, she took stock of the surviving crops. The tomatoes, peppers and eggplants were shielded under bird netting weighed down with stones. A determined soul or two had prodded the stones, got annoyed, and chosen easier targets. The potatoes thrived inside their vertical bed, growing fat as Elaine mounded the soil ever higher during their season. Her potted berry bushes were safe inside the enclosed porch, faithfully locked in each night. She would survive. They had enough supplies preserved to last them at least another year. The crops that lived would supplement her diet well enough as they ripened. There was always spare to put away for longer, replenishing their stores.

Elaine hugged Christine, whispering in her ear, "Mummy's work is never done."

• •

The turn into fall brought cause for celebration. The *Lycoris* was blooming. Elaine made Christine a brand new dress in bright red sateen, this time with a matching cap edged in black ribbon. As she arranged the cap on Christine's head, she said, "Look at you, all growing up. You're a proper little lady now."

She'd laid out a picnic blanket in the flower garden, overflowing with platters of fresh cut tomatoes, baked aubergine, and potato pie. At the center was a cloud of berry pavlova topped with powdered sugar. A pot of tea kept warm under a knitted tea cozy made to look like a strawberry. Elaine served tea from precious coral-colored china with gold edging—only two teacups and two saucers—the first time any of the set ever been taken out of their boxes.

Christine sat upright against a stack of pillows, her knees covered in a baby blanket. For her part, Elaine wore her best dress, a pink and white striped number in linen, edged in crocheted white lace. She paired this with pink ballet flats and her reddest lipstick, red as her thriving *Lycoris* plant. That morning, the first red petals had spread their wings, tipped with elegant, whiskery stamens that floated outwards in soft curls. The best time to appreciate the red spider lilies was by the light of sunset, when the world was set aglow with warm rays. And so, their picnic tableau was timed to take in that golden hour, which they intended to make full use of.

She poured out tea for the both of them, two sugars with a bit of cream, and cut herself a slice of pie. Although only twenty red spider lilies made up her flower bed this year, she reckoned in a few years, they would carpet their designated space. She would keep feeding them, season after season, with whatever meat she could find.

"The bulbs have plenty to eat, you see," she told Christine. "So they'll spread and spread, while Daddy sleeps until he's ready. And every summer, we'll watch them bloom together. Won't that be nice?"

Then she took a bite of flaky pastry, afterwards dabbing her mouth with a paper napkin that stained crimson from her lips.

fortunato, after

p.g. streeter

After revelry, after promises. After winding tunnels and insinuation. After chains and brick, perfect dark and utter stillness.

After all of this fails to end him, Fortunato takes a single step.

It is a small, stuttering thing; he allows himself no thoughts but of the cold stone against the calloused soles of his feet as he staggers forward like an infant learning to walk. He concentrates on his footfall, on the precise placement of feet on the musty floor, as his palms brace against the granite walls that line the narrow passage.

His second comes, hardly sturdier than the first, and he dares to lift his gaze, ever-so-slightly, forward. The narrow arch of light that lines the door ahead is like a hundred suns to the pinhole apertures of his eyes. He recoils, casts them downward, and sees the tattered skirts of his absurd costume. Sees knees caked in ancient dirt and saltpeter. Sees bleeding feet and remembers, unbeckoned, the curled points of his felt shoes catching on rock. Remembers clumsily kicking them off, feet scraping on knifelike stones. Remembers crawling.

A third step—and here he attains something like balance. He takes strength in the knowledge that now he walks, when so recently he could do nothing but slither—serpentlike, bestial.

Earlier, in darkness and despair, he found the passage—unknown, he suspects, even to his captor—a weakness in the rock foundation of the cell's rear wall. Gathering what strength he could, he crawled on his belly, squeezing through, tasting dirt and damp in the feeble suspiration he managed between hacking coughs. After some time, he collapsed entirely, certain he'd abandoned one tomb only to dig himself another—but then he saw it, a faint glow at the tunnel's end. This was the passage of his birth; life, not death, lay before him. So, he continued, ever forward. And now, already, he stands, a man on two feet. Already: three steps closer.

Four, now, and he considers lowering his hands, letting his legs take the full burden of his weight. *It is less than before*, he reflects, and he wonders how many days it's been since his lips tasted food or drink—tasted anything but acrid air. In the darkness of his cell, night and day were indistinct. Ages seemed to pass before that single torch gave its last, sputtering breath of flame—and after, ages more. In the absolute dark, the rectangular pattern of the brickwork before him remained burned into his retinae.

Five. His arms fall to his sides and the cold iron links that dangle from his wrists swing in pendular arcs before striking against hip and thigh. The chains hang, intact, from manacles that still chafe his wrists; no strength of man could have broken them. But, in the blackness of his prison, he felt the pins that held them to their brackets begin to give way. Minute by dogged minute, hour by hour, he threw the weight of his body forward—until he felt a sudden weightless pull and found his knees and elbows digging into layered dirt and crushed bone.

His sixth pace brings him nearly within arm's reach of the door. His eyes, by now adjusted to the pale light, fix straight ahead. He reaches into the folds of his tunic—into the pocket sewn into the piebald fabric of his carnival attire—and clasps at the weapon that might save him. It's there, still intact: a broken neck of glass, riven uncleanly from the flagon the other man had bade him consume mere moments before his betrayal. Fortunato could still hear the echoing of the carnival's revelry as he took that final swig. Was that to be his last taste of sweet grape and bitter tannin? For a time, he mourned that he had not savored it, that he had instead anticipated the superior drink that he believed would come.

A seventh step, and he pauses at the door. He grasps the bottleneck and vows silently that those final sips will indeed be his last. His tastes, it seems, have been irrevocably altered. He presses the tip of a finger to the point of jagged glass, where a welling pool of red liquid (the only tonic that will now give him heart) informs him that this blade will suffice. It will end Montresor's life.

No more steps. He extends his right hand to the door's latch as his left still grips the bottleneck. He pulls.

The open door reveals a cross-hatching of dusty wooden boards; the sight of it causes a ripple of laughter to course through him.

His laughter crescendos, and its accompanying thought courses through his veins, imbuing him with a preternatural strength of purpose. No matter about the boards: he kicks, and they shatter.

He strides, upon freshly bleeding soles, into the room—a servant's lodging, doubtless, in some forgotten corner of the palazzo. Pale moonlight streaks in through a lone window, a narrow crenellation in the chamber wall. Festival music echoes through the night, as if no time has passed.

The mad strength that flows through him now is more intoxicating than any wine that has met his lips. In this moment, consumed by this giddy rush of power, he experiences a revelation. *It is not enough to end him*, he decides, dropping the shard of glass. *I must become him.*

After all, it's carnival season, he thinks, and he unbuckles the belt that holds the tattered suit of motley to his skin. His tunic falls away as he rolls his shoulders back. It coils on the floor, and he stands, naked as a newborn, almost free.

Forward, he strides again, and his skin begins to slough off; it trails behind like the long sleeve of a serpent's molted husk. Gout-inflamed joints, arthritic bones, and rheumatic lungs melt away and dissipate into the air. He becomes a vapor, nitrous and thick. He will seep into Montresor's bones, he decides—will wear his skin like a fine suit. Buried deep within the brickwork of sinews and tendons, the architect of Fortunato's misfortune will be chained, helpless but to observe as his erstwhile captive lives the life that once was his.

Behind him, Fortunato's discarded skin forms a perfect circle on the stone floor. It is an autophage, an ouroboros—a corporeal sign of the single, echoing thought he has become:

A single injury deserves a thousand more.

goat's blood hymnal

josh hanson

> *HE IS LIFE'S LIBERATING FORCE.*
> *HE IS RELEASE OF LIMBS AND COMMUNION*
> *THROUGH DANCE.*
> —EURIPEDES

It's full dark on the midwestern plains, and the moon hangs like a silver fishhook just above the horizon. Row upon row of corn or wheat or barley stretch along the roadside, all standing dark and silvered in the moonlight, all hulking like a wall. Everything is still as a photograph. Not even a breeze shakes the corn or the wheat or the barley. The night is a long-held breath.

Hear the road rising. That beehive hum comes from that place where the road is gripped by the whitewall tires of a shining black 1951 Nash Statesman. It rockets through the night at a steady fifty miles-per-hour, a sleek, chromium-accented lozenge, and where it passes, the corn or the wheat or the barley waves gently on its stalk, as if in reverence.

It's too late for any signal on the radio, so Bromius "Big King" Little hums to himself as he lights a cigarette, drawing the blue smoke down and releasing it in twin plumes from his nostrils, where it is whipped out through his open window. His face is so black that it's blue in the reflected light of the road and the dim light of the dashboard, and his hair is long and straight, swept back in a massive pompadour that shines oily in the dark. His big eyes are dark and gentle, cow's eyes, but quicker, full of laughter and also rage.

He takes the cigarette between his thick fingers and taps a slow beat on the steering wheel, humming a low, church organ note. He smiles, and it's a cat's smile, all teeth and sneering mischief, one gold tooth showing near the back. He takes another pull from the cigarette and lets out the smoke with the lines of a song. It's a new song, but an old song, too. He's constructing it right there under that fishhook moon, but he's building it out of old, old materials. It's a traveling song. It's an *I'm coming home* song, even though home is a thousand miles and many years behind him. It's an *oh, baby, won't you please open up your door* song. And underneath all of that, down in the bedrock, it's a holy song, a song of worship, straight from the church doors, tripping bleary-eyed down the church steps, and kicking up rainwater through the gutters in its best Sunday shoes.

He'll call it the "Leaving St. Louis Blues," even though it's been a long time since he left that city, and it's hardly even a blues at this point, twisting as he shapes it into a tool to fit his hand, and as he rolls past the corn or the wheat or the barley, he sings, smoke rising from his open mouth like a volcano belching fire above some Pacific island.

I'm a lightning strike, baby.

Gonna hear the thunder 'fore I come.

Even as the words spill out through the open window and whip out across the plains, a bluewhite line sizzles across the horizon.

It's too far off to hear the thunder, but the thunder is there just the same.

A storm rolling in.

And your trouble's just begun.

The tail lights of the Nash Statesman glow like red embers through the midwestern plains. *And your trouble's just begun.*

• •

Deliah True rolled off of her bed to return the needle to the beginning of the record. She'd bought the 45 in its paper sleeve at Harvey's the week before, picking it almost at random. There was only a four color photo of an electric guitar leaning against a chair, and the name: Bromius "Big King" Little in big red letters. The A-side, printed in small black type read "Chuga-lugga" with a B-side reading "Sweet Wine and Honey" in even smaller type.

She'd spun "Chugga-Lugga" a few times. Liked it. It sounded just like the name suggested, a lurching blues with a striding piano, and the big growling voice of Big King Little chanting non-sense words and guttural noises. But "Sweet Wine and Honey" was something different. It was a slow groove, with almost imperceptible drums and a simple piano line. Little's voice was so smooth, slipping into falsetto and then dropping back down into his gruff baritone, but always soft, always pleading.

The song seemed to entrance Deliah. It made her feel warm, like she was soaking in a hot bath, and muddled, not quite able to concentrate. She'd already set aside her geometry homework, giving it up as a no-go, and for some time she'd just been lying on her bed, feet up on her pillow, staring at the ceiling, listening to Big King Little plead with her to come back, promising that he would treat her right, that he had a river of kisses for her, sweet as wine and honey. She felt herself drift, swooning in the heat of her close room.

The record ended again, only two and a half minutes of mysterious enchantment, and then the scratch and bump of the needle on the runout. She rolled once again from the bed, moving toward the record player where it sat beneath her window.

She re-set the needle at the beginning of the song, hearing the hiss and crackle and then the first chords of the piano.

Looking out her bedroom window, out through the branches of the locust tree, she saw the sky in the distance grown black. A solid wall of dark clouds approached from the east, and even as she watched, the wind was rising, shaking the branches of the tree, its leaves rattling, and the light gone yellow as a bruise.

Big King Little cried low, and Deliah True leaned on the window sill, watching as the storm approached.

• •

Deliah came down the stairs in a blur of speed, feeling the pull of the sky. Her mother was in the kitchen, preparing dinner.

"Where are you off to?" she said.

"Just running downtown," Deliah said, already at the front door.

"Dinner at six," Mother called as the door swung shut.

Deliah walked briskly down the sidewalk, the trees above beginning to whip back and forth in the wind. It was late afternoon, but the sky was already darkening with storm. She turned right at the corner, went up a block and turned again onto Main Street. Just three blocks of shops and restaurants made up Deliah's whole world. There was Harvey's, the five and dime where she bought her records and magazines. Two doors down, the theater.

She stopped, almost stumbling.

There, on the marquee, black letters against the orange glow of the backlit display:

BIG KING LITTLE

TONIGHT ONLY
8PM

How could it be? Here? She'd never even heard of Little before picking up the single, and now this?

"You going?"

Deliah startled and spun. Jacqui Thomas stood there, pulling the bubblegum from her teeth in a long pink string. Jacqui was Deliah's oldest friend, though over the last months, that had seemed to mean less and less. Jacqui spent most of her time with Billy Duncan, cruising downtown in his rust bucket truck. Still, Deliah was happy to have someone to share this development, if only to establish that the marquee's promise was real, that she wasn't imagining it.

"I had no idea," she said.

"Just went up today. Guess he's passing through. Simmons called around town, putting together a band. Apparently he travels alone, playing with local guys. Billy is playing drums, so I'll be there."

Deliah tried to imagine Arlo Simmons putting together a rock and roll band. The old man was deaf, hunched, with a neat white beard.

"Really? Billy?"

"Yeah. They've been practicing all afternoon." Jacqui pushed the gum back into her mouth.

"With Little?"

"Nope. Mystery man is expected soon. Isn't it wild?"

"Wild," Deliah said, turning back to the marquee.

"So?"

"What?"

"Are you coming?"

"Oh, God, yes. I'll be there."

"Good," Jacqui said. She smiled and turned on her heel, heading up the block.

Big King Little, in Thiva, Kansas. It was like a dream.

Deliah ran all the way home.

••

The storm keeps pace with the Nash Statesman all the way across the plains, all through the day. It is a sky of rumbling depths and sharp crashes of light, swirling winds and roiling clouds. Bromius Little guides the storm into Thiva like a shepherd leading his flock.

The sleek black car pulls to the curb before the theater, the lights from the marquee reflecting sharp off the lacquered hood.

He steps out into the street, swinging the door shut behind him, striding around the back of the car, running a comb through the slick hair at his temples. The town lies quiet, nearly sleeping.

He stops just beneath the marquee and breathes deep. He'll wake them up, the residents of this sleepy little corner of nowhere. He'll shake them out of their stupor.

He lights a cigarette with a silver lighter, lowers the sunglasses on his nose, looking into the dark of the theater's interior.

He drinks in that darkness. It's his natural habitat. In the dark, everything is possible, nothing is sure.

He'll welcome them into that darkness, into that world between the worlds. Some of these people will be transformed by it.

The rest will burn.

••

At dinner, Dad was reading the newspaper while Mom was trying to talk to him. This was a familiar display. Deliah couldn't complain about her father. He wasn't overly strict, didn't have much of a temper, and didn't talk to her like a child. But he never really seemed wholly present in any given space. He was like a shadow or a ghost. A kindly apparition. But Mom wanted him to be something more.

Deliah just ate her chicken and tried to find a way to slip into her mother's one-sided conversation. She needed to tell them about the concert. That was the plan: not to ask but to inform. *Mom and Dad, I'm going to a concert with Jacqui tonight.*

Simple.

Before she could say anything, the phone rang. Dad grumbled and snapped his paper. One thing he hated more than being forced to interact with people was being forced to speak on the phone. Mom pushed back her chair and went into the living room to answer.

Deliah heard her mother say hello and then questioning sounds stacked between long pauses. She thought maybe she could try getting her father's permission—no, she'd inform him. He was certain to ask fewer questions than her mother, and once Deliah obtained his consent, she'd be home free.

"There's a concert downtown tonight, and Jacqui and I were thinking of going." Not exactly a demand, but not a question either.

Her father looked over the top of his paper, his forehead wrinkled up.

"Concert?"

"Some singer passing through. I haven't seen much of Jacqui lately, so I thought it would be nice to go. For her."

"Hm," he said.

She was trying to decide if that 'hm' was enough to count as assent, when her mother hung up the phone and strode back into the kitchen.

"That was Mary Yeats. She's in a tizzy."

"Again," Dad said.

"Well, there's some singer in town, giving a show tonight. Race music. Mary says it's Devil music."

"Course she does," Dad says.

"I mean, Mary Yeats is high strung, but that doesn't mean she's wrong. I mean, all these people sing about is S-E-X."

"Mom, I can spell."

"It's just shameful, and it shows what the world is coming to. I can't imagine what a show like that would even be like." She looked off into the distance, and Deliah thought her mother was absolutely imagining what it would be like.

"They're meeting at 7:30 to counter it."

Her father lowered his paper.

"Mary Yeats going to *pro*-test?" Dad's smile was wicked.

"Yes, I suppose that's what you'd call it. And so am I. We don't need that kind of lewdness in our community."

"Ah, lewdness," he said, going back to his paper. "Pitchfork's in the shed."

Mom stood up and came around behind him, kissing him lightly on the top of his head.

"Aren't you just the funniest man that ever lived," she said, and then she was off, bounding up the stairs.

Deliah looked down at her plate. Her father folded his paper, slapping it down on the table.

"Well, Dee, I think that's your answer."

"But, Dad."

"You're not going to cross your mother's picket line, however ridiculous it may be."

Deliah stared at him across the table. He stared back. Deliah had never argued with her father about one single thing, and she wouldn't argue now.

There was nothing to fight about, anyway—she was going.

••

Deliah met Jacqui at the corner. They peered around the drug store's window display to see the little cluster of women walking in a tight circle under the theater marquee.

"How we going to get in?" Deliah said.

"I mean, I can walk right in. My mother's not parading around out front."

Jacqui marched up to the crowd of angry women. Mary Yeats was holding a placard that read "Save Our Children," and Jacqui moved right past her. She walked up to Deliah's mother and started talking to her. Her mother stepped out of the circle, and while it looked like the conversation was civil, it was certainly animated. Deliah's mother gestured wildly, apparently infected by Mary Yeats' hysteria.

Deliah walked down the sidewalk, eyes down, pace regular; as she approached the protestors, some of the women started to call to her, but she didn't look up, she just turned into the shadows of the theater entrance and pushed through the door.

The box office was a little phone booth-sized thing just inside the doors. Betty Goode, an ancient, shriveled woman, seemed to live inside that little box. Deliah bought two tickets and then darted aside, out of sight from the darkened windows. Soon, Jacqui pushed in, bringing the cries of hellfire with her.

"What did you tell them?"

"Told them we're going to hell, Dee."

She took Deliah by the elbow and they entered the theater. The interior was shockingly ornate for the dusty little town, all red velvet and gold painted scrollwork. The stage wasn't hardly big enough for a three-piece band, but the theater had a balcony and red curtain that was two stories high.

There were quite a few kids inside already, but the room wasn't even a quarter full. No doubt, Mary Yeats' little campaign would scare a lot of people away.

They dropped into seats in the second row and slouched down so that their knees pressed into the seats before them. Deliah watched the big red curtain, certain that when it parted, her life would be changed forever.

• •

Big King Little feels the familiar thrum, like thunder coming up through his feet. He checks his hair in the mirror, though half the white bulbs around the vanity are burnt out, casting irregular shadows on his face. The thrumming rises to a rumble. He flashes his reflection a smile, showing that gold tooth. There is a smell like roasting meat, and the lights flicker, the ground shaking. He slips on his coat, white satin with black velvet lapels.

It's time.

• •

When the curtains parted, the music was already playing, the trio of musicians all dressed in black. The drummer was almost invisible in the back, just beating out the one tempo, vamping. Jacqui pulled at Deliah's arm, pointing toward Billy, though there was no real way to know that it was actually him sitting behind the snares and toms. It could have been anyone. It was as if the boy they knew wasn't even there. He was just a piece of the music, a ripple in the sound, an extension of whatever febrile pulse was snaking its way through the theater, wrapping itself around Deliah's head, slipping into her mouth.

As showtime got closer, the audience pressed up toward the front—still seated, but straining forward, transfixed, waiting for the epiphanic moment when Big King Little would appear.

Yet it didn't come. The band vamped. The audience fidgeted. The music seeped into their bodies, shivering their skin and freezing their genitals. The chill took them into anxiety, then doubt. All at once, the idea that this set-up was all a fake, that Little wasn't there, seemed to ripple through the theater, unspoken but clear as can be, and people started to shout. They called out the singer's name. They demanded satisfaction. Some stood up, shaking fists toward the stage.

Deliah sank lower in her seat, feeling the eerie frisson of barely contained violence. One boy started to climb up onto the stage, and Deliah was certain that he was going to attack the band.

Then a spotlight came on with a deep "chock," and a blinding oblong appeared in the center of the stage, bright as the sun, dust and dander caught in its beam. The boy at the edge of the stage fell back, and the room hushed.

The band fell silent.

Bromius "Big King" Little stepped into the light.

There was a long hush, and then he stepped just out of the spotlight, pulling a big chromium microphone on a heavy stand into the center of the stage. Feedback shrieked, and the reverberations of the stand sliding across the stage rumbled through the speakers like distant thunder.

He set the mic upright and cupped his hands around it, putting his mouth up close to it and letting the spot catch the sheen of his eyes and the smooth black carapace of his hair.

"Good evening, children," he said, his voice low and breathy. "I'm so happy you took time out of your evening to join us here. To drag yourself away from all the petty cares and those things that you worship. Yeah, yeah, you heard me. Worship. We all worship every day. But tonight, we gonna worship a little—bit—different."

He raised his hands up above his head, crossed at the wrists.

"And this is how we do it," he said. Deliah heard horns, though there were no horns anywhere on the stage. The band hit on the beat, the guitar frailing away, high up on the neck. Big King Little dropped his hands. The theater lights went out.

••

They were destroying the place. She could barely hear the music over the roar of the audience ripping up the chairs and throwing them toward the stage. In a frenzy, some climbed over row after row of seats, flinging themselves against the edge of the stage. Only the aisle lights, set behind metal grills in the end-seats, offered any illumination. All Deliah could see were black shapes hurling through the darkness.

Despite the dimness, the band played hard. The sound of the music was omnipresent. Little wasn't even singing. The band was just lurching through a slow blues, no frills, just chugging away, while Little stalked the edge of the stage, waving his hands, egging the crowd on to further mayhem. A match's momentary flare lit the front row, and then a bundle of papers were afire, waved in the air like a torch, flaming scraps drifting down into the dark. The smell of smoke and sulfur pushed against Deliah's face.

Then, the back doors all opened at once, as if kicked off their hinges. Blinding light flashed through the theater and Deliah turned to see a lawman's shape silhouetted in the doorway. The band continued to play, but the audience members froze just as they were, with upholstered seats raised above their hands and burning paper in their fists.

"I hereby declare this gathering unlawful!" Chief Howard's voice boomed from the doorway. "Disperse at once!"

If the sheriff was here, it meant Gene was probably at the other doorway, hands shaking on the handle of his gun. Big King Little shrugged off this outside authority, walked back to center stage, circled around the microphone stand, and turned to the front again. He breathed into the mic, a low, smokey laugh.

"Y'all don't have any power here, sir. We're at our worship."

"And you're gonna be sleepin' in a cell tonight, son," Chief Howard called out, his voice going up toward the end of the sentence.

"Oh, my," Little breathed out. "Boys and girls, how about we show these men how we worship?"

The doors slammed shut, and Deliah just made out a cry of surprise from Chief Howard that was immediately swallowed up by the roar of the crowd. They screamed with one voice and in one movement their bodies, become one body, one hand, one fury, rushed toward the back of the theater. Under the thudding bass, they shook the whole building.

Deliah stood, looking back and forth between the faint shadow that was Big King Little and the deeper shadows, where there were screams of joy and pain and the thunder of feet. She felt Little's eyes on her, could sense him smiling in the darkness, and she knew she had to choose.

All those hours in her room—what else could she call that but worship? Playing "Sweet Wine and Honey" over and over again, letting it caress her. How many times she had lost herself in the rhythmic, soft velvet of Little's voice. She was a worshiper. A believer. A maenad in Big King Little's royal train.

She stepped out into the aisle and walked toward the sound of screams, into the pit where bodies slapped against each other. Hands out before her, she felt naked flesh, slick with sweat. Something smelled raw and earthy, and she knew it was blood. She pushed forward, pressing between the bodies, toward the center of the mass, and then her hands were slipping into a wet, warm mass that smelled like shit and iron. Slick ropes and puddles of gore seemed to suck at her and she pursued them, wanting to vanish further inside. When her hands came upon something solid, she grasped it and pulled it to her. The thing was dense and heavy. One part of her mind knew that it had hair.

She stood to her full height, lifting the thing high, and then the spotlight came on again. Its fierce glow illuminated dozens of dancers writhing to the now-silent music as Little stood over them, stark in the center of the stage. Both boys and girls were naked to the waist; the girl nearest Deliah had long scratches down her back, rough cuts that broke her skin. Faces and chests were marked with bloody handprints. Caressed or slapped, it was impossible to say. Deliah scanned the delirious pit for Jacqui—forgetting, then remembering that she was holding her hands up above her head.

She held her breath as she raised her eyes to the treasure she'd wrested from the audience. Both knowing and not knowing. The thing between her palms looked back at her. Looking down at her from between her hands was the head of Chief Howard—one eye socket empty, tongue swollen and lolling, an unholy fruit plucked by violence, lust, and song.

Little rumbled into the mic. "Oh, yeah. This is how we do it."

The band started up again, and this time, Little sang the lead. Deliah knew the tune, felt it in the deepest, most hidden parts of her body: "Sweet Wine and Honey." She swayed with the music, squeezing Chief Howard's head against her breast. Wrapped both arms around it. Her chin brushed against the ragged edge of the stump of his neck, where the head had been clawed from his body, and the blood, already gone sticky, smelled delicious.

As the rest of the crowd danced and writhed, climbing over one another in an orgiastic, sweaty embrace, fingers and nails in each other's ears and noses and cheeks and mouths, Deliah lifted the head and tipped it up, pressing her whole tongue into the tattered gore, sucking and swallowing, swooning as the syrupy blood ran down her throat.

••

It's full dark on the plains. The fishhook moon hangs still above the darkened fields. A black car rockets along the straight line of the highway, and in the driver's seat, Bromius "Big King" Little slaps the steering wheel to keep the beat, as he sings.

It's an old song.

A *baby, I'm leaving song.*

An *it's been so long song.*

A song of the gathering storm and the lightning strike, rumbling out from his smiling mouth, sweet as wine and honey.

sophia

claire rudy foster

McNab was the first of us to come into his money and quit work, and therefore in the best position to host our small reunion. He was a good host of the old school type and took pride in the house he owned upstate; its glassed-in porch faced the sea and gave a view of a half dozen islands, each trailing a spangle of lights, buoys, and fishing boat markers. When we came to visit at the end of that summer, we found him waiting at the end of the long, gravel driveway, smoking a pipe under a Maine apple tree. He was in his late 20s and the picture of early retirement. He wore an old college sweater with the school's name peeling loose, one letter at a time; his ankles were bare, and instead of shoes he had shoved his feet into a pair of battered tartan house slippers. He looked, we thought, as we turned in from the road, as though he was sitting by a fireplace, but there was no fire; there was only the tree, and the unruly box hedge, and the salt-stunted blue crab grass that bristled like a lobster's spiny antenna. McNab put his hands on his knees and pushed himself upright to greet us, raising a hand as though it had been years, not weeks, since we last crossed paths in the city.

Although we were all the same age, McNab was born old—an old man, with an old man's taste for comfort. We piled out of the car, carrying sleek polyester-sided bags packed with dry clean only garments for the weekend. McNab beckoned us into the massive, two story house that slouched like an emeritus after too many glasses of port, heavy with self-importance.

We knew the type. The five of us were friends at Groton and then, by some miracle, all matriculated to schools around Cambridge. Keith and Sutherland got stuck at Harvard, McNab finished a finance degree at Boston University, and Halston quit MIT after one semester and went to rehab instead. Constance, the richest one, had the car; he'd learned about jazz at Berklee and punk in the city and took great pleasure in subjecting us, his middlebrow friends, to his mixtapes on the long drive up to Maine.

The house was too big for McNab, but as we filed through its comfortable, clapboard rooms we saw how he matched its grandeur with his own, filling each room with conviviality and sound, even when he was alone. The house was solely for entertaining, he told us; he was going mad all by himself out here, and had taken to chasing the mail truck like a dog, desperate for something to chew on.

"You should get a retriever," Keith. "Even less trouble than girls."

"Smells," McNab said. "Tears up the yard."

"Like women don't?"

"Tulips," Sutherland intoned. "Cabbage patches."

"What do you really need them for, anyhow? Creature comforts?" Constance said.

"Everybody ought to have a maid," McNab quoted, and walked us up the stairs, whistling. He bounded down the hallway, pointing each of us to a room. The phone was on the second floor and there was a separate, locked office at the top of the stairs.

"You're keeping the best view to yourself," Sutherland said, jiggling the handle.

McNab laughed, a sharp bark that bounced off the ceiling and back into our ears. It was his private room, he said. You needed the skeleton key to get in or out, and he told them he'd gotten in the habit of locking himself in during the day, to work, when he needed to concentrate. We dawdled across the landing, unloading luggage onto the neatly made beds and changing out of our shiny city shoes.

"You'd better not be writing a novel, McNab," Constance said. "I'd have to publish it."

There were a few hours of daylight left, so we walked together toward the paltry beach along the narrow, gritty deer trail that led through the low shrubs and stunted balsam firs. As we got closer, the grass turned from soft pale leaves to hard rushes, dark blades that stabbed from the sliding, mica-flecked sand. A flowering quince clung to a handful of shriveled fruit, and on a whim, Sutherland snapped a twig from it and put it in his pocket with the white oak leaf he'd found, perfect as a mariner's map, in the middle of the path.

We were raised on estates in the valley or nearer town, knew how to fly fish, canoe, camp, pack, hike, and row, but in the city, nobody had time for that; there, we mixed with people who were ignorant of the tide tables and the magic of tying a trout lure. In the city, we forgot our summer selves and talked about the stock market instead. None of us would ever need money but we felt the pressure to do something with our lives, which usually meant earning a living. We had been unhappy boys but became exuberant men; we were drawn together by the rare bliss of having survived our familys' expectations, undergraduate anxiety, a culture that celebrated binge drinking, and the unique, miserable tanning process that every upper class white boy was subjected to: ears lowered, face scraped raw, extremities bound in sedate shades of wool, and shoved into a cold world populated primarily by other men, where the common language was rooted in competition.

But standing on McNab's beach, we contemplated the shallow, muddy inlet and the waves that slouched over its surface and wondered when we had forgotten the salt-rotten sweetness of decomposing plant life and fish and the animals that ate them, mixed together in an irresistible broth that we could nearly live on, when we were young. We put their hands in our pockets and faced the water, inhaling, and felt the city fall from us with each breath. The fishing was skunk, McNab said, but he'd gone out a few times and sculled when it was flat and if you went out toward the mouth of the cove, you could see mackerel fry in the warm water right before it dropped off into the dark Atlantic shelf.

The mackerel he was making for dinner, he said, was caught by someone with more time and talent than he had; and Sutherland teased him again about his novel.

"If I *was* writing a novel, I would write it about us," McNab said gamely. We knew he was telling the truth. We picked among the rocks, looking for mementos—a horseshoe, some sea glass, a stone. In minutes, we forgot that we were the well-educated elder sons of wealthy families. There was nothing for us but the beach. By the time the sun had receded over the western ridge, we were hungry; Keith had beat the rest of us in a rock-skipping contest and was elected to be our wine steward for the evening.

We crossed the lawn again, noting the apple tree. (Yes, it gave fruit. No, it was bad for eating. Yes, good for cider.) McNab laced on a massive white chef's apron and produced several bottles of white wine and a large parcel of groceries, which he dispatched with a long, sharp knife. Keith poured the first round and we sat in the kitchen while McNab fussed. We felt unbelievably grown up, with these glasses, this house, the sense of pleasure in taking our leisure together. McNab coated both sides of the mackerel in egg and bread crumbs and dipped it into a pan of bubbling butter. The kitchen filled with fragrant steam. Keith went around with the second bottle.

"I'm glad you aren't married, McNab," Halston said. "Wives fuss over everything. You're self-fussing."

"Auto-fuss," Constance said. We agreed that independence was more desirable than marriage and soon we were comparing near misses and narrow escapes from girls who'd hoped to bag us in the past. There was nothing worse, we agreed, than watching a date's eyes light up when she realized you were one of those Sutherlands.

"After that, you never go Dutch again," he complained.

"And you pull out and pray, too," Keith said. "That's how Allie almost got me. She said she was having a pregnancy scare and then was furious when I demanded a test. I caught her in my sock drawer with a pin, pricking holes in the condoms."

"That's got to be illegal."

Keith shrugged. "If I hadn't caught her, we'd be married now. She still writes to my mother and tells her how much she misses us all."

We contemplated the selfish wickedness of female people in silence, which was broken by McNab's announcement that the fish was ready. We trooped into the dining room, which was set with white linen and crystal, carefully polished for the occasion. McNab whipped off his apron and set the dishes out: a massive salad dotted with pickled radishes and blueberries, the perfectly crispy mackerel, homemade yeast rolls, roasted carrots sprinkled with balsamic vinegar, and steamed sweet peas with creme fraiche and honey.

"The last thing I ate was a drive-thru cheeseburger," Sutherland intoned as he loaded vegetables onto his plate.

"Two granola bars and a sugar-free Coke."

"Leftover lasagna."

"A handful of gummy bears and my morning cigarette," Constance said, and since we agreed that was the absolute worst, Constance was elected King of the Feast and given an extra helping of peas. We were no longer growing boys, but in each other's company, we reverted with pleasure to our younger selves and the customs that predated our entry into adulthood. Looking around the table, we noticed how the candle light smoothed each other's faces, erasing a decade of wear. Our cheeks pinkened from the wine and as we laughed together, dredging up old jokes and stories, we seemed to recede through the years, becoming underclassmen again. Outside, the weather picked up and by the time McNab pushed back his chair and brought in the tray of lemon bars, the panes were rattling in their frames and a persistent howl pressed against the roof as the sea wind blew across the mouth of the chimney.

Constance listened, head tilted. "That's a G sharp minor, I think," he said. "Is there coffee, McNab?"

"Or cocoa," he said. "And it's my house, so you can smoke at the table, you savage."

Storms were not uncommon in Maine in the late summer, but all the same, as we listened to the wind's fingers scrape over the roof and test the house for weatherproofness, forcing its way between the boards, under the shingles, and past the glass, we hoped it would not linger. Perhaps it was only a wind; but the first patter of rain, which hit the windows like a handful of gravel, was the sign of something more serious—a spoiled weekend, and although the atmosphere inside was still convivial and warm, we were all separately hoping that the squall would roll back out to sea overnight. After all, we could have stayed in the city if we wanted to be stuck indoors. The point of this trip was to be away from constraints, the forces and laws that confined us, as men, and squeezed us down and down into airless, dreadful cells where there was no sunlight, no air, no sea. Nothing we wanted to do was permitted in polite society, and when we indulged in the freedoms of our boyhoods, we were chastened by shrill voices who expected better of them. Here in the country, we could shed our neckties—those nooses we wore voluntarily, as though dragging a leash, demonstrating to anyone who wondered that yes, we were good boys, we were very good boys, the leash was snug, we could obey, we were trained and to be trusted. Away from the city, we shook off the duties that collared us and let ourselves be beasts again.

Halston pushed the wine away and rose from his chair. He knelt by the hearth and began to arrange a few pieces of wood on the iron rack in the fireplace. The wind whistled, and the newsprint under his hands stirred as he held his lighter to it. Within a moment, though, the kindling had caught and a vivid yellow flame was chewing its way through the paper-dry, curling bark on the logs. We drifted toward the bright, leaping fire and settled around it in various postures of repose. Constance lay on his back with a cigarette between his teeth and a saucer balanced on his chest.

"I might be desperate enough to hire a housekeeper," he said, and we groaned.

"Just get married," Keith said.

"Live-in help is cheaper," Halston said. "And you can get rid of them any time you want."

McNab's eyes scanned each languid figure before returning to the bowl of cognac in his lap. In the mellow light of the fire, he looked both ancient and younger than his real self; the golden glow erased the wrinkles that crept across his forehead and at the corners of his expressions. With his old-man clothes, he looked like the tintypes of our distant ancestors who slouched with their ankles crossed, gazing into nowhere. He was elsewhere in our midst and as he drifted we sensed the subtle change in him as a grain emulsified into a dark misshapen pearl.

"You've already got one," Constance intoned, catching on to the clues at last. "You dog. Where are you hiding her?"

McNab shrugged, embarrassed. He enjoyed playing the confirmed bachelor, always had, and the house by the sea and the deliberately old fashioned clothes and old-man ways were part of that. Girls came and went from his room in college, but only lingered long enough to collect their panties and slip their shoes on. None lasted. These girls said McNab was a brute, which made no sense, because having met him, nobody could take him seriously. And there was no proof, aside from anxious rumors, whispers. Girls departed—not a mark on them, no screams, just the usual rumpling of bedspreads and the sock on the door as a formality to unexpected visitors. If no girl stuck around, that meant women simply didn't appreciate McNab's finer points. Show us a nineteen-year-old girl who can appreciate aged brandy and hand-rolled imported Turkish tobacco; a girl who reads Joyce unironically and loves madrigal singing and movies with sleek Italian cars in them. *We* weren't in love with McNab—not even dear Constance, who treated Fleet Week like homosexual yuletide—but we loved our friend. He was no brute. His arms and back were thick from chopping wood and lugging wheelbarrow loads of stone up from the beach but we could more easily imagine him wrestling a bear than raising his hand to a girl, even one who might have deserved it.

It *would* be a bear, not a girl, who might be charmed by this place, which was beautiful but barren the way that coastal Maine is, with its delicate tones of gray and the ripe silence that surrounded the house. We knew from experience that girls preferred chatter, music, and dramatic fights, and this place sucked the sound out of everything but the fire that drew us closer than we have been in years. Even the sea birds' cries were muffled and the wind against the house was a fine wool batting. You could scream and scream here and be heard by no one.

"She's alright," McNab said stolidly. "She does well with some hard limits. Our arrangement isn't exactly romantic."

"Who is it? Local fishing?"

"Just old Sophia," he told us, and we growled in approval. Sophia was at school with us and inexplicably took an art degree at MIT. Halston remembered her. They'd shared a dorm before he dropped out to kick the cocaine habit that was incinerating his trust fund. There were stories about Sophia there; her reputation from Groton held steady, which suggested there was plenty of truth to it. To our knowledge, she wasn't among the girls who flitted through McNab's cave, but we couldn't watch at all times, and McNab was notoriously tight-lipped, another fuddy-duddy habit that we teased him for. McNab, our clam. He insisted that a gentleman never told, which only stoked our curiosity.

Sophia, however, was no gentleman. Her exploits were well-known and frequently discussed as a group and—if we were honest—in the privacy of our beds as well. Sophia, with her hazel eyes and buzzed head, terrified us. She wore tight clothes and drew macabre figures on her arms with permanent markers. She was a freak, people said. Sexually voracious. She was fearless and indiscreet. We wondered what was under her stretch-leather skirt. Tentacles? A wolf's hairy britches? A sea-slick animal with horrendous fangs? We saw no reason for her to be interested in McNab, but we also understood that she was what was known as polymorphously perverse. An anemone in isolation will clone itself out of boredom, just to have a globular partner to fuck. Sophia must be bored to select McNab, we thought. Or maybe she knew something that we didn't.

"Slut-hunting?" Sutherland teased. "I don't suppose she put up much of a fight."

McNab smiled. "Not much."

We considered the implications of this: Sophia, stepping across the dewy grass in her high heeled Mary Janes toward McNab. We imagined the two of them in the house, miles of nothing but farmland and coast in any direction. Although Sophia terrified us—her sexuality as cold and coiling as a serpent—we wondered how it would be to have her on our terms, our turf. Without other women watching or the strictures of feminism, we could do plenty of things to Sophia—things she wanted and things she didn't, but then it wouldn't be up to her, for once. We considered Sophia, with her sassy laugh and ever-present, unrestrained breasts—we could see the imprints of her nipples through her shirt and we could see halfway down her neck when she laughed at us—and we couldn't help but imagine our hands around her slender throat or tearing open her thighs and squeezing that laugh out of her, making her scream with the parts of our body she mocked and our tender boy-bodies that were disobedient and unmanly in her eyes. We could be dangerous too, when we chose, and who would believe her anyway, a slut like Sophia. She asked for it with her eyes, her miniskirt. She was the kind of girl who belongs in a trunk for a long drive to the middle of nowhere, because after all, if a girl is alone with you in the woods and nobody hears her, did you really do anything wrong?

"Watch out for that one," was all Keith said, the clear-eyed wife-seeker. We lolled, mentally fingering the holes in Sophia's fishnets.

"How're you going to keep this one around," Constance teased.

"I don't think she has much of a choice," McNab said.

The fire burned low in the grate and the coals blackened at the edges. We breathed up the air in the room and all got tired at the same time. It was hard to believe we'd been in the city only that morning; less than three hours away, Cambridge stretched its grassy arms out, gathering in the white colonial facades that sprawled across the commons toward the Charles River. We were smart in Boston, snappy. Young. Promising. Yet, the sweet gravity of Maine softened us. We forgot what we'd said, exactly, and only remembered that we'd spoken. It was good to eat and talk without worrying, for once, who was listening. We cherished this temporary freedom, which we realized for the first time was a type of luxury, too, like this house and these friends and this time away. We had lapped up McNab's cooking and his booze and we limped up the stairs like puppies tired from play, each to our own bed and plump, inviting pillow.

For the first hour, we slept soundly. The hungry wind had found something to chew on and stroked the apple tree's branches, sated. The rain softened to a constant thrum that reminded Constance of typewriters and Sutherland of distant traffic. City creatures, even natural sounds rasped mechanically against our ears.

Even so, the metallic grinding was loud enough to wake Keith. He rolled over, snarling the quilt around his legs. It must be the septic tank or the boiler, he thought. But as he lay in the dark, the irregularity in the sound tugged his ear. No machine moved this way, even a broken one.

He wrapped himself in the sheet and edged off the mattress. His feet were cold. The strange sound led him to the door and as he started across the sand-smooth floorboards hallway he caught the distinct tones in it. Metal on metal, metal on something soft and alive. It was the languid, arrhythmic clanking of chains. He came to the door of McNab's private room and brought his ear close to the wood of it and listened, certain that whatever was inside could not hear him, mere inches away with his breath held. He ducked his head and a bead of sweat darted down his temple and into his ear. Coldness and salt. He put his hand on the door knob and it turned against his palm and before he could stop himself he flicked the handle and swung the door open in the darkness. The window, open to the pulsing night. A cadaverine musk. He could see part of a garment hung from the foot of a narrow bed. Floor covered in wadded towels and a crumpled camping tarp. A second mattress against the wall, innards spilling from its stained cover. He stumbled and stepped forward and flipped on the light.

At first it was only a form, not even a body, because how could a body be in such disorder. Ruckled against the back wall and folded on itself was a naked female thing, bent in half and chained ankles to wrists and neck to knees, ass up on the bed and both holes leaking a dark fluid that seeped into the bed in a trail of stains that slithered past the gagged mouth. Wide open, horribly white eyes. She was not trying to hide or shield her face but pleading with Keith to see her and know her name, remember who she was. Ugly shapes in black ink were scrawled across her and red blisters raised in patterns meant to be words, some blasted open with infection and others pressing against their crust of wax as though there was some other escape. The gag was coated in slobber and her face was half sealed by a rind of spunk and tears. On the bare bed, she lay with her legs split open and the stump of her body defaced and burnt. The smell was vomitous. As Keith looked at her she made the smallest mew, like a kitten that has been stamped on.

"Sophia," he whispered.

Her eyes focused on him one at a time, left then right they turned on him and found his face and blinked pitifully.

"Help," she mewed. "Please help me."

If she had said his name he could not have borne it because it would have made them equals, both too human, and he could not accept that in the stronghold of McNab's house, their chosen bastion of culture and old-boy tradition, something like this was possible. He extinguished the light, wrapped the sheet tighter around his shoulders, and edged out of the room with Sophia's eyes clamped onto him.

He closed the door and it was quiet again, the night as pure as milk. He heard a distant rattle—the glass bottles jostling one another in the refrigerator door as it closed—and spirited himself back into his bed in an instant. He rolled his face on the pillow and found he was crying icy tears that soaked the goose down and crisp linens. He squeezed his eyes shut and squinted through the wavering film, willing his pulse to slow and his breath to slacken into the rhythms of sleep.

Before Keith could drift off into sleep and forget, McNab came up the steps with an object in his hand. He was still wearing his college sweater and old slippers. He paused on the landing, listening. Keith was rigid in his bed. The object was thick as a rolling pin and blunt on one end. A cluster of wires dangled from the other end, catching one another's barbs. It was the length of McNab's forearm. Keith remembered how casually they'd joked about their cocks, envisioning the horrified expression of a girl suddenly confronted with the inflamed cyclops she'd spent all night teasing as it became a monster that rose up like a pillar and bludgeoned her into submission, taking the satisfaction she'd withheld as we rammed into her, because wasn't that what these tight bitches all wanted anyway? Keith shivered violently under his quilt but McNab did not notice. He went into the room and the skeleton key slid into the lock and sealed him in with the broken girl.

Time pressed on Keith for what seemed like hours. His own room had a small window and he counted the stars as they appeared through the vanishing clouds. The solitary stars became constellations as their connections were revealed and they became more than themselves against the terrible void of the universe. He could not hear what was happening in the next room and somehow that made it worse because his brain provided every soundless gasp the girl would make as the blunt thing stabbed into her. He closed his eyes and her pale, miserable face wobbled in the darkness there, too. He thought of the broken skin on her haunches and the putrid fluid running like piss down her thighs. The infection she harbored.

After a while, McNab left the room empty-handed and locked the door behind him, whistling gently through his teeth. He went down to his own suite on the first floor and the house was truly silent. Maybe she had fainted. Maybe Keith would have to look at her again; maybe McNab would offer his friends a turn with her, insisting they share his toy. He would encourage them to help themselves, the way a good host should. The door, opening and closing, as they each did their best to tear Sophia in half, to prove that they'd always meant what they said. It was too late to turn back. Keith knew that he would join the others, when McNab invited him. He would have to; he was beholden to them. Keith retched at the thought of the girl's wounds and their sulfur stink. He rolled onto his belly and spat off the side of the bed, not caring that the bile landed on the rug. His face was beaded in sweat and tears and the tiny muscles in his brow ached. She was on the other side of the wall; maybe McNab had let her have some water.

He drifted off to sleep for an instant, then snapped to awareness. The stars had rotated an inch or two past their starting positions and if Keith had not been so intently watchful, he would have missed the feeble keening that sought his ears. She knew he was listening. She sensed his presence as he was alert to hers, and knew he would do nothing—as any of them would have done nothing, in Keith's place. McNab gave him the room at the top of the stairs. That was the only reason for this. Keith was sensitive to the vague snuffling coming from his friends' beds and the tilting movement of the sky outside his window. Soon, it would be dawn and all of this would be erased, as though it was a dream. He screwed his eyes shut. The weekend was half over. He would not wreck it by dwelling on this issue of Sophia. McNab said she came willingly. What they agreed to was nobody's business. Perhaps she liked it, he told himself, and this dreadful lie was enough to lull him into a deep and restful sleep.

••

Death is a black wave that swallows you up, but Sophia was still swimming in circles on the midnight colored sea, unwilling to sink. The moment Keith abandoned her in the cell at the top of the stairs, Sophia decided she would not die in this room, at the hands of these boys. After play time, she was given a dish of wet cereal with a sedative mixed into it and a dog bowl of tepid gin. McNab, who was everyone's friend, let her out of the restraints so that she could eat and then shit in the dishes she'd licked her food from, and then try to clean herself with the rags of her old clothes. She welcomed unconsciousness; in the morning, the friend woke her up with a bucket of cold water or simply pissed on her so that the acid on her skin scorched her out of sleep. He had new ideas every day, each one worse than the last. She had lost count of them. But this was the first night that he had left the window open.

She could no longer smell herself, but she sensed that parts of her were infected. She peed on the floor sometimes and fouled the bed when she was too tired and afraid to be a person anymore. The friend would not want to ruin his charming house with vulgar odors. He had wedged the sash open a few inches and propped it with a block of wood the morning the car came from the city.

The fresh air intoxicated Sophia: she had forgotten that there was a world beyond the private room, with plants that bloomed and sent their spores and pollen grains into the breeze and tantalized the birds and insects with their undefinable scents. She caught a whiff of shoreline and it made her dizzy with desire. She clung to that shred of *outside* while the friend worked her over, then revived her, then rechained her in new and horrible poses. While his guests kept him busy downstairs—she smelled their food cooking and heard their varied, male voices afterward in the sitting room—Sophia rotated her head by millimeters inside her collar and assessed as best she could with her bruised eyes the stiffness of the window frame, which was partially painted shut, as well as the height of the drop. The friend was careful to keep his skeleton key in his pocket, out of reach and on a fob clipped to his trousers and therefore impossible to lose. She dreamed of finding that key in her cereal or seizing it in her teeth when he came close, but the window was open now and a second floor escape was both more likely and safer than hoping he would make a mistake that allowed her to get away. When she was unhooked for the night, she slunk to the end of her chain, which was long enough to let her put her nose out the window.

The physical longing rippled through her as she coveted the night, the beach, and the hundreds of species of shore plants she could taste individually. The chain was rigged to a heavy duty eye screw, fastened to the bed frame. If she jumped with the collar on, she'd snap her own neck and dangle against the side of the house, throttling. He would like that. She set her swollen palms to the screw and ignored the oven-mitt dullness in her hands. If she could feel this, she would have stopped, but the nerves had been battered and burned into submission and she was beyond pain, so she twisted it and trusted the wood to give up before she did.

The screw's loop moved so slowly it seemed at times to be going backward, riveting itself in place against her feeble efforts to loosen it. After what seemed like an hour, she wriggled it out of its socket like a rotten tooth. The shank was sharp at the tip and the eye was generous, the size of a ring. She slipped a puffy finger through it so the spike pointed out from her knuckle. She gathered the chain around her fist, careful to stifle the metal links. She was naked and he had taken her shoes. Her clothes were unrecognizable scabs, saturated with the fluids and excretions she mopped up at the end of each day. However, there was a hunter's coat in the closet; she reached past his collection of implements and snatched it from the hanger. The lining was silky and immediately adhered to the open sores on her back. Her hands were too inept to zip it up, but she wrapped it tightly around herself and stood at the window, contemplating the twenty-foot drop. She would have to land feet-first in the pile of cut brush and apple branches that had been left near the house, and then sprint toward the road. Maybe someone would see her, she thought, though it was futile to hope anyone would find her as she limped along the shoulder way out here, with the nearest neighbor over a mile away. She was a fast runner before this, but her body was shrunken in its wrapper now and her muscles cramped even just holding her upright. She could not outrun five fit young men who had never missed a meal or a night's sleep in their lives. She swayed. Perhaps the fall would kill her. They would like that, too.

Her hands were flabby and useless as half defrosted filets, but she stuck them under the window frame and hauled on it as hard as she could. It shuddered and, with a jolt, opened another two inches with the ghastly shriek of peeling paint. She repeated the movement and earned another inch. That was all she needed. She slid one leg out and the air caressed her bare body and it was as delicious as water. She was fumbling with her chain and trying to get her other foot out through the narrow gap when she heard a familiar, beastly voice on the other side of the door and a sound that made the hair on the back of her neck prickle with fear. It was the fob, withdrawn from his pocket—the tinkling sound that signaled the beginning of *play*.

The keys jangled in the friend's hand and he laughed, making a joke to someone Sophia could not identify. He could hear her struggling now, chain flapping loose and the panes rattled as she frantically tried to stuff her lower half past the splintered frame into the vast, empty space beyond it. The coat scrunched against the wood and made her too thick to slip through. She fought harder with her awkward, unfeeling arms and stiffened legs, easing herself backward bit by bit until her legs both swung free and down and her toes landed against the house's siding so she felt the lip of the shingles as a ledge that would not hold her. She hung by her hands, fingers wrapped into numb fists. The skeleton key clicked into the lock.

He was on her faster than she expected, grabbing her forearms and half-dragging her back into the room. His face was close to her and his breath was around her like a cloud, choking her with its rich scent of cigars and Scotch, peat and leather. She bent her knees and set her feet against the side of the house and without thinking struck out with her free hand and the steel point of the screw on her finger impaled his cheek and he screamed as though for both of them; the screams she could not release through those days and nights of wet cereal and beatings and fuckings all came out of the bloody puncture wound as though from the mouth of hell and she pushed hard with both feet and in a whoosh she was out into the late summer dawn and the mist and fragile dew on the blades of the grass rushed up to meet her as she fell feet-first into the yielding body of the earth.

Her legs buckled under her and her left leg jammed up into her hip and wrenched as she landed and rolled through the brush pile. A tearing inside her. She sprawled face down in the grass with the coat open. Her knees were stained with mud and her bare feet made deep imprints in the turf. She felt the mud between her toes as she clawed her way forward, grabbing handfuls of the ground because her hip would not cooperate but she had no time to find out why because there were more voices now, coming through the house, and the thunder of feet in shoes and she had only her steel ring to defend herself as she scrabbled in the direction of the road.

She reached the end of the driveway just as Keith shouted her name. She did not turn, but lurched sideways in the gravel, not minding how it cut her thighs and belly, and seized the door handle of Constance's car. She pushed the latch and the door swung hard, nearly hitting her in the face as she dragged it open and threw herself into the driver's seat, thrashing against the fawn suede and slamming the door and locking it just as Keith's big stupid pink face appeared like a moon against the window. His hands rested for an instant against the glass and he stared in at her, where she shrank away from him with the emergency brake prodding her guts. His lips moved rapidly and his finger jabbed toward the glove box.

"Spare key," he mouthed. "Stay low."

She slid into the space under the steering wheel and ducked her head low. He turned back to the house. The boys filed out, pulling their jackets on. He waved his hands over his head and then pointed toward the beach.

"She went this way," he shouted, and took off at a brisk jog across the yard, drawing the other boys along in his wake as they picked up his pace. They disappeared one at a time into the chokecherry bushes with McNab following up the line, one hand pressing a white bandage against his face.

Constance kept a second key in a small magnetic box inside the compartment and although her body was shaking so hard she could barely slide the plastic plate aside and extract the key, she did it and yes, it was the right one and slid into the ignition. Her left leg was useless but she pressed the brake with her naked right foot and cranked the starter. The tank was full and she threw the engine into gear and floored the gas.

She was several miles down the road when she realized she was crying and another few miles by the time she found she was shaking too badly to navigate her way back toward the city. Her hands were at ten and two on the wheel. Outside the house, it was loud and bright. You could buy things. Make choices. The radio was on and the shock of strangers' voices and the Top 100 made her wince. Each jingle promised you could leave for better pastures.

Everything hurt. She pressed the accelerator.

Sophia had no plan. All she knew was to drive south, fast, before her old friends could ever catch her. Her hip ached. She could last a while longer.

She rolled down the driver's side window and let the land-scent roll over her, refilling her body with the wholeness of the world and all that survived outside that house in the country and the little room at the top of the stairs with the best view of the apple tree. The apples would be there in another hundred years, just the way Sophia remembered; a sour, gnarled tree that pushed its blossoms out into the season's chill, transforming the salty fog into fruit that could be collected, and pulped, and bottled for those days when summer was far away.

flu season

keith lafountaine

1

Something is wrong with my husband.

It's flu season. First, I asked him to get the shot. Then, I implored him, and when imploration didn't work, I begged him. *It's just one quick prick. One quick prick and you're protected.* But he refused. Sure enough, he came home from work sneezing into his sleeve.

Now, he is sitting in the shower of our apartment's second bathroom, watching the hairs on his thighs writhe as the water hits them. His nose is bright red, and his nostrils are clotted with thick, green mucus. When he breathes, a faint whistle escapes his lungs, as if an ancient wind is yearning to burst free. Or maybe, to suck something in.

He watches the hairs on his legs, and he wheezes, and he sniffles. His expression is that of pure satisfaction. Of sickened delight.

2

He let me put him to bed, and when I wrap him up in the covers, placing a washcloth on his head, a piece of my heart snaps off from the base—in the same way my Uncle Ted says California will rip away from the mainland in a few decades.

"I love you," my husband whispers.

I smile at him as I rub Vicks onto his chest. "I love you, too."

3

I wake up in the middle of the night, some demented nightmare about computer viruses racing through the dark with cackling glee. When I turn on the mattress, I see my husband standing in front of the apartment window, looking out. His hand is crusted with snot and his skin is pale.

Is he humming? I think he's humming. Or maybe he's muttering to himself.

I lay in bed, hesitant to ask him what's wrong. Afraid, even. For some reason, I feel as if I've descended into the dream world yet again, or, rather, risen from one dream to pierce another's membrane.

What was it Mom always told me? *Don't ask questions you don't want the answers to.* So, here I am, not asking questions. Huddled in bed.

He turns, seeming to sense that I'm awake. The moonlight slashes across his face with vicious, blue ribbons. In that light, I see his left eye is shot through with crimson. It's practically leaking out of its orb.

"Go back to sleep," he commands. I turn over.

He doesn't return to bed, and I don't fall back asleep.

4

"Hey, Fred. Yeah, I just feel like shit. Appreciate it."

His voice sounds different, but I convince myself it's just the way the shower is distorting my hearing. He is my husband, the man who held me so long ago when the world seemed huge and frightening. We'd been young, but our youthfulness allowed us to pull the tender meat from each other's hearts. Maybe that was what entwined us when everyone else pulled apart.

He's posted up on the couch when I finish showering and dressing for work. "Doing okay?" I ask.

He nods. "Just gonna relax."

"Good thinking." And it is—he is not the kind of man to visit a hospital unless he has a limb missing, or if his lungs lay on the floor in a puddle of vomit. A little R&R is the most I can feasibly convince him of.

I steal a final look at him after I slide on my flats, and I press my fingers to my lips, blowing him a kiss. He catches it. But that bloodshot eye looks worse today, and it holds a sinister leer.

A chill runs through my teeth. I smile again, and then I turn to leave.

5

All the paper is gone when I return that afternoon. We had a couple reams by the printer in the living room. I have a few journals and notebooks tucked away in my nightstand drawer— gone. Even the grocery list that was held to the fridge with a guitar-shaped magnet has disappeared.

The toilet flushes and my husband steps out of the bathroom attached to our bedroom. I turn to him, my hands in my pockets. There's no denying how sweaty they are.

"What's wrong?" he asks.

I try to ignore that the bloodshot has flowed into his other eye. "You need paper for something?" I reply.

"Huh?"

"I need some scratch paper," I lie, "but I can't find any."

He shrugs, smiles, and walks toward the couch, where he plops down and picks up the remote.

"Baby, you should go to the doctor," I say. "Your eyes are bloodshot."

"I'm fine," he says, waving me off.

My feet hurt. My head hurts. Fatigue pulls at me.

I'll call his doctor tomorrow, I think. *He'll help.*

6

My nightmares tend to come in threes, like the newly deceased; as such, I wake up in the middle of the night once more. The bedroom is quiet, *too quiet,* and when I slide an arm to the other side of the bed, it's cold and empty.

I turn over onto my elbow, propping my body up. He's nowhere to be seen. I turn and glance toward the bathroom, but the door is open. There isn't much light beyond the milky moon, but that offers enough luminescence to confirm he's not on the toilet—or hugging it. I crane my ears, but don't hear the floor creaking under his weight, or the fridge opening as he rummages for a midnight snack.

My stomach coils tight.

The moon is heavy and full, hanging in the sky like a scuffed, forgotten marble. The stars stare through the darkness, and in that moment they suddenly seem very much like millions of eyes, and the dark expanse little more than a protective covering to shield our nascent minds from the impossibility that lurks just behind.

I slip free from the covers. The rug does little to comfort my cold feet. I pad over to the window, staring through the glass. Our apartment building's parking lot is filled with sedans and SUVs and annoyingly large trucks. The F-150s never park right. They always take up multiple spots or block the sidewalk. Sometimes both.

The ground is glistening, and a thin trickle of standing water lines the border where the road meets the curb. I wrap my arms tight around my body, holding each elbow with the opposite hand. My shivering has nothing to do with the temperature of the night.

My husband is standing in his boxers and his tank top. Snot is crusted around his upper lip and streaming from both nostrils. His face is turned up toward the shining moon. Suddenly, in three swift motions, he strips his clothes off and tosses them aside. They are violent gestures, more *tearing* than pulling, and as soon as he is nude he goes running across the parking lot. As he approaches the main road, he goes down on all fours and sprints like a rabid dog, racing into the darkness.

Even up on my floor, with dozens of feet separating us and a few panes of glass deadening the sound, I can hear him snarling. I stand there for a long time in shock, feeling horror creep up my bones like a river parasite. We learned about those in a documentary, he and I, the organisms that can climb up your urine stream.

I half-walk, half-run toward the front door and snap the lock into place, stepping back from it, expecting him to come shouldering through anyway. The thing I saw outside, the *man* I saw, did not resemble my husband in any fashion. And yet, it is.

An hour or two later, I hear a soft knock on the door. The rounded glass of the peephole distorts his face. The mucus is gone, but his eyes are as crimson as ever, and he's smiling. No, he's *grinning*—there is a difference. And he's grinning wrong. Like something is looking through those bloody eyes and cranking open the sides of his mouth with fishing wire.

"Hi, honey," he says. "Can you unlock the door?"

My hand hovers above the deadbolt, and I hesitate.

What if he's sicker than I realized? What if he dies out there in the hallway and I didn't let him inside? Can two days of horror strip away a decade's worth of memories? Of kindness? Of love? My fingers grasp the deadbolt. I grit my teeth as I unlatch it.

I back away from the door as he opens it. His clothes are damp, but he's wearing them. He stares at me, and then he moves to his left and enters our bedroom. I stand still, frozen, and I hear the bathroom door snap shut and the lock snick into place.

I grab my pillows from the bedroom and I retreat to the couch. My exhausted mind forces me to snatch at sleep like a toddler reaching for plastic keys.

But it's never enough and it's never too long.

When morning sunlight streams through the windows, I climb off the couch and ignore the pains in my back. I creep toward the bedroom door, and I peer inside. The bed is empty. The bathroom door is locked.

Everything in my chest screams at me to run, but I think about the trip we took in Iceland. He got food poisoning and we spent a night in the hotel room wondering whether we'd have to take him to the hospital or not. I spent that night beside him, stroking his back, while he forced everything from his gut into the toilet bowl.

He's sick, I remind myself. *He's probably burning up with fever. And when people burn up with fever, they do strange things. Horrifying things. But it's not his fault.*

I approach the bathroom door, and I rap on the wood as softly as I can while still making my presence known.

"Honey?" I coo.

A rancid smell slips between the door's cracks. Not vomit, not shit, but something worse. Something that smells like a rotting corpse trapped within a vat of tar.

Silence. I almost decide to return to the kitchen, to find the spare key that will open this damned door, but then he responds in his nasally, stuffed-up voice, cracked through with phlegm and weaker than I ever remember hearing it.

"Just didn't have the energy to come to bed," he says.

I grasp the knob and turn it, but the lock prevents my entry. "Baby, let me help you."

"I'm fine. Don't come in."

For some reason, it sounds like a warning. And, though it pains me to do so, I obey.

7

I call out of work and spend the day trying to reach my husband's doctor. I start out confident, calmly explaining his symptoms to the scheduler, but then I get transferred around half-a-dozen times and end up speaking to some oncologist. They say they can't help me, so I start the process over again.

I finally reach the correct scheduler at eleven. She promises me that Dr. Flushing will return my call in a half-hour or less. I wait on the living room couch, occasionally wandering to the bedroom to confirm that the bathroom door is still closed. It is. A half-hour turns to an hour, then an hour-and-a-half. After two hours, I call again. The scheduler and I do the same dance, and she iterates the same promise, and I wait another hour before tossing the phone aside with a huff and plucking the bathroom key from our kitchen island's drawer.

I return to the bathroom door and knock on it again. "Honey? I'm coming in, alright?"

"No!" he shouts. His voice is barking. Harsh.

"Baby, I know you don't want me to, but I'm worried and your doctor is giving me the runaround. We—you need to see someone."

Even as I say the words, I find myself losing speed. What would I even say to the ER nurse? *My husband has the flu, but his eyes are also so red I think he's going to start crying blood and yesterday he took a nocturnal sprint down our parking lot in his birthday suit.* But I think about Iceland, and I think about that first night when he was huddled under his blanket and shivering from fever. Biting my bottom lip, I stick the key into the lock and open the door.

My stomach does a flip, and then one more for good measure.

112

Black slime drips down the walls. It coats the tile floor. A small pool of it, chunky and thick, like sewage, sits in the sink, clogging the drain. It *plinks* from the shower head and slides down the shower walls. And there, in the middle of the mess, is my husband.

For a moment, I think I'm seeing things.

For a moment, I think I'm having a nightmare.

But, no—this is real, even if it is cruel, and what I see is *there*, even if I wish it wasn't. Half-a-dozen eyes have sprouted out of his neck, and they stare at me, blinking. His chest is beet-red and swollen with bumps. As are his legs. And his arms. He looks up at me like a scolded child. His eyes are still scarlet amid the rash of new bumps on his cheeks.

"Baby," he whispers. "I told you not to come in."

I sprint out of the bathroom, through the kitchen, to the living room where my phone lays on the couch. It's ringing. I recognize Doctor Flushing's number, but I reject the call and dial three numbers. *9-1-1.*

An operator picks up, but when she asks where I am and what the emergency is, all I can do is scream.

8

Health officers in hazmat suits arrive with a stretcher, and one of them, looking every bit like the government scientists that came to put E.T. away, starts to ask me questions. I ramble through explanations and answers. The man, who doesn't give me his name, nods along in his suit and he listens. Honestly, that earns him a few points in my book.

A scream rips through the apartment, and I jerk my head in the direction of the sound.

The man listening to my story is gone, rushing toward his colleagues, and even though his face is shrouded I can see a horror leaking into his gait. It's there, like he's a child again, and when I approach, I understand, too.

My husband's bumps have sprouted into eyes; now, they line his skin like scales. Each orb weeps that stinking black sludge, and the eyes blink on his arms, his neck, his legs, his chest. He's ripped open one of the hazmat suits, and the health officer's face—a younger man, I realize, no older than twenty-five—is bare to the world, kissing wind. My husband's head rears back, his throat bulges, and he sends more of that vile, black substance into this poor man's face. The health officer falls to the ground, screaming, clawing at his throat. My husband—the *thing* that was my husband—turns to the nearest hazmat suit.

I don't wait. I sprint to the door of our apartment and into the building's hallway. I forget about Iceland. I forget about who this man once was. I forget about the tender nights in bed, and the way he promised he'd protect me, and I forget about the fights and making up after, and I forget about our vows that said *in sickness and in health*. I forget about everything that isn't pure, animalistic instinct.

I run to the elevator because it's closer than the stairs, which are at the other end of the hallway. I stand there, smacking the button, feeling fear climb into my throat. More screams echo from outside, and then our apartment door slams open, cracking against the wall. I hear the echo of bronze on wood. Clomping, wet footsteps follow. A shadow spills onto the cream-colored walls like vomited coffee. I smack at the elevator doors again.

The shadow grows, and the footsteps quicken, but the elevator doors ding, and I fall back into it, jamming my finger into the close doors button. And it works! Halle-fucking-lujah, it works. The shadow is large and lurking, but the doors slip closed. I lean my head back against the wall.

Fingers poke through the doors' closing gap. Eyeballs pop and black sludge spills to the floor. I think I hear small screams as the elevator doors pull open slightly, enough that I can see my husband and the eyes growing from his body staring through at me.

"Ellen," he growls in a voice that sounds like he's speaking through a grinding garbage disposal. "We have so much to show you, Ellen."

His breath is rancid and stinks of meat. It's then I notice the blood spilling down his chin. I hope it's just a split lip or an awkwardly bitten gum, but I think I know what it is. I think one of the men in the hazmat suits turned into his dinner.

With a wild cry, I rear back a leg and kick his fingers. More of those tiny screams. He jerks back, shocked, and the doors slam shut. The elevator is descending. But I hear him laughing as I retreat. Laughing like someone just told him an inside joke.

9

Alaska seemed cold and distant enough. I hope never to see him again. A part of me hopes never to see a *man* again. But Gerald at the grocery store is kind enough, and Mark will fix my plumbing on occasion. So, I guess, I hope never to see men other than Gerald or Mark again.

It's snowing outside, frost on the windows. This rental came with a fireplace, and flames are roaring as I sit at my kitchen table and wonder, endlessly, what happened to the man I once loved.

As usual, I've locked the door: the deadbolt, the push-button lock on the knob, and the sliding gold chain. I don't trust anything—not after seeing my husband and those eyes. Not after watching him hold the elevator doors open.

Truth be told, I'm not sure I trust myself these days.

I've been sneezing a lot. I check my tissues every time, looking for any hint of black bile, and when I shower I spend an hour in front of the mirror, prodding my skin and looking for welts. I stare into my eyes until I see purple spots.

Nothing yet.

But as I dress in my pajamas, I think about something Gerald told me a few weeks back, a casual remark that turned my blood into a mushy, frozen slurry.

"Better safe than sorry," he said, holding up a box of Emergen-C. "It's flu season, after all."

I climb into bed and stare up at the ceiling. I don't like looking out the window. The sky is too clear here. The stars are plenty. The night before last, I dreamt that the moon was a giant eye, and a massive lid came closing around Mare Tranquillitatis. And my husband's million tiny laughs echoed as whatever hung behind the night sky stared through and waited for me to understand.

malcom strickland's dreams

ethan warren

The first film, completed late in the fall of 1968, lasts only three ragged minutes. Entitled *Meeting*, it begins with a middle-aged, pot-bellied man, dressed in an argyle sweater and dingy boxer shorts, entering a plain gray room that seems to balance on the edge of existence. The ceiling is slanted dramatically, and though there are no windows, light appears to come from inexplicable angles, lending the film an over-exposed, blinding quality.

The man—played by the director himself—enters with a clear sense of purpose, and approaches something seated on a plain wooden chair. To call this something a person doesn't seem quite right—its arms and legs are just a bit too long, and its joints seem to follow biological urges utterly alien to our own; its facial features are all either a bit too large or a bit too small, either a bit too close together or a bit too far apart—and as pot-bellied the man approaches, the something seems to smile, both welcoming and ominous.

The man goes to the creature and cups its cheek with a lover's tenderness. The creature touches the man's face as well. They hold the pose for a long moment, and then they move to touch each other's shoulders, and then arms, before finally clasping hands; his, marked by four decades of life and the creature's moving with the lurching quality of a body in perpetual seizure. It's hard to say quite how, but we know that an understanding has passed between the man and the creature.

And then the man begins to cry hot and violent tears, his sobs yanked from his chest by an unseen thread. The creature stands, calm as ever, while the man grabs the chair and uses it to beat the walls, gouging plaster and raining splinters, the rough wood shattering in his hands.

Those hands start bleeding, staining the pulverized wood. And all the while, a buzzing like thousands of bees operating on thousands of frequencies slowly overtakes the soundtrack, mingling with the man's howls until the tones are indistinguishable.

A static shot of the creature's hands—its fingers just a bit too long, its knuckles perhaps just a bit too pliable—comprise the last thirty seconds of this brief, stark film. It's impossible to discern the significance of this shot, much though cinephiles have tried in the ensuing decades. The peculiar hands just sit in the frame until the viewer's mind starts to reel. Only then do we cut to black.

••

"I suppose there must have been something about Malcom's dreams that made me fall in love with him. Something about the passion with which he described them to me. I don't know what else it could have been. And I *have* wondered."

This is one of the few direct statements offered by Cilla Alfredson in her 2011 Q&A at New York's Angelika Film Center. This rare public appearance was moderated by NYU Professor Lloyd Ramsay whose monograph, *The Fathomless Vision of Malcom Strickland*, was published alongside the digital restoration of the four short films Strickland produced between 1968 and 1971. In a video available on YouTube, Ramsay is patient and warm as he tries to coax Alfredson into reminiscing on her relationship with this most inscrutable of artists. But she is evasive and cold until he happens to ask how the couple met. Only then does the ice melt for the length of one memory.

"We were at a party—it was at my advisor's house, actually—and I had probably overserved myself a bit on the red wine, but this *man* walked in." The video, seemingly uploaded directly from a smartphone, is shot from a preposterously bad angle, but still we can see a smile flicker across her face as she recalls the spring night almost sixty years earlier when two young graduate students who would soon be husband and wife became acquainted at a party in Cambridge, Massachusetts.

"He wasn't much to look at, back then," she says, and as she recalls the story, her speech is nostalgic but halting, as though she's both excavating and still processing this long-ago meeting. "He needed a haircut, he needed to lay off the fatty foods, but we got to talking and he started to tell me about these dreams he had. Every night, all night, these—and I said, *Those sound more like nightmares.* They were really quite ugly. But he described them with such detail, and such passion, and he said they didn't frighten him. Not at all. Which is quite—well, you've seen the films. At any rate, maybe it was the wine, maybe it was his passion—I knew he would be an artist, had the soul of an artist, and I always did have a weakness—yes, I fell in love with him that night. And I just kept falling for eighteen years."

Alfredson, who reverted to her maiden name in the 1980s after personally declaring her marriage void, tends to be defiantly silent when asked to discuss Strickland, but details have been pieced together over the years. We know she spent the first ten years of their marriage assisting in various research projects at the Harvard Museum of Natural History, while he did menial work at local TV stations, seemingly unable to hold down a job. We know that when she received her grant in 1964 to travel to the mountains of Virginia for her work with the Ash People, he was entirely available and eager to make the journey with her.

The attendees at the Angelika Q&A in 2011, though, have little interest in the marriage, little interest in Alfredson herself at all. The young men who line up at the microphone—the type of slightly awkward, obsessive overgrown boys who think deeply about a body of work that totals only sixty minutes and has never been commercially available—are here for any shred of an answer to the myriad questions that have lingered around her husband's work for decades.

The first young man who steps to the microphone is shy, his voice quaking. "Do you think it's possible the masks, do you think it's possible it could be a kind of breathable latex? Did you ever see him working with anything like that?"

"Malcom was private about his work," she answers.

The second young man is more assertive, willing to badger her. "There are no puppeteers listed in the credits for *Lifespan*, but the Mantigo has to be—"

"Technical questions about Malcom's work can be addressed to his collaborators," Alfredson snaps.

"All due respect, none of them—"

"I'd prefer to answer another question." Her voice is firm, and an usher hustles the young man aside.

A third young man steps to the microphone. "So nobody's ever wanted to try and finish *The Barrels*, I guess?"

"I'm sorry," Alfredson says, standing abruptly, "but I'm a very old woman and I need to get some rest."

And then the video ends. Alfredson has not made a public appearance since.

••

If there's a thematic throughline in Malcom Strickland's scant filmography, it might be a primal dismantling of social norms. In *Meeting*, we can infer an upending of the very idea of communication. *Punch Card*, his third and longest completed film, is clearly a satire of mundane bureaucratic rituals, even as its last quarter spirals into Grand Guignol hysteria. But his most evocatively enigmatic film, the fifteen-minute *Lifespan*, offers the richest density of detail, and seems the closest Strickland came to volunteering his perspective on relationships. If you were looking for textual evidence to suggest Malcom Strickland may have been an unfit romantic partner, *Lifespan* would seem to offer an abundance.

The film is narrated in voice-over by a young girl, who opens the story by informing us, "This is the story of what happened when I was a grownup." Before we've even begun, we know we're in a world that operates on rules quite different from our own.

Lifespan—shot in sickly, under-saturated 8mm—begins on the stony banks of a calm, rural river. A young woman walks along in peasant clothes, as the narration offers mundane but confusing details: "I was twenty years old and at the bottom of a well. When I got that way, I always had to cry, even though they said I wouldn't." The girl's voice has a detached quality that makes it feel almost like she's learned the script phonetically.

The young woman encounters a creature on the riverbank; it looks much like the one in *Meeting*—the same too-long limbs, the same mismatched facial features that seem to have been smashed on haphazardly—though significantly larger, and it moves with a jerking fluidity so unearthly it's stomach-churning. This creature (whom the little girl refers to as "the very nice man," leading to its classification in Strickland studies, along with the *Meeting* creature, as "the Niceman") appears to be on the verge of death, gasping and clawing at the ground. The young woman digs a hole in the earth and pulls out two handfuls of red slop, which the Niceman devours with disgusting abandon ("I liked to smell, and

I liked to wrap my eyes," the little girl says wistfully). The little girl sings a nursery rhyme about eight spotted dogs as the young woman and the Niceman begin a rough, carnal encounter that's as alarming as it is sensual.

For a long stretch, the woman and the Niceman enact domestic rituals on the riverbank— the Niceman brushes the woman's hair, the woman rubs the Niceman's feet—and we come to understand that a great deal of time is passing as they build a life together. At this point, the Mantigo enters.

The Mantigo (so nicknamed by Strickland scholars as a portmanteau of the mythical beasts Manticore and Lampago) is a quadruped that bears similarities to the Niceman, though the main point of comparison is how unaccountably *wrong* both look. The Mantigo's knees appear to bend backwards, and its mouth is distended and drooping. Its eyes roll independently of one another and it seems perpetually out of breath, but it moves with tremendous speed and force.

No other figure in a Malcom Strickland film has invited nearly the discussion that the Mantigo has, merely for the question of how this effect was achieved. In the late 1960s, characters like these could only be rendered through stop motion animation, or puppetry, but the Mantigo seems to be neither. For that matter, as alluded to by the first Angelika questioner, the Nicemans (or Nicemen) are similarly inexplicable; if the actors wear masks or prosthetics, they're shockingly advanced for their era. Whatever visual effects Strickland employed were decades ahead of their time, while evidence suggests he was operating on a shoestring budget.

The Mantigo is apparently jealous of the riverside relationship, so it murders the Niceman and takes its place—both domestic and carnal—in the woman's life. We see the same routines enacted, and at this point, the little girl's narration ("I didn't like the way things seemed, but the way they seemed was the way they were, so that's everything") is joined by a sort of droning hymn sung by a guttural chorus. The young woman is visibly miserable, and finally she kills the Mantigo with her hands, a scene of violence so terrible that it begs to be peeked at through fingers. We cut to a shot of the same woman on the same river-bank, now aged into a grotesque, lonely old crone.

"And that's what happened so now I died," the little girl says as the film cuts to black.

Lifespan has been the subject of furious scrutiny and debate over the past fifty years, due in large part to the scarcity of information on its creation. The lead actress, who'd recently graduated from Boston University's School of Theater, tragically took her life within a year of shooting, and the actress who voiced the little girl, now in her sixties and the owner of a chain of fast-casual restaurants in the Southwest, learned only years later what she had been working on. The few credited crew members who ever admitted to working on the film have refused to discuss the experience, and none of them pursued a career in the arts.

But this much is clear: if this is Malcom Strickland's thesis on relationships, it seems a remarkably cynical one. As with all his work, everything from language to action is stripped to a point of elemental bluntness, and we're left only with a romance marked by physical roughness, passionless coexistence, and sorrow. The presence of an animal figure with sexual and emotional needs equal to a humanoid one only layers a transgressive ugliness onto the proceedings.

So yes, based purely on the evidence presented in *Lifespan*, one could imagine why its creator struggled to maintain a healthy marriage.

• •

It's very difficult to visit the Ash People of Virginia, and they have little interest in visiting you. Located in the Blue Ridge Mountains, at the end of a dirt road so long that anyone interested in driving in must bring along an extra tank of gas for the return trip, this community of just over 300 residents was founded in 1586 by a group expelled from the Roanoke Colony. Details as to the community's history are lost to time and blended with legend, but a few facts are clear.

The Ash People (they dislike the nickname, but it's stuck for better or worse), possess a unique genetic trait amplified over centuries of closed-loop reproduction that lends their skin a deep gray tone; a photograph of an Ash Person taken in monochrome or color shows no substantial difference.

A persistent myth claims that the early settlers were expelled from the Roanoke Colony for some sort of religious transgression, though the community vehemently maintains that this has been debunked by historians.

Due to their social isolation, the Ash People speak in a sing-song patois that has roots in both rural American and extinct European dialects, as well as their own unique slang. The language also seems to be constantly evolving—and, some claim, decaying—at a faster rate than most any other spoken tongue. And this is what led a young ethnographer named Cilla Strickland to apply for a grant that allowed her and her husband Malcom to spend six months with the Ash People in 1965.

It would be a gross understatement to say that the Ash People have not kept up with the modern world. Travel is so time-consuming and treacherous that the community is largely self- sustaining. They grow what they eat and purify what they drink; there's neither electrical power nor plumbing, so the nights are lit by candles and the homes and furnishings are rough-hewn. Socially, the Ash People are neither primitive nor puritanical, and they aren't particularly ignorant of modern culture. They're simply happy with their lifestyle and disinterested in a world that rarely intrudes.

During their time with the Ash People, the Stricklands were hosted by a young man named Adonijah Bean, whose wife and son had recently died, leaving him with an excess of space and an abundance of loneliness. Cilla Strickland was the first researcher to attempt a thorough documentation of this isolated culture, and with only half a year to accomplish the task, she was by her own account distracted and harried, leaving little time for her husband. This left him plenty of time to strike up a close friendship with their host; correspondence between the two men continued in the years following the Stricklands' return to Massachusetts. As Adonijah wrote in 1966: *I be plum bored since thee go. A good darklark be zim interesting wee a buddy. A fellow can't get to aught mischief he be alone. Yet I be pondering aul yourn ideas, and I conclude thee hafta make it true. Don think too much, don queer theez head up. Thee vrien sent supplies for thee aid. No vear, plenty zim fid that come vrom.*

Parsing the language of the Ash People is a challenge; their vocabulary and grammar seem in constant flux, and no comprehensive glossary has ever been attempted. From their letters, we can surmise that Malcom and Adonijah were in the habit of taking nighttime walks to discuss some sort of inspiration Malcom was experiencing (as well as possibly getting into some vague type of "mischief," presumably of the innocent variety rather than the malicious) and that Adonijah was urging Malcom to follow through on whatever ideas he was cultivating.

As for what supplies Adonijah might have sent "for [Malcom's] aid," no answer has ever been confirmed. But Strickland enthusiasts have their pet suspicions.

The abstract and surreal nature of his films has led to a natural assumption that Strickland had a fondness for psychedelics. However, Alfredson describes her husband as having a puritanical disdain for the era's drug culture. The child of two inveterate alcoholics, he never even drank in her presence.

But one paragraph in Alfredson's 1969 book, *The Singular Tongue of the Blue Ridge Mountains*, has long been the basis for a common interpretation of Adonijah's reference to supplies:

THE COMMUNITY [Alfredson took great pains to avoid using the term Ash People] DISTILLS A UNIQUE LIQUOR, USING THE SAME RED WHEAT THEY USE IN THEIR BREADS AND CEREALS. THIS SUBSTANCE, WHICH HAS AN ALCOHOL CONTENT WELL IN EXCESS OF MOST COMMERCIALLY AVAILABLE LIQUORS, IS COLLOQUIALLY REFERRED TO AS *ZINHAINT* (A TERM POSSIBLY DERIVED FROM THE FORTH AND BARGY TERM FOR "SUN," AND APPALACHIAN SLANG FOR "SPIRIT" OR "GHOST"), AND DISTILLED FOR A PERIOD OF TEN YEARS IN BARRELS THAT HAVE BEEN USED CONTINUOUSLY FOR OVER THREE-HUNDRED YEARS, MAKING THEM, AS ELIHU PUT IT, HARD AND SCARRED. THE DISTILLERY IS APPARENTLY LOCATED A FEW HUNDRED FEET ABOVE TOWN IN A DAMP AND TEMPERATE CAVE. ELIHU REFERRED TO SEVERAL SPECIAL BARRELS KEPT RESERVED FOR A SURPRISE VISIT "VROM DHICKA [from that] ANGEL." HOWEVER, THE COMMUNITY IS QUICK TO DENY ANY SUCH SUPERSTITION, MUCH AS THEY PREFER TO AVOID ANY TOPIC THAT MIGHT LEAD TO RELIGION.

To quote one post on the Malcom Strickland discussion page on Reddit, "Pardon my French, but come the fuck on. Anyone who thinks he wrote those movies not tripping balls is an idiot.

The supplies were special-reserve zinhaint, case closed, I'd prefer to answer another question LOL."

· ·

To be blunt, *Punch Card* is Malcom Strickland's worst film. It's not a controversial opinion. At 40 minutes, it could be cut down by at least half. For most of the runtime, the imagery is pedestrian, and it lacks the cinematic eye of *Lifespan* and *Meeting*. *Punch Card* is Strickland's third film in as many years, so perhaps this pace was just too trying for such a singular, insular artist, and his inspiration was flagging.

Shot in a black cube with spare set design and props, *Punch Card* tells the story of a workplace that bears similarities to both a bureaucratic office and a sweatshop (even for an artist who painted in broad strokes, this is a bit on the nose). About half the runtime is taken up by the abusive relationship between The Boss and The Worker, as The Boss berates an employee who seems to be doing his best at whatever this job is. The Boss hurls invective at The Worker, criticizing his every move, and whenever The Worker attempts to get a word in edgewise, The Boss steamrolls him with another diatribe.

It's the first Strickland film to feature synced dialogue, which has been the main focus of critical discussion of *Punch Card*. And that's because the copious reams of dialogue were written in what's been dubbed "Stricklese."

Stricklese is a seemingly constructed language. Linguists who've studied *Punch Card* agree that it has phonology, grammar, and vocabulary, but while there have been extensive attempts to translate the film, all have come up short. No written screenplay has ever been recovered, so there's nothing to decode, and Stricklese includes several sounds that bear no resemblance to sounds in any other natural language, sounds that linguists have struggled to even reproduce, much less classify.

To make matters worse, no extant print of *Punch Card* includes any credits, so no actors or crew have ever been identified. With nobody to provide background or context, there's nothing to prove Strickland didn't simply conjure *Punch Card* out of thin air.

And then, of course, there's The Herald.

Though it bears similarities to the Nicemen who appear in the other two shorts, The Herald is much larger (at least eleven feet tall) and seems to emit light from an inner power source—to say The Herald glows would understate this dazzling effect. The Herald's face is disproportionately large, and its features are disproportionately small, but there's a compelling grace and beauty to the imbalance that render this creature unnervingly breathtaking.

The Herald appears to The Worker just as he reaches the point of collapse, and they begin a clandestine relationship, including erotic encounters that seem to draw on some sort of psychic link to achieve sexual satisfaction—The Worker's pleasure seems very much unsimulated, though it's difficult to identify exactly what's happening between the pair. The Boss, naturally, is unhappy with his employee's newfound joy, and with the film nearly over, we seem to be headed for one of a few conclusions.

But the film's final moments are utterly unpredictable. The Boss utters one syllable to The Worker that apparently seals an agreement between them, and without another thought, the two of them savagely murder The Herald and then spend an agonizing period of time desecrating the corpse as the light source flickers and goes out.

For such a bare story told in a made-up language, the sequence is oddly heartbreaking, and we begin to hate the two men and long for their punishment, which makes it all the more satisfying when the ink-black walls around them sprout ink-black arms—first dozens, then hundreds—that use their ink-black fingers to caress the two sadists, overwhelming them until they collapse into shrieking tears, which we observe over the course of a long fade to black. It's the only spoken sound in *Punch Card* that viewers can fully understand. Shrieks of existential pain and terror need no translation.

To suggest Strickland was experiencing existential pain of his own at this time would be presumptuous. But we can surmise that, on some level, all was not well. In the fall of 1970, buoyed by the success of her book on the Ash People, Cilla traveled to the University of Illinois at Springfield to spend a semester as a visiting lecturer. By her own admission, she visited home rarely and was consumed by her work. Malcom, for his part, had managed to convince student film societies at Boston-area colleges to host screenings of his work. These screenings occurred late at night; word quickly spread that they were not for everyone, and best enjoyed under the influence.

If Cilla was, for the first time, seeing signs that her husband might be on the verge of finally breaking through to professional success, she would have had every reason to think he would be occupied and fulfilled in her absence.

Evidence, however, suggests that while he may have been occupied, he was less than fulfilled. Around this time, Adonijah Bean's correspondence with Strickland picked up. Adonijah sent at least 12 lengthy letters between September and November of that year, an impressive rate given the difficulty of getting any mail in and out of his remote community.

Nodhing come to thee yet? Adonijah wrote in early September. *Be patient, aul comes trugh soon or late,* he wrote two weeks later. *Gotta sleep. Liketa come when thee sleep,* he wrote in mid-October. *No vear. Reckon it gets quare better with sleep,* he wrote in late October, closing the letter with, *Biya!*, the typical Ash Person expression of excitement and encouragement.

Fade about thee get more buddies? Wee oree, might get simpler, he wrote in early November. Weeks later: *Thee's in mine thoughts, and thee's in mine heart. Fade theezil's head is plum special, buddy. I swan, I knew dhicke since I met thee.* Then, a two-month gap in the records of their correspondence.

Through the thick dialect, we can glimpse words of support to a friend whose self- confidence was failing, and a suggestion that he might open himself up to collaboration with others.

It would appear Strickland took this advice, at least in a fashion. After a brief reunion with Cilla at Thanksgiving, he featured in a brief item in an early December issue of daily student newspaper *The Harvard Crimson*:

LOCAL UNDERGROUND FILMMAKER MALCOM STRICKLAND STAGED A BIZARRE DISPLAY ON THE QUAD TUESDAY EVENING, BEGGING PASSERSBY AND ONLOOKERS TO "DREAM WITH [HIM]." THE FEW STUDENTS WHO ARE FAMILIAR WITH MR. STRICKLAND'S WORK SUGGESTED HE MIGHT HAVE BEEN EITHER ATTEMPTING TO DRUM UP PUBLICITY FOR AN UPCOMING SCREENING, OR RECRUITING ARTISTIC PARTNERS. BUT ACCORDING TO FRANK DENHAM '72, WHO HAS HOLLYWOOD ASPIRATIONS OF HIS OWN AND APPROACHED HIM HOPING TO TALK SHOP, MR. STRICKLAND EVADED FRANK'S ATTEMPTS AT PROFESSIONAL DISCUSSION, INSTEAD BEGGING HIM TO DESCRIBE HIS PREVIOUS NIGHT'S DREAMS IN AS MUCH DETAIL AS POSSIBLE, THEN ASKING WHERE FRANK SLEPT.

"I THINK HE MIGHT HAVE BEEN LOOKING FOR INSPIRATION FOR A SCRIPT." FRANK SAID. "BUT IT WAS A TENSE CONVERSATION, IF YOU CAN CALL IT A CONVERSATION, AND I WAS SORT OF RELIEVED WHEN SECURITY MADE HIM LEAVE. BUT IF THERE'S

EVER ANOTHER SHOWING OF ANY OF HIS MOVIES, I REALLY REC-
OMMEND IT. MAYBE THAT'S JUST WHAT GENIUS LOOKS LIKE."

• •

By the Way of the Sunsetting, Malcom Strickland's fourth
and (as of this writing) final short film lasts 98 seconds. Filmed,
like *Punch Card,* in a black box, the film's first 84 seconds comprise an unbroken shot of a Niceman, its face painted black, and
its body painted white, shrieking as the camera moves in, the
frame jerking and shaking as though the camera operator is in
terrible distress.

At the 85th second, another Niceman (this one about a third
taller than the first, with a gaping wound in its torso) lurches into
the frame. It goes to the first Niceman, grabs it by the ears, and
wrenches its head from its body. The headless body falls with
a ragdoll gracelessness; rather than blood, what appears to be a
thick and endless earthworm slithers from the severed throat.

The final second is thought to be the middle part of a longer
Stricklese word, but the beginning and end are cut off abrupt-
ly, leaving only two nearly unpronounceable syllables. As with
Punch Card, there are no credits attached.

This, at least, represents something like a consensus version
of the film's events. Perhaps due to its brief length and current
unavailability on home video or streaming services, descriptions of the film are strangely divergent, even among audience
members at the same screening. The provided description is close
to that offered by Prof. Lloyd Ramsay in *The Fathomless Vision
of Malcom Strickland;* however, this author has altered Ramsay's
analysis slightly to incorporate some personal experiences of the
film. To be candid, this author has always found it more than a
little bit eerie when another viewer denies having seen the earthworm, given how clearly visible it is. But, as differences in color
acuity demonstrate, every eye perceives the world uniquely.

131

The title, which has no clear connection to the events of the film, was seemingly drawn from *Visio sancti Pauli*, a third-century apocryphal gospel purporting to be a first-person description of Hell. According to the translation by British scholar M.R. James:

AND I WENT WITH THE ANGEL AND HE TOOK ME BY THE WAY OF THE SUNSETTING...I LOOKED AND THERE WAS NO LIGHT IN THAT PLACE, BUT DARKNESS AND SORROW AND SADNESS: AND I SIGHED.

Apparently, Adonijah's letters weren't doing the trick in lifting his friend's spirits. And so, he did something extremely rare for an Ash Person: he came to visit.

At the time, Adonijah's trip was ostensibly to assist Cilla Strickland with updates and addenda to her book, so all travel and accommodation expenses were approved by The Keflavík Fund (since renamed The Hilmarsson Foundation for Ethnographic Research). With the passage of time, though, it's come to seem much more likely that this was cover for a furtive collaboration between himself and Malcom.

Adonijah kept up his end of the bargain with Cilla. Over the course of the Ash Person's six-month visit, the two of them completed extensive appendices to her book, leading to the publication of a new and updated edition only two years after the initial one. The tone of her notes, and her acknowledgement section, suggests a warm and satisfying partnership, to the extent that she considered Adonijah part of her family. She has even mentioned having worked on a draft of a more informal article detailing the experience of introducing Adonijah to metropolitan life, documenting his awed reactions to everything from supermarkets to an unforgettable visit to Fenway Park.

Around this time, Cilla has since alluded, Malcom fell into what she perceived to be a deep depression, marked by spending most of the day asleep. She blamed herself for not taking his distraction more seriously, but claimed she chalked it up to his artistic temperament—though never explicit, some of her comments do suggest she was growing frustrated with a husband prone to what looked like "moping." Struggling to manage this disconnect during a time of professional pressure, she moved into the guest room after Adonijah offered to sleep on the pull-out sofa downstairs.

In large part, this is our picture of the summer and fall of 1971: three people sharing a house but passing like ships in the night. In her acknowledgments, Cilla does mention Adonijah often "burned the midnight oil." We know that in this period, Malcom Strickland wrote the screenplay and shot the raw footage for the feature film *The Barrels*. Was Adonijah conspiring with Malcom while Cilla slept? We can't be sure, but even if Malcom was depressed, it's not conceivable that he slept twenty-four hours at a time.

It's at this point that it becomes most frustrating that we know so little about the biography of Malcom Strickland, because it means we know even less about *The Barrels*. As of this writing, *The Barrels* exists only as canisters of celluloid. The sound has never been synced, the 21st century has seen no effort to digitize the footage, and there has been no attempt to begin a rough assembly.

Descriptions of the footage are vague at best. It would seem Strickland intended the film to run between 90 and 120 minutes, and it does seem there was an attempt at conventional plotting, with a protagonist on some sort of journey. By one account, the footage could be compared to, "A sort of *Alice in Wonderland* or *Wizard of Oz* kind of thing, but a lot more..."

This quote, from a post-production expert specializing in film restoration, trails off because the individual (who preferred not to be named) suffered what appeared to be a brief attack of stress.

Prof. Lloyd Ramsay, who was granted a look at six out-of-context film cels, has described the imagery as "in terms of ambition, leaps and bounds beyond [Strickland's] short efforts" featuring "landscapes and creature design to rival the 21st century's most accomplished fantasy efforts."

"Each cel almost seems like it was taken from a different film, the stylistic differences are so striking," Prof. Ramsay said in a 2017 interview with the online film journal *Bright Wall/ Dark Room* promoting the new edition of *The Fathomless Vision of Malcom Strickland*. "It's impossible to guess what the story might have been. It looks like it might have been a nauseating watch, that's for sure, much more so than the shorts. But it also might have changed the course of filmmaking, at least in the cult world of your Lynches and your Jodorowskys."

In 2019, a crowdfunding campaign was launched to raise sufficient funds to complete and release *The Barrels*, with a stretch goal of finally making the short films commercially available. Donor rewards included new limited-edition Mondo wall art and T-shirts to be produced by vintage clothing company Junk Food. With the help of a grassroots social media push, the campaign was fully funded within weeks. It looked, for a brief moment, as though Malcom Strickland's dreams were on the verge of crossing over into the mainstream.

But there is currently no plan in place to complete the campaign's objectives. Every post-production and restoration professional who's viewed the footage has declined the project immediately and refused to discuss the film's content.

"I like to sleep at night," one expert said (also preferring anonymity), "so I don't think about what I looked at. And I consider it my social responsibility to make sure nobody else does. I'm sorry if that's frustrating to people, but I wouldn't want to burden them with having to know how right I am."

• •

Malcom Strickland left Massachusetts without a trace in 1972. If he's still alive, he would be over 90 years old.

The most significant update to the 2017 edition of *The Fathomless Vision of Malcom Strickland* is a new interview with Cilla Alfredson, her first since her 2011 Angelika appearance. In this interview, she is candid in a way she's never been, seemingly bolstered by a trust built between herself and Prof. Ramsay:

CA: Yes, he does live with Adonijah now. Well, I don't know that for sure. I should say, Adonijah knows where Malcom is.

LR: But you haven't spoken to him?

CA: No. I tried to reach him a few times early on. Adonijah made it clear that this wasn't in Malcom's best interest.

LR: Did you ever go back to Virginia to try and find him yourself?

CA: I got the distinct sense this would be a futile efort, and to be honest, not one I was sure I wanted to put forth.

LR: And did you attempt to obtain a divorce?

CA: Again, effort was required. I was fairly certain I wouldn't be getting married again, so I just think of myself as a widow. Legally, the marriage can't be declared void, but to me, it's void.

By her own account, she did receive one letter in 1991, written in Adonijah's handwriting and purporting to be a transcript of a message from Malcom. She burned it upon reading it and claims to have erased its content from her memory.

"You want to leave memories as they are," she said. "You don't want anything new and—complicated, or—you just can't…"

As seems to happen so often when people try to discuss Malcom Strickland and his work, she trails off into dark contemplations.

The 2017 interview between Alfredson and Prof. Ramsay ends with a discussion of what she knows about *The Barrels*, and her memories of its production. As with all of her husband's films, she knows very little about how it was made. "It was *his* career," she says. "He didn't ask to come to work with me, I didn't ask to go to work with him. We were both so consumed with work that home time was sacred." However, when pressed, she offers her impressions.

"I found a few pages of the script one day. They were under the couch […] And I read them while he was sleeping, and when he woke up—I was shaken and I said to him, *How do you know all this?* And he was so agitated, he didn't want me to see the script. I don't know if script was the right word, it was more of a treatment. A detailed description of scenes. Very, very detailed."

Prof. Ramsay prompts her to explain what she means about the content of her reading.

"Oh, I'm so sorry. My mind sometimes—especially about all this—it was *my* dreams. He had written down *my* dreams. […] And I never told him about—it wasn't only that, of course, there were other images written down, and they were numbered and coded somehow, I've chalked it up to a formatting—something."

Prof. Ramsay addresses the elephant in the room: does she put any stock in the theories that obsess some corners of the fan community suggesting the Strickland filmography is, in any way, influenced by legitimately supernatural abilities or forces?

In the interview transcript, this question is followed by: [EXTREMELY LENGTHY PAUSE].

And then Alfredson offers a memory.

"One night, about three weeks into Adonijah's visit, maybe four, I was sleeping in the guest room. I woke up one night. There was a pressure. It was very late at night. There was a pressure, right—[indicates sternum]. And I woke up—with great difficulty—and Malcom was sitting on me. Not with all his substantial weight. He had his knees by my sides. But with enough. And I couldn't move. And he was looking at me. And he didn't seem surprised, he seemed dazed. That's not quite right. He seemed focused.

"I heard something moving around out in the hall. I thought it was Adonijah. I think it was. And Malcom left. Calmly. And I didn't say anything. But later he told me he'd been sleepwalking recently. He said it casually. But casually, in that way you talk when you want someone to hear you, without—but he was awake. I could always tell the difference. I always knew when Malcom was dreaming."

fecund

rajiv moté

It was more than the usual disrespect of youth for experience: Jerry wanted me gone.

I couldn't take it personally. We'd tussled in meetings, chats, and email chains, but ultimately, it was about the work. Even the older generation of business pundits claimed that the past wouldn't fit in the containers of the future. I was dead weight, too slow to change. It was implicit: everything needed to be challenged, disrupted, and reinvented. In fact, "ReInvention" was what Waterman, Inc., my employer of twenty-some years, called our annual innovation brainstorm week.

Jerry attacked during the ReInvention kickoff, aiming the conference room camera at the top of my head, showing Chicago, Austin, Toronto, and Mumbai the thinning, scalp-exposing hair at the crown of my head.

New ideas were synonymous with youth. Jerry was an up-and-comer out of Technology, and I was a balding, middle-aged man in Customer Engagement.

"Is that a blow-hole?" he asked four cities, zooming in on a pucker of skin at the center of my crown that I'd felt, but never investigated. The blown-up image on the main monitor was an obscenity. I covered my head with my hand, drawing focus to the untanned groove where there once was a wedding ring. The years do leave their marks. Three nations of laughter burned in my ears.

If you show vulnerability, the youth will tear you apart. I pulled my lips into a smile, grunted in what could be taken as a chuckle, and leaned back in my chair, moving my loss of hair and marriage out of frame, leaving the camera to focus on the paunch straining the buttons of my dress shirt. I missed the days without cameras reminding me how others saw me. It was better for my confidence, and easier to concentrate on the work.

The global laughter died, our Head of Business presented her slides, and ReInvention commenced. Over the course of this week, the ship that was Waterman, Inc. would chart a new course. Again.

Ninety minutes later, I rushed to the restroom. If you've ever tried to look at the top of your own head in the mirror, you'll understand the unsuccessful contortions my neck and eyeballs made. I positioned my phone, took a picture, and zoomed like Jerry had. Holy shit. Jerry pulled his punch by calling it a blow-hole.

"I need this like I need another—" I couldn't finish. It wasn't funny. Long ago, going through puberty, I was comforted by my father's reassurance that my alarming bodily changes meant I was becoming a man. What was I becoming now? Was there a word for it, other than old? It was nothing to look forward to. And I'd never heard of *this* before.

I couldn't blame Jerry for wanting me gone. But I had no place else to go, at least none that would pay for medical insurance—which I'd need to take care of the new hole in my head. To Jerry, I was old, but for retirement benefits, not old enough. Somehow I had to keep going.

Back at my apartment, I sat at my dining table that doubled as a work desk and wondered if my new hole was an entrance or an exit. No, that's a false dichotomy; I'd been through enough tolerance training to respect all orientations and lifestyles. A human orifice could be whatever its owner wished. Still, this hole was, to my knowledge, unprecedented, and perhaps its biomechanics predisposed it to certain usages over others. Sure enough, I had new musculature that allowed me to flare or clench the aperture, but nothing emerged. No spray of seawater. No mental excretion. No brain-child. Not an exit, then. At least not now.

Unbidden, I imagined Jerry standing on the conference room table, holding me by the ears and displaying his dominance on my hole while tears rolled down the bridge of my nose. *Goddamn, Jerry.*

It had to be considered. I traced the pucker on the crown of my head with my middle finger, circling the hole, a decaying orbit to the opening. I pushed my finger in. There was no pain. Nor, to my relief, pleasure. I expected to hit skull or brain matter, but my finger kept going in, without resistance, to the knuckle. I pulled it out, and it came out clean, if moist.

Experimentally, I sniffed. It was too light to be an odor, too earthy to be a scent. It reminded me of gardening with my mother. Learning to grow things. What was her word? "Fecund."

I ought to call my doctor, I thought. I still had health insurance, after all. I wouldn't have time to see him during ReInvention Week, but the responsible thing at my age would be to get my new hole looked at. It probably wasn't worth a trip to the Emergency Room, unless it started to hurt. I decided it could wait.

The next morning, after strange, fingery dreams, I woke to pressure in my head. Not pain, precisely. But my new cranial musculature was spasming, and I had a sense of what might happen. I went into the bathroom and bowed my head to the toilet as I hadn't done since my 20s. Something slipped out of my hole and plopped into the water. It was moving, curling and straightening, propelling itself around the bowl. A finger.

Not *my* finger: the skin tone was off, it was a little slimmer, its nail beds were shallow, and it had an extra joint bending the wrong way. Where it would have met a hand, there was smooth skin. Not a copy of the finger I'd inserted, but certainly inspired by it. I watched, uncertain how to feel. In a social context, this would be repulsive. In the privacy of my bathroom, it was fascinating. Maybe a little wonderful. I'd created something, and if it wasn't entirely original, it wasn't a throwaway commodity, either. Maybe it wasn't marketable, but it was worth thinking of as a proof-of-concept, a new way of making things. I fished the wriggling digit out of the bowl and vigorously washed it along with my own hands.

I took to wearing caps. People commented, but it was easier to talk about caps than a puckered orifice at the crown of my skull. Jerry, of course, told me I ought to air out my blow-hole, and played the National Anthem on his phone to get me to take off my cap, but ReInvention Week was in full swing, and there wasn't much time for razzing and banter. We had futures to imagine, presentations to prepare.

Privately, I experimented with inserting things into my hole. My dreams became vivid and strange. I dipped things in and out, and later, similar—but different—things emerged. A red jelly bean produced a mauve cylinder. (It tasted of bourbon and swagger.) A buffalo nickel inspired a silvery seven-cent piece, stamped with a Viking head on one side and a rhinoceros on the other. I rolled up a page from *The Pocket U.S. Constitution*, and I later extruded a page with three new Amendments about reversing hair loss. I produced three more middle fingers and fixed them to the television stand, constantly curling and straightening.

ReInvention continued.

"You ready to wow leadership tomorrow?" Jerry asked me. "Because I sure am. I don't think you're going to like it much, but if you're curious—" He tossed me an object. It was a flash drive. "Here's the future." He smirked. "I'll bet you know where you can stick it."

He'd put his presentation on a flash drive just to make that joke. Hurtful. But I'd been openly blocking and challenging Jerry over the last several months, so we'd established an open antagonism that leadership called "a productive push-and-pull dynamic." It showed we both cared. Still, hurtful.

I didn't stick Jerry's flash drive in any bodily hole. I did stick it into the USB port of a loaner laptop, since I didn't trust Jerry enough to use my own. In broad strokes, what I found was what I expected. Every problem was a technology problem, and it could all be solved with more technology. Lots of buzzwords, lots of machine learning. Nothing specific about our business, but plenty to suggest that it was all just a matter of feeding the right data into the magic solution-box. How to get there was a patchwork of hand-waving and dubiously relevant case studies, but the implication was clear: Waterman, Inc. would no longer need me, the Customer Engagement department, or any institutional knowledge at all. The new tech would take care of everything.

Data was like money: once you had enough, it would just start sustaining itself, and the business along with it.

It was bullshit, but convincing bullshit, using all the language and aspirations that resonated with the industry articles that leadership read. Cutting human costs through automation. Marketing-friendly trends. A blend of new and familiar, balanced to feel both exciting and safe. Leadership would love it. I thought back on every year at ReInvention. The week always seemed to inspire a pivot, but we never actually did anything new besides reorganize departments and "right-size." ReInvention wasn't about innovation, but making waves and surviving them. This time I wouldn't survive Jerry.

Unless.

That night, I laid out my clothes for the next day, brushed my teeth, and inserted Jerry's flash drive into my hole. I didn't know if it would work this way. I had no idea how my hole worked, and maybe it didn't matter. If ReInvention was really just magical thinking, well, my thinking was the most magical of all.

My dreams that night had the character of Revelation. Burning bushes, a great stone sphynx speaking backwards, storms where lightning burned shining letters into the firmament. The proof came in the morning: the flash drive was still there, lodged in my hole, but its contents had been replaced. I grinned as I reviewed the slides. It was nonsense. Lunacy. No business case, just "vibes," as the kids say. But so was Jerry's. The only difference was who came out ahead.

••

I could barely pay attention to Jerry's presentation. Watching it twice wouldn't make it any less depressing, or more coherent. Not that I'd prepared anything close to coherent. My hole could only produce a parody of what tech offered. At best, someone would get the joke. That was my bar to clear for this year: successful satire.

Jerry's presentation got applause, mostly from engineering, but enough people could extrapolate the "right-sizing" that would result from the proposed systems. So the response was tempered. It gave me the perfect segue to my presentation.

"Jerry showed us a compelling future of automated systems that know our business and will let us—well, *some* of us—ride on their coattails," I said, bringing up my first slide. "But you've been hearing about these solutions for years now, and where has it taken us? What promise, made year after year at ReInvention, has it fulfilled? We're still chasing a horizon that hasn't gotten any closer."

The tech folks across two continents looked exasperated. These things took time, they always said. If only the Old Guard would get out of the way and let them deliver.

"The problem is strategic. Year after year, we've tried to lead with a new idea around silicon intelligence, but we're always catching up. It's not our core competency. What do we do better than any start-up, than any hot new tech firm? Only one thing, really. *We know our customers.* We have a relationship with them. We know what they need, through decades of experience. It's time to pivot from artificial intelligence to organic wisdom."

"Take your hat off!" Jerry said. Laughter.

"Thank you, Jerry. I was about to." I took off my cap and unclenched at last. I felt my new hole release... something. The fricative feeling of silent, continuous cerebral flatulence. Through the room's main display, I saw a golden nimbus radiate from me like a halo. Uplifting music chimed from somewhere, probably my own head. I wasn't sure what would emerge; my only thoughts were to win over my audience and *sell it*, regardless of what "it" was. It was the first time I'd tried extruding an intention. *It was lovely.*

"Organic wisdom. It isn't something new," I said. "It's going back to first principles. What Waterman was founded on. Knowing our customers." I caught a whiff of new-office smell: a bit of sawdust, new paint, fresh toner for the printers.

"The future is organic," I continued. "Organic production. Organic growth. You can almost smell it." Now, the air was suffused with that garden-smell. Fertile soil where plants could grow. *Fecundity.* On the monitors, I saw employees across three countries look up, their nostrils flaring as they inhaled. Impossible. Nonsense. But I went with it.

The music swelled, and the nimbus transformed into a spray of stars in a limitless sky. I kept speaking from my slides. Even I lost track of where it was going--if it was even going anywhere at all. Sometimes a bad movie can be saved by its music and visual composition. This was similar. There was a sense of a grand future unfolding, a sense of awakening from a digital dream and feeling, once again, the earth beneath our feet and the heavens above. I never thought such things could come out of my head.

"This is the year when Waterman—when we—find our way back to what we once knew to be true," I said.

Abruptly, I turned to Jerry who was searching the walls and ceiling for the source of the light, music, and scents. "Of course," I said, "there will need to be some tweaks to our organization. We have to bring our feet back to Earth. Technology will have to be subordinated to Customer Engagement. *Structurally subordinated.*"

The two words hung in the air. Gravity seemed to increase. The galaxy of light coalesced into a spotlight on Jerry. The conference rooms across the world were silent and still, as if the video feed had frozen.

It was far more dramatic than my parody warranted.

Then, our Head of Business clapped. It was a slow clap, the kind at the end of movies, the kind that declares the winner. It was joined with applause across four cities, swelling to the sound of a storm.

"That was some bullshit," Jerry said, packing his desk up to move to a lower floor with the rest of the right-sized tech department. "I don't know how you pulled off those special effects. But that presentation made zero sense."

Jerry wasn't wrong. But apparently it didn't matter. I shrugged. "It seems this year, the future is organic." Then, I fished in my pocket and tossed Jerry something I'd made especially for him. "And I guess you know where you can stick it."

Jerry screamed when the newly-made finger wriggled in his grasp, and he continued screaming, far longer than the joke warranted.

nightmare diaries

k.m. parker

To Mrs. Fotia,
St. Petersburg, Russia September 29th, 17—

Dearest Cousin, I hope this letter finds you well and in good spirits as the winter season commences. I intend to honor the promise I made to correspond regularly throughout my time in the Americas. I am yet to arrive, and so I imagine this and several other letters I will send at once when we make port.

If we make port.

Our voyage has taken an unexpected turn. An unseasonable storm has blown us north, well off our course, and now the ocean is covered in ice in every direction. The sailors I have spoken with have assured me that we can tum southward and resume our voyage, though I can sense their unspoken apprehension. Our voyage is in peril, and we must make haste to get back on our intended track or risk being crushed by the ice. As I cannot in any way affect this outcome, I have tried to tum my thoughts from it, with limited success. The situation weighs on my nerves, and the dream I had last night has compounded my unease.

I dreamt I was afloat upon a plate of glass smooth and polished like mirrored silver, surrounded by walls of ice so high they blocked the shape of the moon in the otherwise inky darkness. The plate moved by some unknown power, and I knew in my dream that I was but a passenger on a voyage beyond the realm of my understanding. It was not a comforting realization. As the ice closed in around me, I screamed. I begged Almighty God to preserve me, even as the echoes of my voice were repeated back to me by mockingly indifferent glacial cliffs.

In that moment before I started awake, I felt truly and helplessly alone. In the light of that dream, the world seems leaner, darker. As if in every angle and curve aboard our vessel and floating out in the ice hides a silent lurking predator. That, even, would be comforting, for what 1 fear most about our predicament is the thoughtless surety of our destructor. Should this ice consume us, it will neither celebrate in victory nor contemplate in guilt. It shall continue on, primordially unaware of the destruction it has wrought, and no memory of our deaths will exist outside these pages.

September 30th, 17—

It is with mixed relief that I relate to you the arrival of something to distract me from my melancholy, and from the increasing vividness of my dreams.

It was early this morning when I saw him. A man, trudging unevenly across the ice. At first, I thought he was a figment of an exhausted mind driven to the edge by contemplations of its own mortality. But one of the members of the crew—one of your countrymen, I believe—called out some warning in his tongue, and as I watched all the sailors at work on the ship came to the railings. A skiff was sent out, and the man on the ice was successfully retrieved. He was tall, and the clothing that covered him made him appear bulky, though what little I could see of his face was sallow. He wore a hood and had a scarf wrapped so tightly that I could make out no features save for two piercing, dark eyes that seemed to penetrate my flesh. The sailors who had brought him over on the skiff believe him to be a survivor of some shipwreck. This is merely speculation, as the man appears to be dumb, though he understands English when it is spoken to him.

Mr. Renselov, one of the sailors who had collected him, said that a mute condition was not unheard of among those who have been shipwrecked and left alone for a great deal of time. Solitude, it seems, can drive one to many different forms of madness.

The stranger was provided a small bunk and the sailors went back to their tasks. I presumed they were merely too busy to ply our new guest with questions, but Mr. Stetler informed me that there is a bit of superstition about madmen on ships. The belief purports that if they are allowed to spread their tale, the madness will spread among the crew. As I am not afflicted with such superstitions, I have taken it upon myself to discover the truth of our visitor's ordeal.

When I first went below to speak with the stranger, I brought along pen and paper, to facilitate communication. I did not know if the man was lettered, but hoped that he would be able to relay at least a partial account of whatever harrowing ordeal befell him. Truthfully, I was so desperate for a distraction from the ice that I hoped the exercise would be laborious and time-consuming.

The space he had been afforded was small, making him appear larger than when I had observed him on deck. It was chilly belowdecks, even out of the bite of the wind, so I was not surprised to find he was still wearing the bulk of his winter gear, including the scarf and hood that leant him his air of anonymity. Only his hands were ungloved and he held them to the heat produced by a small lantern, the sole flickering light that cast the room in oddly unsettling shadows.

In that light, his hands appeared strange and mismatched. His right was stout, tanned and calloused, while his left appeared smaller and paler. I wondered for a moment whether some strange vocation may have caused the imbalance or if a disease had perhaps weakened one of his limbs, but thought better than to ask. I sat down on a cot across from him and asked if he would relate to me what had happened to leave him stranded on the ice.

For a moment, my mysterious companion made no move to respond or to reach for the papers I had proffered as a means of recording his tale. I worried briefly that whatever infirmity had driven him mute might have affected him more greatly than I had originally supposed, to the point that I would not be rewarded my answers.

But then, it happened. The man reached into his coat and withdrew a small bundle of papers, which he reached across to offer me. The edges of them were damp from melted ice, but the pages were covered in writing in a firm though unpracticed hand. They appeared to be a set of entries for a journal, though they were not bound into one, and as I read them the shadows in that cramped belowdeck space seemed to push in on me, and by the time I finished the heavy coat I was wearing was far too light to suppress a shiver down my spine.

I have transcribed the paper's contents below for you, both to present them as part of this dialogue and to preserve them. The entries read as logs, so I have included the dates provided.

••

September 21st, 17—

I have passed beyond the furthest reaches of human exploration—the frozen landscape in all directions is barren to the horizon. The relentless arctic wind drives any offending mound of sleet or snow down into the icy surface like a frozen mallet, beating endlessly against the lifeless landscape. And yet I forge onward, leaning into protesting squalls, heedless of their warnings to tum back, seeking the place where my compass needle spins uselessly.

My possessions are meager now. On one hip I carry a cutlass, on the other a pistol with one predestined bullet. My compass I keep in my hand, closed tight in my mittened fist. Since the death of my dogs, I pull the sled myself through this glacial purgatory, as I cannot afford to lose the cargo it carries: A man bound up in furs and leathers, delirious but alive, and the strange tome that served as my guide to this place. My salvation or my destruction, we have yet to see.

Beyond these earthly tokens, I bear a heavy isolation, one that I have been cursed with since the moment of my birth. I carry a burning question, one thing I must know before the moment of my death. But most importantly, I drag along in my soul the intangible wound that was left by the sudden loss of the man I have hated my entire life; the one who plucked me from the void of concept and gave me this wretched, cursed existence, only to abandon me to it. The man whose death I thought would bring me peace, but instead I am more empty without my hate.

The winds have become too strong to continue tonight, so I have stopped to rest. I write this in the utmost hope that when I lay my body down tonight I will pass into death, not the dreams that have tormented me so. Should this prove to be my last entry, simply destroy this and anything else you have found in my camp. Leave our bodies to the frozen wasteland, and do not read the book I carry, lest you too learn to fear the act of sleep.

September 22nd, 17—

Last night, my dreams brought me to the abandoned barn where I had taken refuge after my first rejection by mankind. It was there I had learned to understand human speech, and how to read and to write. It was the closest I have been in my miserable, short life to happiness. But those times are not the times I dream of when I dare to sleep. Instead, I return to the day that that happiness came to an end. For when I told my creator of what had happened there, I lied.

The day had begun as I had described to him: the family had gone for a walk, and old blind De Lacy had stayed home. From the other side of the wall, I grappled with the urge to go and speak to the man, to introduce myself in the hopes that I may slowly acclimate the family to my presence, to make them know that I was not a threat to them before they saw my horrid countenance and recoiled in terror. But despite what I said later, I never shook that fear of rejection that paralyzed me.

Instead, it had been a stranger who knocked on the door of their little hut that day. In my dreams, I can hear the man introduce himself. I watch through the chink in the wall as old De Lacy offers the traveler some warm broth and engages him in conversation. I remember the feeling of jealousy at this interloper. I recall the pang of fear that this man would take credit for the acts of charity I had been performing for the family. But in my dreams, I do not replay these emotions, only the growing dread of hearing each of the man's revelations, knowing what will come next: He told De Lacy he was just passing through the area. That no one was traveling with him, or knew of his travel plans. De Lacy was like a fly in honey, drunk before he realized he was ensnared, as the traveler wove a web of the man's own doom around him.

I was so engrossed, I did not see De Lacy's son, Felix, sneak up behind the stranger until the younger man clubbed the unfortunate traveler over the head. Even in dreams, I still feel the pang of shock to see the family, only moments before so precious to me in the innocence of their joyful cohabitation, tie up this stranger and drag him down the hatch to the small cellar below the hut. I had never seen them go down the hatch before that day, and in truth had almost failed to notice its existence.

Trapped in Sisyphean recreation of that horrid day, I wait several long minutes before curiosity overwhelms fear, and I creep out of the ruined building that had been my home and in through the front door of the adjoining cottage. As I stride uneasily across the cottage floor, I begin to hear muffled sounds from below; voices raised in a repetitive rhythm. As I throw open the cellar door, the sound becomes clear, a chant in some ancient and horrific language that even in memory drives a cold spike into my gut.

In my dream as in my memory, I walk heavily down into the cellar, my height leaving the scene below obscured until the moment my feet touch the cold earthen floor. No matter how many times I dream this same cursed dream, what I see at the bottom of that staircase sickens me to my unnatural core.

The dirt floor in the center of the room had been inlaid with a silver chain, winding in some sort of profane symbol that I could not make out, because over the center of it was bound the body of the traveler. He had been tied down to stakes, and a figure in tattered black robes was leaning over him. It had taken me a few moments to realize that this cloaked figure was in fact biting at the traveler, sinking his teeth into the man's arm and tearing ferociously like a wild dog while the man lay stupefied. Three other dark figures stood over the scene, chanting the dark arcane chorus I had heard above, with one holding a book bound in dark leather.

My fear is overcome with hatred and revulsion. This place was sacred to me, that family had been under my protection. In the litany of ugliness I had seen in my short life, this perversion was elevated in that it threatened to desecrate the only thing I had ever held dear. Against one cellar wall was a shovel, and

I took it in one fist and brought it down hard upon the nearest robed defiler. I shattered the shovel fully against the second. The one holding the book screamed. It did not stop me, and I drove my weapon's splintered end through their body, pinning them to the wall like wine-stained laundry hung upon a clothesline.

At the noise, the last figure looked up from his ghastly feast. It was then that I saw his face, old man De Lacy, his lips stained red with fresh blood, his sightless eyes searching for the source of the commotion. I hesitated only a moment before bringing my mismatched fists down like hammers, consigning the old man to oblivion.

As I laid the bodies out along the floor of that place, I wept. Not just for the sinners' lives, but for my own shattered reality. They destroyed the ideal of what I believed good, decent people were like. I wept for the cruel fate of a cold cosmos, the cursed existence my creator had thrust upon me. The traveler shivered on the floor in his fugue, and I ignored him. Instead, I collected the leather bound book and began to read its pages. Oh, how I wished I hadn't! In every silent moment, every horrid nightmare, every creeping hour of solitude since, I have wished for any other outcome. For what I saw in those pages drove me to a madness that no other fact of my wretched life had forced upon me, and drove me to unimaginable depths of depravity to escape the silent, lonely moments when those terrible pages might be called back unbidden to my mind.

September 26th, 17—

The wind has finally subsided, and I have reached the place where my compass quits, spinning like a convict at the end of a hangman's rope. The only feature in this wasteland is a small rise in the distance, so I made my way towards that, and I found what I was looking for.

The object is large, a metallic cigar-shaped construction at least 100 meters across. It angles away from me, out of sight into the ice, and so I cannot rightly tell how long it is end to end, but where it bulges the ice above it there is a mere two meters separating me from the object.

I set to work with my cutlass, chipping away at the ice until I reached a place on the mirrored surface of the object where I could see a shallow inset. I knew this must be the place of ingress. No sooner had I cleared the ice from the grooves' circular shape than it gave way in a corkscrew movement, disappearing under the edge of the mysterious object.

Beyond this hole was perfect darkness, and a warm air wafted out from the recess, seemingly immune to the arctic chill. I went back to the sled and pulled back the covers. The man strapped to it was the traveler whom I had saved back in that small cellar when I was fleeing the havoc I had wreaked upon my creator, when this plan to cement my own oblivion was forming in my head. He did not know it then (nor did I until I read the book), but that day Old De Lacy had promised his soul to some dark and unforgiving being, and now the traveler barely breathed at that creature's doorstep. It seemed his mind would never fully recover. Without proper attention, the arm that De Lacy had bitten became permanently afflicted, withered and slight compared to his healthy one. He came with me meekly enough, but developed a fever on our journey that resulted in my bundling him against the cold. That he remain alive was integral to my plan, so I took care to monitor his condition.

I undid the ropes holding him to the sled, and with a single mighty swing I drove the cutlass into the ice. I tied one end of the rope to the cutlass, the other to the cursed traveler, and I carefully lowered him into the aperture I had discovered. Once he was gently placed on the bottom, I took hold of the rope and tested it against the piton of the cutlass. When I was confident it would hold, I climbed down carefully until I was standing beside my doomed companion.

The inside of the mysterious vehicle was unusually humid. We were standing upon a shelf set into the nose of the cigar shape, a ledge only a few meters across. The majority of the interior appeared to be vacant, though the opening above did not afford much light. One other feature I could make out near the edge of visibility was a corpse, ancient and mummified in a strange case whose exterior was designed in a repeating geometric pattern of teal-tinted glass that appeared to tremble when beheld, like it was on the verge of flying to pieces at the mere perception of it. The images I could see emblazoned on the corpse's flesh I recognized from the tome, signifying the corpse's status as some sort of high priest, a vessel whose very being had been scooped out so that some great and terrible thing could speak through him.

As I watched, transfixed in horror, the corpse's mouth opened just a fraction of an inch, wide enough to allow a hoarse whisper, a pained moan made words by the will of some science beyond even the profane workings of my own design.

"Who treads upon the sacred tomb of Azak-thura, the Eternal King?"

In the darkness I felt I could almost make out some giant, obscene shape crouched outside of the light, surrounded by a sea of writhing tentacles. Whether that shape existed, or is a conjuration of my tortured mind, I will never know.

"No name has ever been given me," I answered, "but you may call me Adam, for I am the only of my kind."

"You are curious, Patchwork Man. So unlike the beings who have come before. Your scent is of decay and sorrow. Have you come for the great destroyer to put an end to your misery?"

I delayed my answer a moment. Though I had sworn that this quest would end in my destruction, here upon the precipice I feared it still would not be enough. All prior attempts to end my horrid existence have failed, even my own. My creator, in his arrogance, made me well. I fear less that this being will try to destroy me than that he would try, and fail.

"I have brought a human with me, Ancient One, whose soul was promised to you by your disciples. I seek to offer you a trade."

"Azak-thura does not bargain with insects. Still, your impudence amuses the Eternal King. What bargain do you seek?" Every respite from that horrid whisper of a voice was a mercy, the sound frayed at my fragile hold on sanity. The descriptions of this eldritch monster's tastes from De Lacy's book returned to my mind in vivid detail each time it spoke, and focusing on the goal I came here to accomplish became harder and harder. I pulled out the leatherbound book from where I had it stowed, and threw it into the dark for the elder thing's inspection.

"The book says that you feast upon the flesh of your sacrifices, while your lord feasts upon their souls. Is that true?"

"You spoke of a bargain, half-made thing, not of questions." The whispering corpse responded. "What do you offer and what do you seek?"

Breath caught in my throat. This was the moment I had come all the way for, the thing that had kept that loaded pistol on my belt from my temple. The one thing that would make the pain and misery worth it.

"Very well." I responded. "Heal and release the human. Take my soul instead. This is my bargain."

The sibliant voice hesitated for a moment.

"You do not want your soul devoured." The corpse finally responded. "No, you wish the great destroyer to tell you if you have one."

Nothing moved in the tomb save the slow descent of snow-flakes that found their way in from the opening above us. I was noticing these snowflakes for the first time. During my long trek through the arctic tundra, the slow dance of snow had been a mundanity, but here it stood out, incongruous with the surroundings.

The voice returned, scratching harshly against the inside of my skull.

"At sunset, the Eternal King shall decide. Wait or flee this place, it makes no difference. If he marks you for destruction, your fate shall be sealed."

I climbed back out of the tomb, and dragged the poor cursed traveler up behind me.

The sun is crawling low in the sky now, and I know that no matter the outcome these are likely my final words. When I began this account, I told myself that it was so that what I saw upon my ascent to the edge of the world may not be lost. But I suppose all along I was writing to you, Frankenstein. Had I been formed by a loving God I would confess my sins now, before the call of oblivion. But I am a monster, begotten as the creation of a monster, I make no amends.

—ADAM

••

As I finished these letters, I felt a cold breeze breathe down my spine, like a rustle in the darkness that made me jerk around to see if someone was behind me. But there was no one. I was alone belowdecks with the stranger, holding the pages of this log he had given me. I tried to hand them back, but if he understood my intention to return them he made no indication. I looked over his large frame again. Sometime while I had been reading he had put his gloves back on, but I remembered my observation about one hand being more slight than the other.

I tried to tell myself that I was unsure if any of what I just read was actually true. And of course questions ached at me. I recalled our strange guest's mismatched hands. Adam had described himself as a patchwork creation; perhaps these hands were his. But the stranger that he had dragged up to the top of the world had suffered an injury, and the writer had identified that one of his arms was shriveled. Which of the two, then, sat before me?

"Are you one of the two men described in these pages?" I asked earnestly. "Do you know what happened? Did the one who wrote this—did he have a soul?"

The stranger did not answer, just stared back at me with those unsettling, piercing eyes. I made several more entreaties in vain, but seeing as he would not be moved to speak or write more, I made a polite exit and came to my cabin to pen this letter to you.

But as night approaches, I am left to wonder. Could a creature made in the fashion of this 'Adam' have a soul? But this same being walked across the ice to trade something he did not even know if he possessed for a cursed stranger.

Could such a person lack one?

the blind curve

taylor dye

I'd guess that everyone's trip home includes at least one blind curve. You know the kind, where absolutely anything could be hiding around the bend—an overflowing river running across the street; a truck that's spilled its haul of Christmas trees, blocking the lanes; a demented clown performing the Macarena along the double-yellow lines; or, if you're lucky, nothing at all.

You never have a clue until you actually make the turn. I would wager at least one of those blind curves is located somewhere within the last mile to your house. I've never checked the statistics—I don't even know if any exist—but I strongly suspect that for the significant percentage of incidents that occur within five miles of one's home, that a not-so-insignificant portion actually occur within that final mile, and a not-so-insignificant portion of those occur in the aforementioned blind curve. But even if that assumption isn't accurate for the general population, I know it's accurate for me.

My blind curve is actually on an interstate—I-5, to be exact—curling under a bridge before heading downtown. I live in an apartment building only a few blocks from the highway, and I can see the upper portion of my building amidst all the towering wonders of downtown even before I reach the curve.

During the day, and particularly during the morning and late-afternoon rush, the interstate is heavily trafficked, with plenty of near misses, sideswipes, and rear-end fender-benders, though hardly any are a consequence of the curve itself. Of course, it wasn't like the curve magically vanished during daylight hours. I suspect it was the presence of so many other vehicles on the road at the same time that had greater impact, negating the more sinister aspects of the curve.

Negating the reason it was designated a "blind curve" in the first place.

It was at night, after the sun went down and the appearance of headlights on the other side of the median divider became only occasional, that the true danger of the curve was revealed.

I arrived just after midnight.

The speed limit drops from sixty to fifty-five approaching the curve, so I was slowing down. There are a couple of streetlights, but even they aren't enough to fully banish the darkness, particularly under the bridge. On this night I had clear asphalt ahead, no traffic, with only the soft orangish glow of the streetlamps and my own headlights illuminating the way. In my rearview, the nearest car was a hundred yards back.

The light shining on the pavement went from pale orange to shadowy black at the bridge. For a moment, even the shine from my own headlights failed to penetrate the void.

Heading into the curve, I began turning the steering wheel. I remember my eyes returning to the road from wherever I had been looking before—I'm guessing the rearview mirror—and then getting the quickest glimpse of a small, white bundle on the ground in the right lane, my lane, just beyond the line of demarcation on the far side of the bridge where darkness became light again.

A tiny, white bundle.

A bunched-up, discarded sheet or blanket, perhaps.

However, it's this next part I'm unsure of. The reason I'm telling you this in the first place. I swear I saw a tiny hand reaching out of the bundle at the last second. Grasping at air.

forever

joey r. poole

The clack of Charlene's heels on the cold sidewalk echoed in the darkness just outside the shifting glow of the stoplight. It was a lonely sound, an empty sound, fit for the cavernous hunger that drove her into the October night like this.

She didn't recognize Senator Raymond Childers when he pulled up in his brand-new 1981 Cadillac, gleaming red like it had been greased, but she knew the instant she laid eyes on him that she wouldn't mind watching him bleed out when the time came later. There were shadows hiding beneath his baleful grin, something sinister in his ease behind the wheel and the nonchalant way he laid a long-fingered palm on her thigh before he'd even asked how much she cost.

"I know a place," she said, shifting her leg under his palm to bring it closer to where he really wanted to touch her and telling him to take a left at the end of the block beside the pawn shop.

The smell of the blood in his veins was rising now, coppery and alive beneath the brass of his cologne and the sweet stench of his whiskey-sweat. The bottomless pit of want in her guts screamed for her to slash him open at one of his thumping arteries—throat, inner thigh, wrist, anywhere blood swished in crimson tubes just below the surface of his skin—but she forced it down and tried to revel in the anticipation. Before the night was over, she'd guzzle as much of that blood as she could and bathe in the rest on the cool luxury of these leather seats.

She'd done this a dozen times now, enough to feel calm and in control, but she still hadn't quite figured out exactly what she'd become. The only word for it—*vampire*—was so ridiculous she could barely think it, much less say it aloud. But it was the only word she had to describe the change in her. Nothing had been the same since the night just a few months ago, one year to the day after her sister Wanda's funeral, when she'd been out of her mind with grief and tequila and let herself fall right into the arms of a stranger she'd met at Jaco's bar.

She didn't remember much about him. There was a cowboy hat, which stood out in a place where men mostly wore mesh-back ball caps festooned with trucking company logos or Gamecocks and Tiger paws, each according to his persuasion. He'd worn a rhinestone jacket like some old timey country singer, or maybe her memory of spangles was just the way his eyes shone in the dark. He was sweet, apologetic, though she couldn't remember for what. She'd awakened alone in her own bed, snuggled into the covers, tequila pounding in her head and a tiny nick on the inside of her thigh, the bloodstain already crusted on the sheets. The hunger didn't begin until days later, and it took her at least a week to realize it was for blood.

That's what you get, she thought. You spend half your life in church, then end up in a bar one shitty night and wake up with the Devil inside you. Something like that happened to her sister, too, except it wasn't blood Wanda hungered for, it was something worse. Charlene might be a vampire, but at least she wasn't a junkie. Or a hooker.

Once the shock of what she had to do to feed this new hunger wore off, she began to embrace it. If she had to stalk the night ripping people apart to feast on their blood, it might as well be the kind of men who'd picked up Wanda when her own hunger had driven her out to sell her body on the streets. The same kind of man as the one who'd strangled Wanda with her pantyhose and left a hundred-dollar bill stuffed in her mouth.

The problem was some of these men didn't seem like bad guys at all. The grandfatherly one who wheezed *I love you* into Charlene's ear as she sliced into his carotid artery. The college kid who'd cried and admitted he'd only picked her up because he was terrified that he might be queer. Those two didn't deserve what happened to them, but they ended the same as the rest, bleeding out in fuzzy ecstasy as she lapped at their gaping throats with lips that spoke dreams into their heads in a way she had only begun to understand. She didn't feel good about those two, but the others all had something wolfish about them, a glint of the eye showing they saw her as something to be used up and discarded. Those kind she didn't mind killing at all.

"Right here," she said, leading the man she didn't know was her Senator to the abandoned cotton mill where she'd been doing her business, dropping the bodies in the river that used to turn the mill's giant grist wheel and ditching their cars wherever she could. They'd wash up on the rocks a couple miles down, or if she was lucky and the water was high, sometimes they made it all the way to the Congaree swamp downstream, bloated and catfish-gnawed beyond recognition.

She almost laughed when he pulled the gun on her, holding it in his left hand, taking his right hand off her thigh and draping it casually atop the wheel. She wasn't going to mind killing this one at all. There'd be no soul-searching guilt tomorrow as she lounged the day away, watching her game shows and soap operas with the blinds pulled down tight against the sun, feeling fat as a gorged tick, the terrible hunger sated, at least for a while.

"Nah, sugar," he said in one of those sighing, old-money Charleston accents. "I'm not stupid. You probably have a man down there waiting to knock me in the head and steal my wallet, maybe even this car. You just hold on while I take us somewhere better to do what we're going to do."

She wasn't sure her influence would work on him from this far away. She was usually so close they could feel her breath in their ear when she spoke like this. But she was growing stronger, and so were her gifts, so she softened her face and let whatever it was that had taken root in her soul into her voice.

"No, baby," she cooed. "We're going down by the river and I'm going to show you things you never seen."

At first he scoffed, but his face slackened a bit as she kept on with the sweet nothings until he belonged to her. He pulled into the shadows beneath a cypress tree on the far edge of the crumbling little parking lot and sat looking at her, quiet and eager for her to use him. She leaned into him, wanting him to fall even more under the spell of her whims, exhaling dirty talk about what she would do to him, how much she was going to enjoy slicing him open.

She was just beginning to learn this went both ways. Often, as she drove her will into a man's head with her words, their thoughts came floating back to her. Usually it was just so much pedestrian pornography, images of what body parts they wanted to violate, or have violated, thoughts of what they wanted to do so badly they'd been willing to pay her for it. Sometimes their desire was spiked with an undercurrent of fear and revulsion. Or it was clouded with guilt, with images of their mothers, wives, daughters. No matter the flavor, though, they all pretty much wanted the same things.

Raymond Childers' desire was different. It ran cold as stainless steel, and deep in his mind she felt what he wanted: to gut her like a fish. A flash of his most urgent want came to her, lazily, a dream, and she saw her own face, bruised and dead, a hundred-dollar bill shoved between her lips. Then the want became a memory, and it was Wanda's face, lips split over cracked teeth, one eye pounded closed.

Charlene's night prowling was first driven by a broad kind of vengeance, aimed at the world in general, at men in particular, a blunt wave of hate, strong in the places her grief had made her weak. She'd never thought she'd find the actual man who'd killed Wanda, but here he was, and she wasn't going to waste this opportunity. She was going to wallow in it.

She flashed her teeth at him, gnashed open the tiniest of cuts in his throat and sucked the blood from it, relaxing into the taste of it on her tongue. It wasn't much more than a shaving nick, but she didn't want him bleeding out too quickly. She'd open another vein, then another, and when he was weak enough he couldn't fight back, she'd release him from the grasp of her mind so he would know exactly what was happening to him. She was going to take her time.

She picked his hand up off his lap and let the pistol slide out and onto the seat beside her as she slipped the watch off his wrist and watched the tiny diamonds studding its face glint in the dashboard light. She wasn't in this for the money, but she still had to pay the rent, and of course she'd quit her job at the diner when she'd become whatever it was she'd become. She slipped the watch into her pocketbook and sank a tooth into his wrist, just where the blood was closest to the skin, the vein snaking from his forearm into his palm. She drank deeply of it this time, feeling it warm her as it poured down her throat and spread in her belly. Then she took off his tie and made a tourniquet of it, tying off his arm so he wouldn't bleed out, not yet at least. She wanted him to be wide awake and aware for what came next so he'd know who she was and exactly why she was killing him.

For that, she'd have to take him home. She'd let him laze away in his stupor until he was chained to the bed in Wanda's old room, then she'd bring him out of it, wake him in his new Hell. But first she was going to have another taste. She bent to loosen the tie she'd knotted around his arm, but suddenly the car was flooded with light as someone opened the door, and for the second time that night, she had a gun pointed at her.

• •

The sudden intrusion of someone opening the door snapped Raymond Childers out of her thrall. One moment, he'd been wrapped in the warmth of indescribable pleasure, his world shrank down to nothing but the tongue lapping seductively at this throat. The next he was jarred back into reality, where there was a gun in his face and he'd been an idiot, letting this hooker woo him into a trap. A thin rill of blood from where Charlene had nicked open his vein slipped down the side of his neck into his loosened collar and he slapped at it like a mosquito, only to find his hand gone pins-and-needles numb.

"Keep yer fuckin' hands where I can see them," the little prick said, waving the gun at him, everything except the arm holding the pistol sunk in shadow.

Childers clicked back into himself at the sound of somebody barking orders. His initial wave of panic gave way to a wellspring of arrogance born from a life of privilege and vigor. Clearly this dickhead had no idea who he was dealing with. He steeled himself like he had when he'd been a tailback hitting the gap in his football days and lunged for the pistol, thinking he'd knock it out of the guy's hand and beat the shit out of him. But he was slower than he remembered, and the bullet hit him harder than any blitzing linebacker ever had.

"Oh, honey," Charlene said, dabbing a finger into the gurgling bullet hole in Raymond Childers' chest and raising it to her lips like a lollipop. "You picked the wrong night for this shit."

She almost hoped the intruder would shoot her. There was nothing a bullet could do to her. She'd already tried to put one through her skull when she first realized what she'd become, but it only cost her a lost hour, like waking up from anesthesia, from oblivion beyond sleep, while her brain reassembled itself. The hole in her temple was tender when she'd awakened, and she'd watched it slowly knit itself back together in the mirror. The pain of a bullet tearing through her chest would be bracing, and it would give her a reason to do what she was going to do to this idiot kid for spoiling both her meal and her plans for revenge on the piece of shit lying dead on her lap.

She reached for the stranger with her mind, figuring she'd gorge herself on his blood even though she could smell that it was absolutely spiked with bitter fear. He was further away than Childers had been when she'd slipped inside his mind, and it was harder to grasp. He recoiled from it like a snake when it reached out to touch his thoughts, and then a bullet smashed into her skull.

• •

It wasn't unlike waking from a hangover. She'd had more than a few of those in the last year—since Wanda was murdered—so she was used to it. Her head was thrumming with pain, but she could feel her body coming back to her. She heard the voices long before her brain had rebooted enough for her to move or even open her eyes.

One of the voices she recognized as the kid who'd shot her. And her quarry, she remembered. She'd gotten her hands on the monster who killed Wanda taken away from her, just after she'd learned who he was, just as the delicious opportunities for her vengeance were laid out before her. Seeing him die was cold comfort. The kid—even though he probably wasn't much younger than her, he smelled so richly of fear and false bravado she thought of him this way—was begging someone to help him out of this mess.

"Goddamn, Terry," the other voice said. This voice was a pack-a-day croak belonging to someone older. "Shut up. Just shut the everlovin fuck up for a second and let me think." Terry tried to shut up, but Charlene could hear his whimpering, coming from just outside the passenger-side door she was leaning against, her head lolling out of the open window.

"The fuck are you thinking, anyway?" the older man said. "You kill two people, and then instead of getting the fuck outta there, you bring 'em to *me*? You fuckin' drive over here across town with a dead woman riding shotgun and another body in the trunk, right up my driveway and into my shop, and you bring your problems on *me*."

The kid just blubbered that he was sorry, that he hadn't meant to do it.

"Fuck, Terry." The other voice paused for the crack of a cigarette lighter. "Tell you one goddamn thing. You wasn't my sister's boy, swear to God I'd put you in the fuckin' trunk with both of them and sink you in the bottom of Lake Murray, is what I'd do."

"I know, I know," Terry managed. There was enough relief in his voice that it was evident he'd expected there was a decent chance his uncle might just kill him.

"Alright. So we just gotta fix this shit, and then we gotta lay low. So listen here: you are officially fired. Don't bring me any more goddamn cars, even if they ain't got bodies in them. The chop shop is closed. We are out of business after this right here."

"We gonna put it at the bottom of the lake?" Terry asked, starting to perk up a bit now.

"Hush. Lemme think."

While the uncle thought and wheezed around his cigarette, Charlene gained strength. Slowly, carefully so they wouldn't see, she tested her legs, gently kicking off her heels and stretching her calves, feeling the life seep back into them. She did the same with her fingers and then tested her tongue, licking the mélange of the Senator's blood and her own from her lips. She was starting to feel like herself again.

And she was hungry.

"Welp," the uncle said. "Guess the first thing is, let's put her ass in the trunk so she ain't waving out the goddamn window while we drive."

Charlene shifted her weight subtly against the back of the leather seat so she wouldn't fall out when they opened the door. She felt rough hands slide into her armpits and pull her out.

"Pop the trunk for me," the older man said, dragging her toward the back of the car. "And gimme a fuckin' hand. This bitch is heavier than she looks."

He let out an animal shriek when she turned her head and bit into his arm. Every kill strengthened Charlene as she gorged on their warm blood, but she hadn't yet had to test this power in a fight; she'd wooed them all into submission and they'd given themselves freely to her. This time was different. She kicked the uncle from where he'd dropped her on the shop floor and his knee buckled inward. She was on him so fast he had no time to scream before she ripped out his throat with her bare hands.

She looked across the Caddy, where Terry stood frozen. For a moment she considered reaching out to the kid with her mind again but decided against it. She didn't want to feel his fear wafting to her in his thoughts, and didn't want to feel sorry for him, to feel anything but his hot blood sliding down her throat. She picked at the gunshot hole, just off center on her forehead, and plucked out the bullet that had been backing its way out of her skull as the wound healed itself and smiled at him.

He turned and ran. She sprang onto the hood and pounced on him as he was frantically pulling the chain to raise the garage door. He was wiry, hard to the touch, and put up a better fight than his uncle. He spun and punched her, so hard she heard her nose crunch, and for a moment she was inside a ringing bell, but then the pain just galvanized her anger. He'd already sprinted away, out into the night when she shook it off. She followed the ragged sound of his breathing and the stench of his bloodfear to find him crouched behind the rusted hulk of an ancient pickup in the weeds behind the shop.

The half-moon hanging like a chipped tooth in the sky lit up the lot bright as noon to her eyes. She stood in the shadows at the edge of the shop, seeing the kid clearly enough to study the tatters at the collar of his sweat-soaked tee-shirt and the wiry hairs of his pitiful mustache. She sprang, covering the scraggly weeded expanse in a couple of leaping bounds and broke his jaw with a swiping backhand slap, knocking him unconscious. She raised his hand to her lips and bit into his forefinger, gnawing on the bone until it snapped between her teeth and then tore it away. She watched his hot blood spray in great spurting gouts into the air, then she stuffed the stump of his finger in her mouth and suckled at it like a baby on a nipple.

• •

The first thing Senator Childers became aware of was the stench of his own shit as he lay cramped in the dark. Long before he was able to move, he felt what he first took to be worms crawling inside his flesh, making jelly of his innards, but soon he realized it was his heart, his lungs, his spinal column stitching themselves back together, the cells driven mindlessly by whatever disease it was that woman had put inside him.

That woman. So much like the first one he'd killed, same frizzly red hair, same gap in her teeth, something haughty in her like she wasn't just some junkie peddling head for money. When he killed *her*, he decided, he'd stuff a hundred-dollar bill in her mouth, maybe even two, for she was worth more than the first one.

Slowly, he became aware of voices, muffled as if coming from far away. An argument, it seemed from the timbre and rhythm of the conversation, though he couldn't make out the words. What came next was hard to decipher. A door slamming, scuffling noises, a shriek so primal and terrified he wasn't sure it was human, then silence.

When he was able to move, he pounded his fists against the roof of his hell, not yet sure where he was, just that it was dark and smelled of his own filth. The claustrophobic terror of being trapped set in, warring with the desire to get his hands around that whore's neck and see the light in her eyes die as she finally resigned herself to what was coming. After a while, he heard a car engine crank, but it wasn't until his prison started moving that he realized where he was.

The thought of being dumped into the trunk of his own Caddy infuriated him. He clawed at the metal inside the trunk lid until his nails bent off and fingers were just ragged wet stumps, then slammed his forehead against it until he nearly caved in his skull. If only he could bend his legs to kick, he thought, he'd find a way out, but he was folded up on himself like a worm on a fishhook.

When he was spent, the rage was gone, replaced with something quieter. He thought of all the wrong he'd done, every shady deal he'd made, every bribe, every crony he'd screwed over. He thought of the first woman he'd killed just because watching her die fed a part of him he'd always been afraid to feed. He cried out for his long-dead mama, for the wife he'd grown to hate, for God—but there was no answer, just the echo of his own voice dying in the dark and the steady hum of tires on the highway beneath him.

He wanted to die then, but the meat was already growing inexorably back over the bones of his hands. Soon his mind cycled back to rage, and he started clawing again, a nameless hunger growing inside him, not from his belly but from somewhere deeper.

••

When Charlene had her fill of the blood gushing from the kid's hand, she let it drop to the dirt at her knees. Fear-spiked and bitter as it was, the blood still soothed her, and now every cell in her body purred like a lounging cat. This reverie was something she still wasn't quite used to. Sometimes she lost hours in it, and she realized that morning would be coming soon, and she had to get back home. She wasn't exactly sure what would happen to her in the daylight, but the instinct to stay out of it had such a pull that she didn't want to find out.

She fished the keys out of the kid's jeans pocket and went back into the shop. At first, she thought the muffled shouting and thumping noises came from the uncle, but his body was still lying crumpled beside the Caddy. Blood leaked from his throat clumping in the sandy oil-dry sprinkled on the shop floor. She paused to listen more closely. The sounds were coming from the trunk. Her heart sang when she realized it was the man who'd killed Wanda—and he was somehow still alive. All she wanted to do was kill him over and over again.

The gravity of the situation began to dawn on her as she backed the Caddy out of the shop and out onto the highway. She'd often wondered if she could turn someone into what she was. She'd been turned that way, it seemed, though she still couldn't remember much about the man who'd been so gentle in bed but left her bleeding on the sheets. But the men she'd killed had all stayed dead. Maybe it was just that she'd drained them completely. Perhaps it was the river; she'd drowned all their bodies when she was done. But she suspected it was just that not everyone had it in them to become what she'd become, that it was something she could only pass on to those with a heart as hateful as hers, as black and withered. Maybe the man she could hear screaming in the trunk had a heart corrupted with his terrible lusts the same way hers was corrupted with all the grief and the knotwork of feelings that came from loving somebody as fucked up as Wanda.

If that was the case, she'd done a terrible thing. She'd gone and made a monster even more wicked, more powerful. But she'd also given herself quite a gift: she could keep killing this monster again and again, forever. She could take him to heights of suffering he'd never dreamed of, and when she was finally bored with it, she'd figure out how to kill him for good. Maybe it was as easy as a stake in the heart, though she doubted that.

Charlene still didn't know exactly how all of this worked. But, as she pulled the Cadillac into the driveway of the house she'd shared with Wanda, she was starting to get a feel for it. She knew now that the hunger which drove her out into the night for blood was just a symptom of what had happened to her. It was a disease, maybe even a demon, that had taken up residence in her body. It was just a hunger that had to be slaked. It didn't define her any more than needing to drink coffee to stay awake for a double shift at the diner once defined her life. But the darkness inside her that dreamed of all the things she would do to the man in the trunk to make him feel the depths of her sorrow—that was *her*, all the way down to the marrow.

in the dark you can't see what's coming for you

chloe n. clark

In the middle of the pandemic, the highways were always empty. It was funny, I'd said once, to Mark, that when the world is falling apart is the one time ambulances made good time.

The first we'd been to was already too late. A woman with her throat ripped out by her toddler. The child escaped somewhere. I don't know if they were ever found, though I've always hoped that they were, that someone kept them locked up long enough for the doctors to do their thing and figure out how to bring their old self back. Finding an antidote didn't take as long as anyone thought it would. But it took probably longer than an infected toddler had.

I wondered sometimes, still, if Mark had worried about the infected. If he would have imagined their lives after they were cured. I wondered sometimes, still, if Mark had thought about it after the bite and before the turn. If he'd imagined all of the infected we'd seen race into the dark, escape through windows. Or if he'd thought of the bodies, all the bodies, we'd called on scene. All I could know for sure was that he'd raised his hand up to me, that he'd shown me the bite above his wrist instead of hiding it, pulling his sleeve down to cover it. He'd shown me so I could back my way to the ambulance, climb inside, lock the doors. We hadn't known then what I knew now.

One of our first rides together, we'd been called to a lake where a little girl had fallen through the ice. Her skin had the lightest edge of blue, where she was laid on top of the white snow. People were gathered around, one man giving CPR desperately. Mark had been so gentle, one hand gently hovering on the man's shoulder. He'd checked vitals, even though he knew, we both knew, that she was long past gone.

The coroner's team was already there, right behind us. As they began to zip the body bag closed, Mark had brushed a strand of hair from the girl's face, away from the zipper, so it wouldn't catch. If I'd been the one to give his eulogy, write his obituary, I'd have said that.

It was a routine call. Or routine for the pandemic. Someone saying they'd been hurt, and us assuming that meant bit, that they didn't want to say. That they were hoping they'd be the miracle who just needed a stitch.

When we got there, we let out a sigh of relief, because it was a woman sitting on the curb. Sprained ankle, swollen. But otherwise she looked fine, no sign of bites or infection. She said she'd tripped. Mark was wrapping her ankle when a group of infected emerged from behind the house, probably drawn by the woman's yelps of pain or the sound of our siren. One rushed me, tossed me to the ground—an infected woman who wore a t-shirt that showed a fat cat that read, "I'm always hungry." I almost laughed. Mark knocked her off of me. The woman with the sprained ankle had already taken off running, fear overriding pain. *Run*, Mark yelled, and I ran.

The police van that should've arrived at the scene before we did rounded the corner. Sirens wailing. That was protocol, police before emergency, but we were always early. The infected turned from Mark to the sound and he could've run to the ambulance, run to safety. But he raised his arm, showed the bite.

The thing was, I'd already been scratched. I could feel the abrasion starting to burn. Scratches took longer than a bite, sure, but it still happened.

As I watched Mark from the window, as I saw them shoot him down—it was too late for him. They made the announcement that night, that the infection could be cured. Mark must've been one of the last ones killed instead of tranqed. Imagine that, if he'd known that there was a cure coming, and he was just a couple of hours too soon, would he have thought it was funny? Funny in the way that the universe is.

If only he'd run to me instead. If we'd had more time, we'd have all the time in the world. I could have opened the door and welcomed him inside. We could've sat there in the ambulance, waiting for the news together.

Maybe, in that version of events, the cure never would've come. Maybe, we would have sat there until the night enveloped us into whatever it was we became.

the intruder theory

kayli scholz

A RECORDED CONVERSATION WITH ROWENA ROVE
AUGUST 9, 2023
INTERROGATION BY DETECTIVE DIANE HOFFMAN
BADGE #JTT0025023
SAINT BERNADETTE HOSPITAL
HOUNDS, FLORIDA, CALHOUN COUNTY

Yes, I know who you are. You're a detective interviewing me because DNA technology might help you help me. My story ain't changed a hair but I can tell you what I know. Yes, I'm doing fine. Yes, the woman dying in that bed there that's my mama. Yes, I can start from the beginning if that's easier.

My name's Rowena Rove. I live in Marietta, Georgia, 312 miles from Hounds, Florida. My sister, Bo, was six when she was murdered. I was nine. The date was June 17, 1996.

Mama's been headed home the last couple weeks in hospice. Back during the trial, a social worker from Victim Advocates set us up real nice so this room is all paid for. The Catholic hospital can't kick us out, and the public hospital won't bill us. You can see on the chart her name is Frances Rove; friends called her Franny, or Fran. Butch Hart was mama's boyfriend. He was one of the few good men, if you ask me. Yes, we got along fine. I don't know any woman alive that doesn't know what it's like to have a man swing at you out of nowhere. But Butch was a different breed.

Yes, me and Bo just called him Butch. He didn't pay us no mind calling him Dad because he had a bad relationship with his old man. We had that in common, us girls and Butch. Our biological father? Roy Johnson. He was serving time at the Tallahassee pen for aggravated robbery. Yes, he was accounted for on the night of June 17, 1996.

The four of us lived in a shotgun house next to a red mud-hill that dissolved into a bog during rain season. It stunk because the sun shined down like nothing you'd ever felt before. It was hot all the time. We didn't have any trees for shade except for a red buckeye covered in pollen. We had rows of chickweed instead of grass. I was afraid of horsetail because it looked like it would bite. Chiggers would latch to the spores. Me and Bo played in what we called the chigger field, behind the house. We climbed the buckeye up to the bigger branches, hang off the side, rip the horsetail out of the ground, scare each other half to death pretending it was poison.

Yes, Butch played games with us. I told you he was a softie at heart. We took turns shooting at old tin cans; *pop, pop,* you know how it goes. Yes, Butch had a shotgun. Yes, it was an old Beretta from the 70s, carved his initials into the comb. No, he never pointed the shotgun at us. Maybe once, playing around.

The field behind us had chickens. They belonged to the old lady that lived there. She had citrus trees me and Bo used to steal from. The chickens would squawk, run over the mud hill when the tin cans got hawked off the timber. Loggers drove ten-wheelers down our street at all hours of the day. No, we didn't know any of them personally. But I suspect—I *know*, Detective

Hoffman—that the killer was one of them loggers coming over the Florida-Georgia line.

I'm getting ahead of myself.

We were broke but not poor. We deserved it; that's how people think about people like us, what people said. When you're broke, everybody thinks you did something stupid to get you there. Maybe you drank too much or crashed your car, maybe you were lazy on the job, or married somebody dumber than you.

Where did Mama work? She worked all over. She was a babysitter, swept at the hair salon, waitress, cashier, and a window washer. She tried working at the sugarcane field about half-ways to ten miles from where we lived, but she had a mean bee allergy. There're always bees out in the fields and they survive the burning season. Butch? He worked at Woolworth's. He worked at the last Woolworth's in northern Florida. It was one of the traditional stores with a diner inside, dusty oranges and rusty brown vinyl booths and a counter. You could still get coffee, two fried eggs, and bacon for a buck ninety-nine. Yes, Butch had that job until Bo died.

Something happened that spring that got everybody in a tizzy over in the Sugar Bends district and in Hounds, too, made for a bad time for all of us. Butch got caught stealing from the Woolworths. It was a Nintendo 64. They'd just come out at Christmas. An N64 wasn't in nobody's budget and me and Bo kept pestering to see the console when his store got them in.

Well, Butch thought of it like a gift. Butch meant well. He worked hard and didn't mean anything by it. He said the company charged too much for a hunk of plastic with some electrical fibers inside. He said it was a rip-off. Us girls about lost our minds when he gifted us that N64 one Friday evening. We were so excited, fighting about who was gonna play first.

Yes, Mama was worried that Woolworth's would press charges. I think Butch stole the thing because he was trying to make up with me and Bo. What happened? It wasn't the end of the world what happened, I'll tell you that. Butch lost his temper, whipped his fist through our bedroom door. He occasionally slammed furniture or punched a doorknob off its hinges. Yes, those photos you've got are damage that Butch did. Yes, he smashed the window by the kitchen, too—yes, the same window that was broken the night that Bo was murdered. Yes, with his fist.

Cut himself all up, stitched it back himself over the sink and put a raw potato on it to stop the bleeding. He was mad at Bo because she was wetting the bed a lot.

No, I can't remember when Bo started wetting the bed. We shared a bedroom and a bed with *The Lion King* bed sheets, and sometimes you woke up smelling like an outdoor cat. Bo just went around with a wet bottom all the time, even to school. It got Mama in trouble with a teacher. Mama didn't have time to haul a garbage bag to the laundromat every day after working on swollen feet and no quarters to pop in the machine because the Winn-Dixie on Cherokee and Banks quit giving out change that year. She was stressed; needed more hours in the day. Mama worried about losing food stamps because she was making good tips. They were real stamps back then; came in an envelope, color-coded by food group. Fresh food was not allowed except for carrots and corn, but Butch always made sure we got any fruit we wanted from the produce bins. He taught us how to check for ripe peaches and sweet pears.

I know what you're going to ask me next, Detective Hoffman, and, no, Butch never touched us girls. The grand jury declared him not guilty for a reason. Look at the evidence. He was a looker, I'll admit that. Butch was a looker. He watched us use the toilet sometimes, made sure us girls were washing our hands and not leaving water all over the sink. Butch didn't like a mess. A lot of men don't. But there was nothing degenerate.

Yes, I know what CPS reported, Detective Hoffman. CPS reported that Bo was wetting the bed to make herself less desirable to the perpetrator. CPS pulled that out of their ass because they needed something to give to the autopsy doctor. You want to know the truth? Bo was pissing the bed because she couldn't stay out of the VO5 that sat on the rim of the tub, using it up like bubble bath, like money grows on trees. No, she had chronic UTIs resulting in an inflamed vagina, not consistent with sexual contact, but by sitting in that shampoo-bathwater and not getting out.

Detective, did I tell you about the chicken pox? One night a few months before Bo died, she told me in secret that she'd had a burning feeling in her crotch. Next day both of us girls got chicken pox. She was splotchy, red, all ballooned up. She was walking around with her hand down her pants trying to stop the itching. There you have it: chicken pox and soiled bathwater.

Butch made sure we didn't get near him that week. He said he could die from the shingles virus if we weren't careful because he hadn't gotten chicken pox as a kid. So, you tell me, how a girl like Bo, climbing trees, throwing limes from the old lady's citrus tree, complaining she didn't get a long enough turn on the N64, was getting abused with no indication except some inflammation? Her medical record for the 1995-1996 year showed she was taking amoxicillin for the UTIs. Look at the evidence, Detective.

Yes, I can tell you about Butch's temper. He was pissed she was pissing on the mattress. Burned a hole right through the cushion because of the acidity. Even the springs unhinged over time. And the day she died, everybody from Hounds came out to watch the technicians confiscate that mattress. Everybody thought one of us killed Bo. As if we didn't have a bad enough reputation, the authorities were hauling out a soiled mattress. Think about that.

Yes, I had a temper, sure I did, but I didn't get as mad as Butch. No, the authorities were never called when I got mad at my sister. This was a sister rivalry you've heard a million times and will again. No, I never hurt Bo. No, I never thought about hurting Bo. When my sister died, all I could think about was getting her back.

We were called white trash by everybody in town, at least from the people that paid attention. People didn't like us much. They had no reason to. Bo went to school smelling like piss, and I was always mouthing off to teachers and got bad marks. Mama had another boyfriend up in Sugar Bends—yes, he was accounted for on the night of June 17, 1996. And Butch, like I told you, had a little history of stealing and fighting. Nobody in old-country Florida cared if you threw a punch to a jit in a barroom, but stealing was something you better pray about.

What you don't know, Detective Hoffman, is I can tell you a lot about love. Mama used to tell us that getting called white trash meant we had to try harder. Girls like me and Bo had a lot to prove and when we won, whatever damn thing we won at, it meant more. She told us that girls like us loved better and harder, and we were a happy family and that counted double. Oh, and did we ever love one another. The only thing people chose to see was the kudzu growing like a jungle over the broken-in porch because we couldn't afford to get it trimmed; the nasty things Butch said behind our backs when he got into a mood. But Mama, Bo, and I, we were always laughing and singing and dancing. Even in the heat. Even when Butch didn't want to hear it. Even when we were broke and had to share cans of RC to make them last. Love can be foolproof, I believe that.

That foolproof love was proved, Detective Hoffman, during hurricane season in September 1995. Hounds had a major hurricane. We worked together as a family to get the lumber tied up to the windows with nylon. The only place that had shutters back then in Hounds was the bank on Placerville. Butch taught me how to tie a perfect slip knot with nylon. Mama got good at it, too, and we didn't get any splinters. Mama said if you know how to tie a knot, you can survive anything.

Yes, I can skip to the morning I found Bo's body. I awoke early because I heard Mama crying. It was still dark outside. The lights were off. Bo wasn't there and I knew Mama and Butch's hysteria had to be about Bo. For a long time, I just lay there thinking. I didn't move a muscle. A psychologist asked me once what else I remember about being in bed that morning besides Mama and Butch, and I'll tell you that I can remember the cicadas buzzing outside my window; loud things. I can remember the smell of leftover Hamburger Helper. I can remember Mama starting the coffee maker.

At some point, Butch opened the bedroom door and asked if I'd seen Bo. I got out of bed and followed Butch into the living room.

Mama had lost all the color in her face, she was crying so hard. Her eyes looked like she'd seen a ghost. At some point, she swung the front door open wearing her nightgown, barefoot, and cupped her hands around her lips to scream Bo's name. Then she returned, grabbed the phone off the hook on the kitchen wall, and called 9-1-1.

Butch watched me check the bathroom and the hallway closet for Bo. He told me to look under the bed.

For all intents and purposes, I will refer to the killer as The Intruder for the rest of our interview, Detective Hoffman.

Mama begged the operator to hurry. Bo had been kidnapped by The Intruder and she didn't know how the hell long Bo had been gone, just that her six-year-old vanished.

I went looking for Bo while Mama was on the phone.

I climbed the stool. We had an attic that was a crawlspace, not insulated, cobwebs, probably rats, although I never heard any. No dormer windows, only darkness. I pitched open the hatch, looked inside. Bo was face-up about two feet away. Her body was covered with a wrinkled white sheet. She looked like a life-size doll. Her head stuck out to where I could see her eyes. They were bloodshot, wide-eyed, fearful. She looked like she'd been frightened to death. Yes, it was unimaginable terror.

The worst part was Bo's pencil-thin, yellow eyeglasses frame. They were upside down on her face above the sheet. From the angle that I first saw her, I thought she'd been disfigured, like her eyes were taken out and laying on top of where her chin should be, but it was proof that The Intruder was hurrying. When he realized he messed up, he didn't bother to fix her eyeglasses correctly on her face. Yes, The Intruder turned her eyeglasses upside down. Blind as a bat, my sister. Even in her death.

Yes, those were the same eyeglasses that technicians confiscated, which disclosed a smattering of my DNA on the lenses. I might have reached out to prod her body, yes, see if she was still breathing, but I didn't call her by name. Deep down, I knew she was dead.

I moved the sheet down some more. Bo's hands were swollen big, like catcher's mitts dipped in grape jelly. I'd never seen that shade of purple in all my life.

Her hands weren't the only thing that turned purple. Her neck was flaming. There was tight-looped nylon garroted around her neck, and a splintered tree branch freshly broken off a myrtle tree twisted up in her loose ponytail. Her wrists were tied together with the same nylon. Horsetail was coiled around her fingers, Detective. *Coiled.*

To this day, big shots like yourself ask me how I could have possibly seen all of that in through the hatch; the sun hadn't reared its head yet. Yes, it was dark—but Detective Hoffman, I played in that crawl space more times than I can count. My vision adjusted. It wasn't a stranger in the crawlspace. That was my *sister.*

Then the police came.

Yes, I can go back to the morning before the murder. Mama was angrier than a wet hen because she'd split the rubber on her shoe. She wore sensible Keds to work and the bottom just wore out from all the walking she did, plus rain puddles. Bo and me, we went outside to sit on the porch. We fed pieces of apple to the chickens, thumbing through old family photos because Mama kept talking about having a family reunion by the lake. She had family in Alabama and they'd never met Butch before. The porch was full of wasps because the crevices in the wood filled with rain water after a storm. Termites had eaten away at the steps.

What were the pictures of? Average family vacation pictures. Butch had taken us all to Brasstown Bald Mountain the year before. We were standing on the rim of the Chattahoochee Trail, arms around each other. Even Butch looking swell and smiling. Chattahoochee wasn't too far from Hounds. It wasn't like the drive to Alabama when we went to see Mama's family.

Yes, Bo is wearing the same eyeglasses in those pictures that she was wearing when she was dead. Glasses upside down on top of the sheet.

The morning before the murder, Butch told Mama not to worry about splitting her shoes and he'd buy her a new pair at the shopping mall. There was a shopping mall in Sugar Bends back then, so it was a drive to get there especially on a Saturday when the mill was closed. The truck smelled like Coppertone. Bo wanted an Orange Julius at the mall, and Mama said we would see. Butch, on the drive, decided to kill two birds with one stone and get his watch fixed. He dropped us off at Sears and said he'd meet us in an hour in the food court.

Yes, that was the wristwatch confiscated by authorities a day later, but I'm getting ahead of myself.

I remember heading into Sears and Mama saying, "It's just to look, not to buy. We're here for work shoes."

But when Mama got that twinkle in her eye, we knew we might end up with something from the clearance rack. She didn't want nobody making a fuss and Bo and I were pretty well behaved when we weren't in school.

That was the funny thing about that day, Detective Hoffman. The rest of the day was so mundane that nobody blinked an eye to our whereabouts. It was just an ordinary day. Butch got us all new shoes, which seemed extraordinary because it wasn't back-to-school shopping, and he got me and Bo an Orange Julius to share. We came home, had supper. Bo and I chased a chicken off our porch. We sat outside on the porch steps looking up at a wheel of stars above us. They look painted-on that night. It was too hot to stay outside very long.

Yes, I can talk about the autopsy results. Bo's cause of death was asphyxiation by strangulation. She also had a skull fracture. Her skull was caved in, and looked like a planet crater from the pictures. The doctor said Bo had a half-apple and horsetail in her small intestine, partially digested within an hour of her death. Who gave her the apple and horsetail? It wasn't me. It was un-likely she got herself a snack, much less ate horsetail out of the fucking ground.

Yes, Butch's DNA was on Bo's underwear. Do you know who did the laundry at our house? Butch. Do you know who made sure Bo got her bath when I was too busy playing that N64 that he gifted us? Butch. Do you know who made our beds and got us dressed before school? Butch. Mama was busy. She had another boyfriend and she had work. Of course Butch's DNA was on Bo, it was on me too, and the whole rest of the goddamn house, the truck, the cupboards, you name it.

Now, Jimmy Ryce had just been in the news. I was scared as soon as I got out of bed, thinking about how I saw his picture hanging up in the supermarket. You couldn't go anywhere without seeing that boy in his baseball uniform. It was very sad and now suddenly it's happening to us.

I'll tell you what really happened, Detective. I'll tell you about The Intruder.

Butch Hart was twenty-eight years old at the time of Bo's death. He loved shooting and drinking, hunting deer, taking us for long drives to the country. The only criminal record you'll find in Butch's name is a citation for hunting gators. Yes, he had a tattoo of an angel on his arm. He always said it was for Mama, even though he got it when he was sixteen.

My mama Franny Rove was also twenty-eight. She loved singing and dancing, especially with us girls. Mama didn't have any criminal record either—not in Florida, not in Georgia, not in Alabama, none of the places she lived in the young years of her life. Mama and me were closest because I was the oldest. She liked Bo, too, and so did Butch. Their relationship was easy-peasy. He was going to teach her softball that summer; teach her to throw like a man. Mama wanted us to grow up to be strong, independent women.

A logger. The Intruder was a logger, Detective Hoffman. The Intruder observed us for months and months. He first observed us when Butch bought plank wood at the side of the road from this logger selling off his truck for the hurricane. Remember the hurricane I told you about? The logger's name was Bill Josephs and he worked the overnight shift at the lumberyard in Sugar Bends. He'd watched us girls tagging alongside Butch, buying sandbags and lumber, and when he realized who Butch was, Bill Josephs got pissed and started putting a kidnapping in motion.

Butch and Bill used to work together at Commodore Plastics. They hauled sheet metal onto conveyor belts and then lifted them onto eighteen-wheelers. Butch had a mean streak and a temper, like I told you. I bet that Bill embarrassed Butch about something; something that really tore him up inside. They got into a fistfight and were both fired for insubordination, made ineligible for unemployment benefits. Butch's reputation got worse moving from Commodore Plastics to Woolworth's. Even Mama, if she wasn't dying here next to us, would back me up on that.

The Intruder watched us for almost a year. He drove by in his ten-wheeler so many times it was as common as seeing the mail carrier. I couldn't have told you one truck from the other back when, but now I think I'd be able to pick out Bill Josephs in a custody lineup. Our killer, Bill Josephs of Sugar Bends, Florida, up the road from Hounds.

It was critical, Detective Hoffman, that The Intruder enter our house while we weren't there. The afternoon we piled into Butch's pick-up, there was a Ford parked at the Texaco four miles away. I think The Intruder came on foot, stuffed some horsetail in his belt, grabbed a myrtle branch that he'd saved for this day, and waited for us to leave so he could get in. I think he came in through the broken window and waited up in the crawlspace flat on his back. He listened to us carrying on about the chickens and watching the stars. He heard me and Bo arguing about having to share an RC Cola.

Tell me, Detective, have you ever seen a myrtle tree this side of Florida? No. There ain't no myrtle tree branches around here and anybody from the Deep South can tell you what kind of branch, along with nylon and horsetail, was used to strangle my baby sister.

Do you know who had myrtle trees in their yard? Bill Josephs. I went out there myself in 2012 to see the place, after he'd died of a heart attack. The place had already been rented out to somebody else, another bum, but that myrtle tree was there, and it was the only one I ever saw around this town. Look at the evidence.

Back to the day of the murder. The Intruder's intention was to lay flat up in that attic until everybody was asleep. He'd kidnap Bo—maybe with some chloroform. He'd stuff her into his lumber truck and take her on a road trip up the 95, and dump her in a river after doing heinous, brutal things to her body. The problem that Bill Josephs bumped into that night was, he forgot the chloroform. Perhaps the broken window wasn't large enough to fit Bo and himself through it; his entry and exit point with a child wouldn't work. How could he do that and keep her quiet at the same time? The man couldn't. It would be impossible. And if he went out our front door, he risked waking us up, risked getting caught by another trucker, leaving footprints, fingerprints, whatever else.

The Intruder didn't need chloroform. Having observed us for months, he already knew we had a Radio Flyer of apples on the front porch for the chickens. We usually wheeled it inside to keep the apples from rotting in the Florida heat. Horse flies were wicked, too. On this night, the night that Bo was murdered, we forgot about the Radio Flyer. I think The Intruder used this to his advantage and scooped a few apples into his jacket and fed half of an apple to Bo when she started getting fussy. But that's not before he crept past me, knocked, picked up Bo, and returned to the kitchen, where he asked if she wanted to eat some fruit while he and Mama and Butch got ready for the day. He was a family friend, worked with Mama, worked with Butch. Who knows what he said to that girl?

The Intruder struck her with his fist. She fell unconscious but didn't die—there's your skull fracture. He left some scuff marks around the kitchen that could have belonged to anybody wearing shoes ever. Smudge marks on the hatch? Those belonged to him, too. Knowing we had an attic, he took her up there, tied her up while standing on the same stool I stood on when I found her, strangled her with the garrote, and left her there for one of us to find, for police to find.

The sheet was already up there in the attic. I left it there. He removed her eyeglasses; like a personal touch some killers leave behind, especially when their victims are children. Then, he left out the broken kitchen window. Nobody saw nothing or heard nothing, it was the middle of the night.

What we have here, Detective Hoffman, is a botched investigation. My story hasn't changed in all these years. Yes, you're right. From your end, there's no evidence that Bill Josephs was ever involved. Yes, they think Bo was killed in the kitchen, due to the scuff marks. Yes, they think it was a struggle. But answer me this: How did Bill Josephs' lumber—the exact lumber he sold to us, flecks of it—end up in Bo's hair? I don't think that's a coincidence.

A long time ago, a social worker taught me something: a word called *pathology*. People don't just snap. People have threads inside of them that unravel, and most of us, keep ours bundled like yarn inside of us, twisted up safely. Somebody like The Intruder, his threads are always coming undone. Some people say we had it coming. These things happen to people like us. We messed up somewhere down the family line. We did something to deserve this. Maybe even Bo did something wrong to deserve this. No, I don't think much about Bo anymore. I moved on with my life.

Detective Hoffman, I'm going to say goodbye to Mama and take the train back to Marietta. Butch left us after Bo was killed; it was too much for him. He moved away after the trial. I haven't seen him since I was about ten years old. Look at Mama now, can't even keep her eyes open. Always worried about dying and now she's dying. She can't worry any more.

Do you know what I remember most about that shotgun house by the red mud hill in Hounds, Florida? The cockroaches. They made all kinds of noise day or night, rain or shine. They didn't care if you flipped the light on. They didn't scurry. That was the scary part, Detective. They didn't care who was watching them.

daylight in the swamp

kate leone

Sarah rose about an hour before legal light. She slipped into the all-black thermals and bib she'd hung over the back of a chair. She walked through the darkened house, closing all the curtains, and flipped on her headlamp. She went to the kitchen and brewed a pot of coffee. When it was ready, she made herself a cup: a little extra cream and sugar today. She sipped as she stared into the yawning blackness of her house. Then she sat down at the kitchen table to examine the rifle one last time.

Everything she'd ever killed, she'd killed with this gun. Deer and rabbits, mostly—a porcupine, once. Her faithful Winchester .243 bolt action, with a Vortex scope. It had sat untouched in the safe for a decade, but when she pulled it out last week, it was as if they'd never parted. She'd set the sight, zeroed in at 100 yards. She cleaned and oiled it, even took it down to the dirt pits one day to test and foul it. It fired clean and true. Now, she gave the gun a final once-over with the flashlight, looking for any cracks or signs of trouble she'd missed.

It was sound. There was nothing left but to do it.

••

Matt had been living in the RV since the summer. He was caught in a tricky situation; he needed to leave Sarah, but he didn't want to leave the land.

Sarah's stomach had dropped when he drove her out to see the property for the first time. He was so excited about the little old farmhouse, the barn, the acreage, that she got her hopes up. As they drove, the pavement crumbled into dirt road after dirt road. There were no streetlights, no neighbors. Her cell phone had no service. He pulled into the driveway of a squat, ranch-style house, the kind on every farm out there. Behind it loomed a barn with its roof caved in—around it, nothing but overgrown grass as far as she could see.

But he took her hand and walked her through the dated, dirty old house and told her his dreams for every room. An open kitchen here, a nursery there. He would make it theirs, he said. She could see it, too. They made love in his truck, right there in the driveway, and then called the realtor.

Three years later, there was no open-concept kitchen. No nursery, no baby. Nothing slumbered in the barn. The only new thing was the leak in the attic that kept her up at night. The leak, and Leanne.

..

There are a lot of ways to drop a deer in one shot. The trick is knowing where to aim.

She killed her first deer with a clean shot behind the shoulder when she was only fifteen. Rut had wound down early that year, but her father still woke her up to trudge out to the deer blind in the dark every morning. They'd paid good money for their tags, and the deep freezer demanded sacrifice. Then, on one of the last days of the season, Sarah saw her. A lone doe stood on the far edge of the cornfield, maybe one hundred yards from them. A long shot, but one Sarah had practiced. She nudged her father and grabbed her rifle. She half expected him to wave her off as he had so many times before: *wait, too far, not a good shot.*

"All yours," her father whispered. "Easy, now."

"Safety off," she said.

Her father still talked about that shot, all these years later. A sniper, he called her. When they cut open the doe, Sarah stifled a retch. She had never seen that much blood while dressing a deer. It was thick, almost black. Steam curled from the entrails.

"You got the heart," her father said.

This was a good thing, she knew. Exploding the doe's heart meant it died instantly: no slow bleed-out while stumbling through flattened cornfields. An ethical shot. And it was her first kill. She'd wanted to take a bite out of its heart, right there in the field, while it was still warm.

••

Of course, Leanne wasn't *new* at all. She'd been sniffing around back when Sarah and Matt first started dating. When they graduated, Sarah went to State; Matt and Leanne stayed in town and took classes at the community college. Sarah sat alone in her dorm room and scrolled through pictures posted from woods parties back home. There was Matt with a beer in hand and, always, somewhere in frame, Leanne.

Sarah asked him about her once, and he threatened to leave because she was insecure. She apologized, but he didn't forget. Whenever they fought or he missed her during the semester, he brought up Leanne as some kind of threat. Eventually, he won. Sarah transferred home. Matt proposed. They got married and moved out to the farm. Everything went quiet for a long time.

She'd forgotten about Leanne altogether until one night in early spring that year. Matt had been spending more and more time away. Sarah didn't mind; she liked being able to watch something that wasn't football and eat whatever she wanted without his running commentary. She created her own routines out there on her own and was often disappointed if he came home before she was in bed. It didn't occur to her that she felt safer, happier, without him. Every married woman she knew lived like this, creating little secret pockets for the things they loved. They couldn't all be miserable, could they?

That was the night Matt stumbled in, drunk and angry. He'd been at his parents' house, he said. They had a big fight, and he was cutting them out of his life, starting now. She hated his parents; they were small, mean people. Bullying was their love language. She leapt up to hug him out of sheer relief. She told him she loved him, and that she was proud of him. He shoved her back down onto the couch and stood over her, swaying on his feet.

"And that brings me to *you*."

Anger is a funny thing. It's powerful, but hardly punctual. By the time you get your Irish up over something, months have passed and there's nowhere to put it all. Once you're holding it, though, it has to go somewhere.

She should've gotten angrier sooner. If she had gotten angrier sooner, people would have understood the plan. Well, they might have.

The RV was still dark when Sarah slipped out into the yard. She walked quietly through the tall, dry grass with the final burn of the moon to light her way. The sky this side of dawn looked and smelled the same as it always did in early November; she was seven and fifteen and twenty-five, all at once. Fathers were dragging crusty-eyed, camouflaged kids into pickup trucks all over the county. It was Opening Day.

Whenever she lost her nerve—which happened a lot leading up to Opening Day, and every few minutes or so on that walk out—she thought of the morning in July when Matt startled her awake.

"Why are you still here?"

She remembered how she'd sat up and rubbed her eyes, trying to wake up more quickly and take in what was happening. She was on the couch in the nest of blankets and discarded socks and bras she'd slowly built since he'd left. She still couldn't bring herself to sleep in their bed.

"I live here, Matt."

"Why aren't you at work?" He threw open the back door, shouted something, and slammed it closed. He bashed down the hallway and ripped towels from the linen closet. Her head spun as he paced.

"I called out," she said. "What happened?"

"Leanne needs to shower."

"Leanne?"

"Get up," he yelled. "Stay in the bedroom or something until she's done."

There. That's when she should've gotten mad, where any reasonable person would have said no—said *something.* But she just sat there, mouth open, looking up at him. This could not possibly be her life. When the back door opened, she scurried off to hide, like a rat. She locked the bedroom door and sat down against it. She heard him open the back door and speak softly, apologetically. She heard Leanne's stifled laugh. The bathroom door closing. The shower running. The dampened sound of water as Leanne stepped under the showerhead. The heavy splat of water against the bottom of the tub, as if squeezed from her hair. The silence after the other woman turned off the shower. More silence as Leanne toweled off, brushed her hair, dressed, probably went through their drawers and cabinets.

The silence went on so long Sarah fell asleep against the door. It was summer, but she dreamed of snow: snow so deep and cold she could fall asleep in it. When she woke, the house was quiet again.

Days later, when she finally forced herself to shower, the drain backed up. She reached down into the ankle-deep water and pulled a slimy clot of coarse, dyed-black hair from the drain.

••

By the time Sarah strapped herself into the tree stand, she was sucking wind. There had been a few practice climbs—clearly not enough of them. Her arms and legs were completely gassed. She felt as if couldn't even hold up the rifle, let alone hit anything smaller than the broad side of a barn. She leaned against the rough bark of the old maple and let her slamming heart gently rock her calm.

Dawn broke as the feeling spread back into her arms. The faintest, grayest light, barely enough to see the deflated old pumpkins a few yards from her tree. Matt had started buying and dumping them in the overgrown field to lure deer the first fall they moved in. *It's not baiting,* he said with a shit-eating grin. *It's farming.* Her father would've been appalled. Every year, she looked out the window and willed nothing to grow. But every year, the prickly, vindictive vines spread.

The sun crept a little higher and the blind came into view, just on the other side of the pumpkin patch. And then, in the distance, the old RV's inside lights came on. She could almost see Matt making himself an instant coffee on the hot plate. He used to bring her a cup in bed when they took the RV camping. He'd always been the first one up—not today. The light looked warm; the bark against Sarah's back, decidedly not. She sat on her hands, one at a time, to warm them up, still holding tightly to the rifle.

The RV lights snapped off and the door swung in. A rush of panic hit her. Had she trimmed too many branches from her line of vision? He was sure to spot her, even tucked up in the canopy.

She'd tested her spot for cover from the angle of the blind, but she hadn't thought about his walk out of the trailer.

But there he went, in blazing orange, without a look toward the edge of the woods. He cut straight along the far side of the pumpkin patch, and she relaxed again.

And then she heard Leanne. Incredulous, Sarah tracked her eyes back along his path to the RV. There she was, drowning in his old camo, crying *babe, babe, babe, wait up.*

Sarah lifted the rifle, took off the safety, and found one of them in her sights. Then the other. Back to the first. She watched them pass a thermos between them. They chit-chatted. They shared a laugh. After a while, Matt leaned forward to watch the field. Leanne pulled out her phone and sank back in the camp chair. They fell into what looked like comfortable, contented silence.

Sarah put down the rifle. She felt sick, as if she'd walked in on them naked or worse. The utter banality of what she saw was so intimate. Her mouth had gone dry. She ran her tongue over her teeth and sat up straighter in the harness. This wasn't a snag in the plan at all; it was a two-for-one. She just had to be real sure of the shots.

She kept taking aim and losing her nerve. The sun began to dip behind the trees, and the cold was sapping her courage. She needed to refuel, and quickly. She let her mind flick through the record of Matt's betrayals. They were so easy to find these days; she'd spent all that time on the couch labeling and sorting them. They were even color-coded by the degree of pain he'd inflicted. What was her poison today? Fresh was best, she decided. So she mined the new releases first: the final break, the RV, the shower. Or maybe she needed something deeper; she reached back to college, even high school, and ran through all the greatest hits.

None of it stirred her, and she didn't understand why not. This had worked so many times. After all, it was anger that had gotten her off the couch and back into the bed. It was anger that called her parents and told them the truth before shame swallowed her whole. And it was anger that awoke her, every day, with bits of this very plan until it all came together. She sat in the tree and picked at every scab she could find, but nothing bled. An amateur at vengeance, she'd miscalculated how deeply her rage ran. She'd squandered this precious resource and, at the moment of truth, was coming up empty.

There was a pretty big hitch in aborting the plan: one she hadn't even considered leading up to that morning. He—they—were still alive. That meant she couldn't get out of the tree, as she so desperately wanted to do, without them seeing her. They would spot her as soon as she emerged from the edge of the wood. And with no orange on, Matt might even mistake her for a deer. If they didn't shoot her, she'd have to walk back to the house while their eyes followed her and she silently begged them to put her out of her misery. Irony didn't give a shit about her broken heart, so waiting them out was the only way. Matt would shoot something or Leanne would get too cold or the sun would set. Only a matter of time.

She settled back and tried not to think about her bladder or toes or the warmth of her bed. She surveyed the breadth of land beneath her. She had never really looked at their property from this angle. The late-afternoon sun and shadows laid it all bare: the moldering pumpkins, the rotting barn, the rust-caked RV. From where she sat, she could even see the hole in the roof her husband never quite finished fixing. Her husband, who was packing a lip beside his slack-faced girlfriend. And there was Sarah, alone in a tree with a gun in her hands and the feeling gone out of her ass. In one final, flailing effort to save the plan, she imagined Leanne moving into her house. Cooking in her kitchen. Sleeping in her bed.

This thought-exercise didn't go quite as Sarah planned; it worked even better. Because what she saw wasn't the sickening domestic bliss she'd anticipated. It was Leanne struggling with the old kitchen cabinet drawer: the one that always fell off its track and dumped spatulas and wooden spoons on the floor. Leanne tripping on the gouge in the bathroom linoleum. Leanne in the bed, wide awake on her back, listening to the roof-hole drip in the dark. Sarah went weightless all over. A seam between timelines slipped open. She didn't know how long she had to go through it, but she wasn't going to wait to find out.

Then, just as she unhooked herself to climb out of the tree, a dark shape snagged at the edge of her vision.

• •

"I was about to climb out of that tree stand—isn't that just the way it is? Anyways, I'm frozen solid, about to climb down, and here he comes, walking right into the pumpkin patch. Beautiful six-point. Once that big boy turned broadside, I didn't waste no time.

"*Bang.* Down he went, right where he stood. I was waiting on him to bleed out when I see Matt come running out of the blind like he'd done something. Well, I couldn't get down that darn ladder fast enough. You should've seen his face when I come out of the woods all in black like some kinda sniper.

"Well, I just knelt right down there and got to work while he was catching flies. *Do you want help*, he says, and I says, *no thanks.* And there's old Leanne standing next to the blind, so I give her a big wave with the bloody buck knife and she runs off and locks herself in that tin can of an RV.

"Beautiful lung shot. I got the heart out and I swear it was still pumping when I took a bite. And I mean a *real* bite, like one you'd take out of an apple or the first tomato off the vine in August. That thing gushed like you wouldn't believe, down my chin and the front of my bib.

"Well, Matt didn't like that too much. He went all green and had to sit down, and there I was just chewing and smiling. So then I finish up and we're dragging the buck to the truck bed and Matt goes, what a lucky shot, and me, I'm laughing too hard to say much of anything."

the botanist

kayla whittle

One gray, muddled afternoon, Madeline spotted the neighbor's gardener peering through the solarium windows. The intruder's hands were cupped around her eyes, smudging the glass. Irritation flickered through Madeline; it was Friday, and she'd hoped to finish early for the weekend. Now there was more work to do and a stranger to chase away.

Bark bit into her palm; Madeline held too tightly to the tree she'd been trimming.

"I'm sorry," Madeline repented, smoothing a hand over the trunk. Thick green leaves wavered near her cheek. She stepped away, keeping her shears in hand, and used the outer door to enter the backyard.

"There's no—" she started, and faltered when she rounded the solarium to see no one. The neighbor's gardener must have realized she'd been spotted.

"No trespassing!" Madeline shouted over the estate grounds, knowing the busybody might still be in earshot. The Griffith property was sprawling, well-maintained by the staff. The property owners were meticulous about appearances, which kept Madeline busy perfecting the grounds. Every pathway was neatly edged and well-laid; flowers were either planted or plucked to maintain uniformity. More than once while trimming the hedges dividing the Griffith land from their neighbors, Madeline had spotted the other gardener from afar. Seen the shape of her sunhat bobbing down rows of scattered flowerbeds, short stature obscured by trellis and vine and shrubbery. They'd never had a reason to meet.

Tightening her hold on the shears, Madeline backed inside the solarium. She shut the door tight, double-checking the lock. With the room secured, she left to alert the staff of their trespasser. A singular incident could be overlooked, justified by curiosity. If anyone spotted the stray gardener again she'd be trespassed.

The untrimmed trees in the solarium waited patiently for Madeline to resume her work.

Each weekday, Madeline unlocked the solarium to sweep the pathways, clean the benches, and polish the windows. There were small plants to be watered and examined and trimmed. On Fridays, the trees were fed.

Outside, the sky was bright and clear, filling the solarium with sunshine. Patches of shadow spread beneath the tallest trees but offered little reprieve from the heat already overtaking the enclosed space. A few fans spun lazily overhead. Madeline sweated quietly as she locked the door behind her, tucking her basket into the crook of her left elbow. Bark strained and leaves rustled, muffling the tinny echo of birdsong that filtered through from the grounds. Despite herself, Madeline smiled. It was endearing when the trees were restless.

With the Griffiths perpetually out of town, Madeline was the only one on the estate with access to the solarium. She lucked into her job when her predecessor chose to retire a few years back; the former gardener had stayed with the staff long enough to ensure absolute perfection in Madeline's training. The trees were too delicate and rare to entrust their care to many hands;

the Griffiths preferred to look after them personally when they were at the estate and left the rest to Madeline.

"I've quite the selection today," Madeline promised the trees, taking her basket to the back of the room where the oldest ones waited. Their canopies nearly touched the roof of the solarium a few stories overhead. Their trunks were irregular, misshapen, and far too thick despite their significant age. She'd spent enough time among them, to know the intimate details of every bump in their bark.

Madeline set her basket beside the first tree and paused to check her watch. It was important to adhere to a fixed schedule, feeding them just before she left for the weekend. The trees were inconsolable if they had an audience while digesting.

From her basket, Madeline removed a small hatchet. A twig poked at her shoulder when she stepped closer to the tree, prodding a smile from her. The grove had grown quite affectionate after they'd acclimated to her presence. She rubbed her hand across the bark; after her own adjustment period, she'd developed a fondness for the unusual, finicky creatures. They were like stiff, unmoving pets. Defenseless.

"It's good to see you, too," Madeline assured the tree before swinging the hatchet, burying it deep in the trunk.

Again and again, she swung. A shallow alcove chipped into the bark, a jagged hole several shades lighter than the protective bark. Madeline set the hatchet aside when she was satisfied with the size of the hollow and returned to her basket, pulling out a dented kettle.

Gently, she pressed the metal against the weakened, exposed trunk. Boughs shifted, straining with the harsh pop of old wood settling. She waited, keeping the metal in place until the twig tapped at her shoulder again. When she released the kettle, it stuck fast to the tree; the trunk had regrown enough bark to hold onto the object independently. Stepping away, Madeline busied herself brushing wood chips from her sweater. A few leaves dropped from overhead, tangling in her dark hair. Madeline smiled again.

"You're very welcome, she said, "Enjoy your meal."

She moved on, feeding the next tree a stack of paperwork showing off the eldest Griffith child's excellent grades. Another trunk received a piece of fencing, nearly as old as the estate itself, broken off during the last storm. Nothing with any monetary value was meant for a tree's meal. Each item had been held onto long enough to absorb quite a bit of memory. Little pieces of the Griffith household kept the grove well-fed. The trees thrived on affection and recollection, had done so since they'd become part of the estate a few generations back. Madeline wasn't sure where the Griffiths had found the trees, or if there were others like them out in the world. She didn't understand the why of them, or the how, and didn't care to learn. The trees liked her, and she liked them, and that meant her job was secured until her own retirement loomed.

Kneeling beside the newest, smallest tree, Madeline gifted it the season's prize tomato, fresh from the garden. The trunk hadn't fed on anything organic before; it took a few long moments for it to accept the offering. The trees would feed on almost any-thing that remained still. Quiet. They weren't dangerous, even when hungry.

She patted a hand over the rich soil hiding the tree's roots; the dirt shifted lazily beneath her fingers.

"Goodbye," Madeline told the trees. "I'll see you on Monday."

By then, new bark would cover their meals. Within a month or so, the irregular bumps created by the trees' digestion would disappear; as they were well-fed, the trunks would never stand completely straight.

Automatic lights turned on inside the solarium; the glow from the ornate sconces felt soft, warm and familiar. Picking up her basket and hatchet, Madeline glanced through a window. Her face reflected in the glass, caught amid her copse of trees.

••

On Wednesday, Madeline scrubbed a fresh set of handprints off the solarium windows, then marched over to the property line. Frustration curdled in her stomach as her mood soured; the Griffiths weren't quiet about their unique solarium, but few were ever invited inside the exclusive space. Part of Madeline's job description included keeping away unwanted guests.

Breath quickening with each step, Madeline's temper flared. There was a small gap in the hedge and Madeline let herself through; if the stranger had no regard for trespassing, neither would she.

The neighbor's gardener was tucked within their rose bushes. Branches rattled as she pulled herself free, clearly having heard Madeline's agitated approach.

"Can I help you with something?" the gardener asked, voice wavering in a way that forced Madeline to pause. Her teeth ground in annoyance at her own hesitation.

"Property lines exist for a reason," Madeline said.

The snap in Madeline's voice made the gardener flush petal pink. It was a fascinating shade, alluring in a way that startled Madeline. Typically, she felt little in the way of physical attraction; she sought the emotional side of a connection, first and foremost. Madeline suspected her immediate intrigue had more to do with the curious intelligence she saw layered within the gardener's gaze, dark as the richest soil.

"I was wondering if—well, you must have spotted me," the stranger admitted, wiping dirt onto her thighs. "I do need to apologize for going about this all wrong. I've studied unique flora from around the globe, and before I was hired on here with the Hargroves, I'd heard of the Griffiths' prized collection. Their accumulation of such a rare species is astonishing, nothing like what I have to work with over here. Although—please don't tell the Hargroves I've said that. I'd love to have more of a challenge when it comes to my work, but I'd also like to keep this position a little while longer. I—I do apologize."

Madeline watched the gardener wring her small hands. She could easily report this to the Griffiths, or even directly to the Hargroves, who had been excellent distant neighbors. But the Griffiths had been so upset when she'd first reported a potential intruder on the grounds. They might begin to doubt her ability to protect their prized property, might begin to search for a replacement a few decades before Madeline was ready to give up the coveted position.

"What's your name?" Madeline asked after a long moment.

"Clara Burnfield," the gardener answered, hands stilling. Her cheeks hadn't lost their acquired flush. She was shorter and slimmer than Madeline; physically, the neighboring gardener seemed to present no real threat.

"Clara," Madeline said, heaving the name from her tongue. "Mind your business and stay away. I won't warn you again." She left the other gardener among the roses.

• •

A series of storms descended upon the estate. The weather delayed the Griffiths' return, leaving the trees sullen. They creaked despondently as Madeline passed, too busy to do more to comfort them beyond offering soothing pats to their trunks.

Wind shook at the solarium windows until they rattled like hypothermic palms. Madeline secured thick, heavy cloths over the tree beds to keep soil in place, in case the glass was breached. Most of her attention fixed upon the youngest, most fragile tree;

the others went quiet as she secured the sapling's trunk to sturdier stakes. Professionally, she would be ruined if any harm befell her charges; emotionally, she would be devastated. The trees trusted her to look after them, and she loved them for it.

Tiny boughs scraped over the backs of her hands as thunder rumbled.

"Just a storm," Madeline said, smoothing a thumb over burgeoning leaves. "Just a silly little storm."

Lightning snapped, lighting the room in a ragged spotlight. The trees shook; the youngest quivered. Thunder vibrated against the glass window panes before the estate's electricity fizzled and failed. Madeline swallowed her unease. The Griffiths paid her well enough that spending the night weathering a storm would be no hardship. A few of the staff were always on property, so she wouldn't technically be alone, though only she could enter the solarium. She wouldn't be able to hear anything from the main house anyway over the noise of the rain.

"It's alright." Madeline rose to her feet, garden stake in hand. "I'll protect you."

Sometimes she thought the trees truly understood her. She'd never cared to push the boundaries of their intelligence. Sometimes it felt like they retained something from the objects they ate, memories or impressions, enough to catch short glimpses of human life. Enough to know there was little a human could do against nature.

Lightning flared. Trees shook. Past the echoing patter of heavy raindrops, Madeline heard something tap against the outer door. Her grasp on the stake tightened. Carefully, she slunk forward. Erratic light guided her. She knew every inch of every path within her small domain; she moved confidently to the back of the room. Rain threw itself against the glass. Something tapped above Madeline's head. Tensed, ready to spring—to defend—Madeline snapped her chin upward.

A twig tap-tapped against the glass. One of the oldest trees had spread its canopy too wide.

"Come on, darling," Madeline chastened. "Don't scratch the glass." She exhaled, part relief, part amused annoyance. The branch tapped again.

The trees behaved as they liked, but they never vexed her without reason. Madeline looked outside. Through the rain and irregular darkness, a shadow struggled by the property line. Madeline's eyes narrowed, grip flexing around the stake. *Clara.*

Madeline wasn't meant to leave the trees alone in weather like this, but wasn't meant to let danger near, either. Indecision weighed her down; anxiety pulsed alongside her heartbeat, pumping faster, faster. The twig tapped again, which decided it for her.

Water soaked her as soon as she pushed outside, struggled to close the door behind her, and forged a path across the wide lawn, fighting against the frantic wind. Grass and mud squelched beneath her shoes.

The figure, of course, was Clara, but Madeline was shocked to find her on the correct estate for once. She wrestled with something on the ground.

"Get inside!" Madeline shouted over the storm's fury.

"The bushes!" Clara protested.

Madeline looked closer. Heavy cloths lay scattered on the Hargroves' grounds near the rose bushes. How desperate had Clara been to keep her job, to risk everything for these roses? Hesitantly, Madeline glanced behind her, toward the solarium. She'd already been gone too long; she should have returned as soon as she'd seen Clara on the Hargroves' property.

"Leave them," Madeline directed. "You—"

Something heavy hit the back of her head, sending her to her knees. There was no pain, not at first; the world blurred in a wash of shadow. Warm hands clasped her shoulders. Small, calloused hands. A voice called, ordering her to stay awake. The grasp tightened as her own loosened, stake dropping into the dirt. Soil-dark eyes focused on Madeline, only Madeline, and they followed her down into the gloom.

••

Clarity seeped back in irregular spurts. When Madeline was able to focus on her longer than a few moments, Clara's hand lifted, pausing a few inches from Madeline's temple. The hospital room's white light made the throb at the back of her skull triple. The pain threatened to engulf her again.

"I feel terrible," Madeline admitted.

Clara winced, nose wrinkling. Her hand found Madeline's, squeezing tight. The pressure relieved some of the tension wrecking Madeline's concentration.

"Let me distract you," Clara said. It was a request, not an order. "You like flowers, don't you? Before I started with the Hargroves, I worked at the university. Botanical research. I'll tell you about my favorite study."

Clara's stories were analytical, and boring, and worked. Time passed in a pleasantly numbed blur.

The main house's report came later, when Madeline had finally been deposited in a room and Clara had left to return to the Hargroves. Part of the gutter had blown apart during the storm. The estate was old, so damage wasn't unexpected, but the Griffiths immediately sent their regrets alongside a demand that Madeline take paid time off because she'd been injured on their property.

The family would return to look after the trees in the mean-time. Madeline flexed her empty hands, clutching tight to the sheets of her recovery bed.

Two weeks later, restless and missing her charges, she returned to work. She arrived at the estate on a Friday—feeding day—and mixed a few of her personal items in with the rest in her basket. The trees wouldn't understand her absence, but Madeline felt the need to explain.

"I'm fine," Madeline assured the grove when branches shifted restlessly overhead. "I promise."

Madeline spent an extra few moments with the oldest tree, feeding it an old school notebook. Every page had been used, filled with reminders and notes and little conversations in the margins between her and old classmates. Ripe with sentiment to devour. While the tree fed, Madeline looked through the solarium windows. It was a clear, sticky summer day, and from her current position, she was offered an excellent view of the Hargroves' hedges. Perhaps Clara was out there, tending to the roses she'd saved from the storm. An old, crumpled leaf fell onto Madeline's shoulder and she sighed.

"I'm sorry," she said. "I don't mean to be distracted. She's just so—"

Madeline tried to grasp for the right word. Frustrating? Fascinating? Clara needed to keep to herself. Clara had saved her.

"Not so bad." That felt inadequate. Clara had kept Madeline calm through the pain. She'd grounded her with stories of previous gardens she'd worked on, places she'd visited, flora she'd researched. Clara was a botanist above all else. She knew all the proper names for the rose varietals grown by the Hargroves.

Boughs pulled closer, a faux embrace of bark and leaf. Madeline leaned against the trunk; it was warmer in the solarium than was natural as the tree digested. Words escaped her again, running together into something new. Madeline looked at Clara and wanted more. Bark pulsed beneath her hands.

"Alright," Madeline sighed. "Alright."

When she'd left the hospital, Clara had given Madeline her phone number with strict instructions to call if she needed anything. Madeline used it now to ask Clara if she wanted to meet for coffee. It would be fitting to thank her in person. Glancing through the solarium windows, perfectly polished and clean after the storm, Madeline smiled.

They met by the hedge. Madeline carried over a pair of mugs lent to her by one of the maids.

"Thank you, Clara," Madeline said stiffly, holding her mug too tight. "Thank you for your help. And, you know, about what I said before—"

"I deserved it," Clara said, tucking her dark hair behind her ears. "I overstepped when I became too curious, wanted to see things for myself. It's nice to see you back on the job. How are things?" Her gaze slid past Madeline, tracking back toward the solarium. Because of the distance and sunlight, it was nearly impossible to see inside.

"It's good to be back," Madeline admitted. "I missed this place." The trees, and the staff, and even the Griffiths, to some extent. It was an unexpected privilege to like her job so much.

"It's been boring here without you," Clara said.

Between sips, Clara spoke about the new plants she planned to import, come springtime. Madeline admitted she was never involved in those decisions, that the Griffiths family rarely introduced anything new, but that was alright with her. Clara's expression twitched when Madeline admitted she was content with their traditional groundskeeping and, if she could help it, never planned to leave the estate.

"We'll have plenty of time to get to know each other properly, then," Clara said. "Meet me here again tomorrow?"

One meeting for coffee turned into two, and then three, always by the property line. It made something warm and sharp in Madeline's chest to glance through the solarium windows and see Clara by the hedges, waiting.

Their time to meet dissipated when the Griffiths returned, descending upon the estate in a flurry of luggage and questions for Madeline. They fussed over her mostly-healed head and repeatedly asked for updates on the trees. Fed on a steady diet of familial memories, the trees were restless in the homeowners' company. They stirred with familiarity, happiness dripping like fallen leaves.

Unable to see her new friend in person while the family was in residence, Madeline called Clara sometimes. The trees edged closer when Madeline turned on speakerphone, leaning toward the new voice.

"What do you think?" Madeline asked the trees one day after hanging up. They remained uncharacteristically still in their response. Pouting, maybe. "I'm sorry you can't meet her."

Madeline loved her job, and the trees, and the Griffiths would absolutely know if she broke their rules. Knowing the trees had some interest in Clara straightened Madeline's back, tightened her grip.

"What about this?" Madeline asked. "When I'm able to, I'll bring her closer. You can hear her properly then, through the windows."

Finally, the trees moved, trunks quivering with an excitement matching Madeline's.

• •

Friday afternoon bloomed in sunlight spilling from puffed white clouds. It was a beautiful day for a picnic. The Griffiths family had moved onward again, visiting relatives before fall could settle in. Most of the day staff had finished their work for the weekend; those left behind kept indoors for a lazy afternoon. The grounds were quiet, filled with the hush of wind through the hedges and the chatter of squirrels in the distance.

Madeline thrilled at the thought of having Clara alone. The other woman let herself in through a gap in the hedges, lifting a hand in greeting. Dirt stained her fingers and thighs. Madeline smoothed the edges of the blanket she'd laid out on the lawn only steps from the solarium.

"I missed you," Clara smiled, dark eyes soft as they met Madeline's. She'd brought a little tray of food, wrapped in plastic, and set it between them.

Over Clara's shoulder, the afternoon sun burned in a gleaming streak. Light flared against the greenhouse windows; Madeline saw her reflection peering back at her, the shape of Clara beside her. She knew their voices would carry indoors to her nosy trees.

Slumping, Clara bemoaned her employers' rejection to her recent rose garden proposal.

"They like familiarity," Clara complained. "Tradition. No excitement. My work at the university was about innovation. Pushing boundaries."

Madeline frowned, wondering if Clara's dissatisfaction would soon lead her into another job search. Reaching for an empty glass, Madeline realized she'd left the picnic incomplete.

"Excuse me for a moment," Madeline requested before hurrying back in through the solarium, down the hall and the stairs to the Griffiths' smaller wine cellar, the one with cheap bottles that would never be missed. Madeline searched for the one she'd painstakingly selected earlier in the day. Everything needed to be perfect. Everything needed to be right.

Hurrying back—up the stairs, down the hall, through the solarium—Madeline didn't bother to lock the door behind her. Clara waited, tying back her long hair, looking out toward the empty grounds. The scent of fresh grass and blossoms filled the air, stagnant on a late summer evening. After filling both glasses, Madeline settled the bottle in the grass beside them.

"I never imagined meeting someone like you here," Clara said, holding her glass loosely.

Flustered, Madeline watched Clara drink deep before she raised her own glass. The sun dropped behind a thick cloud; Madeline shivered, fingers twitching and numb with anticipation.

"I have to say, for a nosy neighbor, you're not so bad," Madeline said.

"You're happy here?" Clara asked, gesturing with her chin toward the whole of the estate.

"Yes, of course," Madeline said, blinking before she took another sip. She misjudged the distance to her glass, nearly knocking it against her teeth. "I'm sorry to hear the Hargroves make you so unhappy."

"I'm right where I'd like to be," Clara smiled.

Madeline blinked again. Clara's smile flickered, distorted—fuzzing around the edges like an overexposed afterimage. The wine glass slipped from her hand; detachedly, Madeline realized she was going to fall, too.

"I've got you." Soft arms caught Madeline as she tipped toward the blanket like an unsteady tree blown over in a windstorm. "I'm here."

Panic lit quick and jolting in Madeline's veins even as her body stilled, refusing to obey her commands. She felt weak, out of control like at the hospital, pliant and numb. Madeline had hoped the afternoon would shift toward this, to Clara's embrace, but her skin felt more pressure than sensation. Though her heartbeat ticked faster and her eyes watered, her limbs stiffened, stilled. Knees locked, jaw loose, skin and bone buckling down into a tight entrapment. She tried, and struggled, but couldn't speak. Clara's face filled Madeline's vision. She could fetch the staff, she could get help—but instead Clara smiled, expression relaxing in a way Madeline had never seen. It weighed Madeline with dread, confusion seeping into questions her jaw refused to voice.

The soft arms left. Bony fingers wrapped around her ankles, dragging her sideways. Madeline watched blue sky pass through unblinking eyes as, inch by inch, Clara hauled her inside the solarium. Grass tugged and pulled at her hair, more resistance than Madeline could provide when locked inside her body. It was bright indoors, sunlight caught in so much glass. The brilliance hurt, echoing the scream trapped in Madeline's chest.

Madeline wanted to know *why*. She wanted to shove Clara out of the solarium, away from her trees, off the property. Not even a finger twitched.

"I'm sorry it's you," Clara said. "I really do enjoy your company."

The hands left, and shuffling started nearby. Madeline tried and failed to turn her head; she could see only the branches wavering above, bending toward her. Madeline felt the muscles in her face loosen and her eyes, staring upward, burned with the need to blink. She remained frozen, even when she heard an ax start chopping into wood. Her heart beat faster, pulse thundering in her ears, wrapping around Clara's gentle voice.

"It took longer than I'd thought for you to notice me watching you work in here."

A few leaves dropped from overhead, settling on Madeline's heaving chest. Hands dug beneath Madeline's arms, maneuvering her upright. Her vision blurred, wavered, encompassed the grove surrounding her. Clara had been a curious busybody. Kind to Madeline, ambitious, intriguing. Madeline had never suspected this, lurking beneath the surface. She thought of the staff, never allowed into the solarium. The weekend that left the estate mostly empty. The Griffiths, not due to return for several weeks. There was no one to help Madeline but herself, and she couldn't fight. Couldn't shout. A tear tipped over the edge of her eyelid, cool against her cheek. The trees couldn't stop Clara, either.

Clara folded Madeline against the new opening on the oldest tree's trunk.

"You don't comprehend the specimens you have thriving here," Clara said. "I've never observed a living sample before. These trees flourish so well on the hand-me-down memories of their owners. Think of what might happen if they could have more, Madeline. Think of what this one might do, with all the memories from you."

Madeline fought against herself, against whatever Clara had fed her to incapacitate her, but her fingers and toes, her eyes and lips, remained still and silent. The tree embraced her. New bark curled around the edges of the newly made hollow, biting into her skin with an echo of dull pain. It stung, matching the new hurt in Madeline's chest, the brittle breaks caused by betrayal.

"I know. I'm sorry," Clara said, smoothing Madeline's hair back. "There's so much untapped potential when it comes to these trees, and you weren't going to do any of the research. You wasted your chance to truly see what this grove is capable of. I need to have this job, Madeline, and you weren't going to leave."

Madeline wanted to look away. Clara's soil-dark eyes softened with pleasure, the kind that came from achieving an old dream.

"I know you cared for them. There's no need for you to worry. I'll look after them for you," Clara promised. "I'll look after you, too."

The botanist reached forward and closed Madeline's eyes.

this is where you loved me

r. lazarus

Today is one of those days where I love you so much it makes me want to vomit. You're not home from work yet, so I wander alone through the empty halls of our apartment, stumbling from room to room. A picture of our graduation sits on the coffee table, covered in dust; we're smiling in it, not because we've achieved something, but because graduation meant we could finally leave that goddamn town.

I lock eyes with my younger self, and I have to look away; it's hard to feel much at all, but I try my damndest, digging my nails into my bare thighs, little tears springing in the corners of my eyes that never quite threaten to fall.

Eventually, I reach the bathroom. It smells like dampness and mold, like something festering; I said I'd keep things clean for you, but I stopped trying a long time ago. I step up to the sink. It takes a second to recognize the person standing in the mirror, but it's me. I can tell in the eyes: dull, brown, and useless. I haven't brushed my hair, and it shows, it's greasy and black and all over me, and everything feels grimy, everything feels like it's covered with slime. I hate you for it. But even as I feel that resentment boil over in me, I know it's not your fault.

Sometimes I make things up about you, but you have to understand, I'm just trying to share the load. I can't hold all this guilt by myself. I've tried.

The old pain sparks again, right through my gums and up the back of my skull. It's a blinding, numbing pain, and light dances in front of my eyes, not quite solidifying. My hands scramble to my jaw, prodding at my cheeks, trying instinctively to dislodge whatever has stuck in my skin and hurt me like this. My mouth hangs wide open, as if that could release me from the coils of pain I'm trapped in.

I slowly, slowly, push a finger into my mouth, breaking through my gritted teeth, and take hold of a small, lumpy mass in the back of my jaw. It releases easily with a small tug. I pull it out and stare at the rotting purple roots. I blink. Hot, metallic blood fills my mouth, and I'm gagging over the sink drain. My face scrunches up like I might cry, and strange wheezing sobs burst out of my throat, and I'm cradling this tiny part of me like it might suddenly disappear and be lost forever—

Something moves beneath my gums.

I run my tongue over the row of teeth in the back of my jaw and find, instead of a harmless molar, a needle point sticking up. It grows quickly, forming into a sharp, serrated thing, stabbing at the roof of my mouth.

Needle-tip teeth push through my gums, pushing my rotted teeth away. They tumble out of my mouth, smacking against the porcelain with small tinks, like rain on a tin roof. Bones grind painfully against each other in their rush to escape the knife-points shooting up out of my gums. I desperately try to catch them before they fall down the sink drain.

My jaw fills up with more and more teeth, crowding in on each other, forcing my mouth open, until I'm just staring into the mirror at the thing that's all needles. All hair. Holding my teeth in its open palms.

I cry quietly, as not to disturb the neighbors.

It used to be different: all kisses under the bleachers, passing notes in the hallways with a smile. We always talk a big game about hating that little town, but if I ever went to heaven, I know it would be high school; a few friends, some acquaintances who I smiled at in the hallways and copied the homework of, but really, *really* it was you and me. It was always you and me. I couldn't remember a time without you by my side: asking for the bathroom pass and holding in giggles as the teacher eyed us suspiciously; whispering into your ear as the gym coach talked his head off; falling in love under the starlight of my alleyway.

The way girls love each other in suburbia is quiet and careful. We laid with our backs against the grassy yard, staring at the power lines soaring across the sky, gripping each other's hands like the lifelines they were.

I gave you a nosebleed once. You came up behind me and I whipped around, excited to see you. Too excited, I guess, my hand smacking into your face. I cried for days. You didn't cry at all, opting to comfort me instead. Always the martyr, always forgiving me.

High school still ended, though, and with it the intertwining of pinkies. But still; we shared a dorm, and it was just like high school, except we were adults and no one could tell us what we could and couldn't do.

Once, in our dorm, you sat at your tiny desk, writing for a project. I laid in your bed, watching you work. I loved it.

"Marry me."

You looked up, startled, like you had forgotten I was there. "What?"

"Marry me." This was not a new concept to our relationship. The plan was to get married after we graduated. We didn't need a big ceremony. Just the legal document, the rings, the kiss. You laughed and shook your head.

"What, right now?"

I shrugged. "Why not?"

You looked at me, eyes wide, like I was suggesting we go lay on the freeway. "No."

It felt like my heart stopped. I sat up, slowly. "Why?"

You stood up and sat on the bed. "We're not kids anymore. We're grown women now. Be realistic." You sealed your spiel with a kiss.

It echoed in my head. *We're grown women now. Be realistic.*

I never felt grown. And it became more and more obvious that I suffered from this lack of maturity, this restlessness, as I violently oscillated between staying awake until the sun crept over the horizon, working on my manuscript, to curling up in bed for weeks. I spat out angry, horrible words at you, and you took them unflinchingly, placing the cold rag on my forehead and kissing my hand.

I hated you in these moments. I wanted you to throw me out of the bed, onto the floor, knocking my head on the cool hardwood like I deserved. But you stayed. Even when I stopped going to classes at all, walking endless loops around our apartment while you studied in your room. Even when I let the dishes stack up and let the laundry sit in the washer and started smoking again.

You did complain about the smoking actually, scrunching up your nose when you kissed me and frowning at my yellow teeth when I smiled. You held my hand and spoke to me about lung cancer and leaving you behind. But cancer appealed to me: something sinister growing under my skin, trying to devour me whole. It made me feel a little less alone.

A knock on the door. You're home. You're home, and shit, look at what I've become. Teeth down the drain. Blood and saliva and sweat smeared across my face. Shame lights a fire in my lungs. You ask if you can come in and I want to say no but the spines in my gums won't move when I tell them to, and my lips are cracked and broken, stretched past their limit, my mouth hangs open, painfully and uselessly, and I can say nothing as you turn the doorknob.

Your eyes, widening rapidly, lock to mine.

"Wait, wait, wait," is your whispered, shrieked litany at the sight of me. I don't like the expression you're making, like maybe this is all one big joke. You want to understand. But there's nothing you can do to understand me; there's nothing to understand.

Terror freezes you to the spot in the doorway, and there are tears rolling down your cheeks, but you reach out, slowly, and I think you're going to hit me, and I'm bracing myself for it, but the blow never comes.

You put your hand on my cheek. "Baby, baby, look at me, it's okay, it's okay," you sob. Your eyes are wide and wet, tears are dripping onto my new teeth, little salty pearls splashing against my tongue.

That kindness again. Forgiveness. It makes me sick. I can't let you do this again. I can't live like this any longer. There has to be another life for us.

And before you can say another word, I bite into your arm. If you cry out, I don't register it. A deliciously sweet, warm taste erupts in my mouth, but I don't stop to savor any of it. No, I know what I need. I carve you right up, ribbons of red flesh swirling around the bathroom like the ballet act your mother took you to when you were three years old and still kicking the back of the driver's seat.

Destroying you makes me *feel* something. It's not quite anger, or fear or joy, but there's something exploding in my chest with more intensity than anything else in my life ever has. It comes to me when I see the scraps of hair torn from your scalp and haphazardly thrown to the ground, when I stare into the dark blue of your eyes. Even as I realize it, I can't seem to stop the onslaught of memory.

It was your birthday, your 21st, and we were happy. You looked beautiful: your hair was a golden braid down your shoulder. (You hadn't cut it in a few years by then. The upkeep drove you crazy, but you told me you just had to maintain what you called "*Princess Bride* Hair.") You wore the dress your parents bought you that year, the white one with lace around the collar and the waist.

I sat on the couch in your parents' house, green twill and cat hair, where we used to cuddle while we watched horror movies, I remember. I sipped on a Cherry Coke, which I always drank at that house and never anywhere else. At that point we *could* legally drink, but being in that town felt too much like childhood to brave it. Once we got back on campus, we drank until we both grasped each other in the big communal bathroom, your pretty yellow hair pulled back tightly as we took turns vomiting.

But that came later. Till then, you sat down on that old couch beside me like you had lived there your whole life—which you had, but it had become so distanced from us at that point that I had almost forgotten—and you curled perfectly into my body, like we, made not as two separate people but one body that had split in two, had just now slid back together. You rested your head on my shoulder, and I turned to kiss your hair, but I was smiling too wide, and I ended up mashing my face against the top of your head instead.

"This is the best birthday I could've asked for." Your breath smelled like heaven, like sweetness, and it made my mouth water.

"Why?" I asked, because I was in love and you were sitting there beside me and nothing was wrong, it was all just soft, even contentedness. I was in love.

"It's perfect." You buried your face in my neck, and I could feel the vibrations as you spoke. "You're here with me."

I love you. That's the simple fact. I don't think I could live without you. Not in this life. So, we must become something else. I'm sorry it had to come to this. But, oh God, what a feeling. The epiphany reaches me as I bite into your neck. *It's an act of love*, I try to say through a mouthful of teeth and flesh and you. *I love you I love you I love you.*

After the massacre, I am alone and with you at the same time. (I try not to think of your death as a killing. I try. I remind myself that I love you. Please remember.) I feel around in the red until I find it.

Your heart. I hold it in my hand. It's beautiful.

It's dripping, viscous and red, and I examine every inch. This is where you loved me. The machine at the center of it all, the source of every kiss, every touch, every stroke of my hair and every time you whispered my name in the dark. I'm not sure I have one.

I hold your still-beating heart, I can feel it thrumming in my hand, and I press it against my cheek, desperately, feeling the warmth fade out, feeling the beating slow and slow until it stops. It brushes against my teeth, and it slides smoothly down my throat, and now we really are one, in holy matrimony, in sickness and in health, until death do us part. I'm all yours. You're all mine. And always will be. Nothing can tear us apart.

wrong rabbit

jeremy horwich

Michael is torturing the rabbits again. We watch him from the bushes. He will be a good soul, and we tremble in excitement. He will be one with us shortly. We will add him to the roster.

The part of us that used to be Jane Franklin is shouting in our head. She was not a kill of lust, unlike with Michael. She was a necessary kill: we had not eaten for weeks. We prefer to kill those who will tend our personality to better directions.

The part of us which used to be Jane wants us to stop. Wants us even to die. Thinks we are an abomination, which we are. But if Michael enjoys torturing the rabbits, he may make us enjoy being an abomination. We long to be without remorse.

Why do we get this way? We are feeling now the murky rush inside that comes before the kill. The little doubt that makes us think about the different ways this could go wrong. But we are practiced. If Michael sees us coming he will see only a huge person whose face is ugly, contorted, the amalgamation of a hundred faces. The sky is clear, the trees are shining, Michael's back is turned, and even from here the flesh on his neck stands out, soft, sweaty, utterly exposed.

We are on the move. Michael has kitchen scissors in his hand and he is cutting the paw off one of the rabbits and laughing.

Blood is trickling down. When we absorb Michael, we wonder how fast it will take for our guilt to drip away. We are coming closer. Step on step on the rough lawn grass. We feel it between our toes like we did when we were kids. We breathe in deep to prepare. The ritual of the moment is something we cannot resist. We breathe out onto Michael's neck. We bare our teeth and lean in close. We are about to suck his soul from the inside out.

He turns suddenly. We should have known he would by the way his hairs raised on his neck but it is too late. He pushes us away, kicks us in our stomach, flees to the front door of his house. We have a chance to get him now—he is shaky, fiddling with the keys—but we cannot get up in time. We are too winded. Pain. Something we do not experience often unless it is the pain of hunger. Michael recognized a killer because he has the soul of a killer. We need him, we are even more sure of it now.

Before we go into the house we pause next to the rabbits. One of them is bound, and he is shaking and crying. We set him free. The other has a paw already gone. We raise our foot up, bring it down onto the rabbit's head and smash his brains into the scorching pavement. Even the part of us which is Jane Franklin agrees with our action. Mercy killing.

The front door of the house is no match for our strength. With our right fist we smash through. We expect to see a den of hatred, a disgusting place. The kind of place where we would live. But the house is ordinary. Michael has a painting on the wall with his wife and children. The boy looks like him. We wonder if his family knows about his tendencies. Maybe Michael's kin is of his like. Perhaps we will absorb him, too.

Light is streaming through the kitchen windows. Some of us remember when we lived in homes like this. This seems like a peaceful place, devoid of danger, but we know the truth. We know what Michael is capable of. We have been watching him for weeks. We wonder where he keeps the rabbits. That is where we will find him.

Upstairs, or downstairs? Michael has left no trace of coming or of going, and we have to watch our back. The house reminds us what we once were: the sooner this is done the better. We hope we will never feel this way again after we finish absorbing Michael's soul. Right now we feel we deserve to die. We go into the basement, because this is where molds grow and pests hide, where we can find the ugly things of the world. The things which survive. We see an empty cage, where the rabbits were kept, but Michael isn't there.

We go up to the master bedroom. We see the king bed. There are a hundred pillows on it. We know we need to move but we cannot, so much of us is thinking about the people we would cuddle with on beds, and sleep next to, and how safe we were when we sank into the mattresses. Next to the bed we see the rabbits. There are two on the floor, hiding near the dresser, petrified.

We pick one up. We will set these free, too.

Something heavy hits us in the head. The rabbits have distracted us. Michael has followed, not the other way around. His yellow teeth glow against the wall. We can do this, we are stronger. We push him down and go for the neck. It is close and the flesh is near our teeth. Michael makes a movement. It happens too fast. We sink not into Michael's neck but the body of the rabbit. We absorb its soul.

Everything is bright and frightening. The murkiness is through our whole body, in our head and in our bones. We have seen what we are feeling in a hundred victims who are us. The body-fear of prey. We are so small and a part of us cannot understand what is happening. Michael is above us, looming over, standing down. Finally the pain is over, the guilt is no longer crushing down. Some of us know we deserve this. Some of us is grateful for his victory.

in the pit of a thousand hags

antony paschos

Every night Climber shuts her eyes, she prays she won't dream again of that paganó that grabbed her brother and dragged him to the depths of the well. And this night perhaps she won't, for someone's banging on the town hall's door.

She springs up from her bunk and sidles around brooms, buckets, a tin trough and a demijohn of sulfur, all arranged neatly in the narrow storage room she squeezes herself inside to sleep. Out of the chamber, her head darts left and right like an animal trapped in the dark hallway. To her right, the town hall's door shudders on its hinges, while to her left, the Mayor clambers down the staircase holding a lantern. The foggy halo lights up his mastiff cheeks, his flaccid dewlap and a small part of his belly.

Climber knows too well, he's no saint. If he were, the policemen wouldn't come calling for him in the dead of night. It's not the first time, but usually the knocks are not urgent and Climber stays wrapped in her mats. What poor soul have they brought him to sentence to death tonight?

"Stop staring, Tásha, and open the door!"

She unbolts the lock and drags the heavy door open.

The Mayor's clogs are clapping on the planks of the floor. The smell of gasoline and garlic fill her nostrils as he nudges her aside. "What the hell do you lazy asses want tonight?"

His barrel of a body shakes as he flinches at the sight of khaki coats, bandoliers, berets, rifles and a submachine gun that should be an MP-what-was-its-number? Pénko, the Mayor's son would know, he chitters about guns all the time.

"We've come for your ass, Krásimir! Heard the news? The plains are on fire. We're throwing you Bulgarians back to your country tonight!"

The Mayor swerves back and the lantern falls from his hand and crashes on the floor, dousing its flame. He skims across the spilt oil, heading to the staircase. Climber prepares herself for the deafening blast of gunshots in confined space, but the guerillas go after the Mayor, soles crunching on the glass fragments. They rumble up the staircase, and Climber is left alone in the dark hallway, door handle in hand.

A breeze ferries in the scent of roses and jasmine and donkey dung. The moon is a clipped fingernail and the rosebush seems to stir in the front yard. The silence is thick tonight, as if the animals respect the Bulgarian curfew. No dogs barking, no cats moaning—their babylike cries summoning the image of the paganó in Climber's mind, though most legends describe the monsters' voice to be akin to a wolf's. She's holding her breath while the noises upstairs are piling up like the quilts that Pénko had once thrown over her to help her hide inside a chest while his father was searching for her.

Fuck this place; she should flee to her parents' house—abandoned since the Bulgarians murdered Mom and sent Dad away to serve as a durduváki, a digger of trenches, never to return. She could creep inside the backyard, hole up under the old wild fig-tree and—

A thump like a dropped sack of grain comes from outside, followed by a groan and the clatter of shoeless footsteps fading away fast.

Shots from upstairs echo outside; probably fired through a window.

"Got him?"

"Son of a bitch's getting away. Get that bastard. Perhaps this will make—"

A woman's cry: "Run, Pénko!"

"Shut up, bitch!" A whacking sound. As the Mayor's wife's scream twists into a howl, a small shape scurries down the staircase. He leaps the last steps and lands on the planks with a thud. Then, Pénko raises his head and eyes to Climber, who's holding the door ajar.

Two guerillas tumble down the stairs behind Pénko in a whirlwind of clatter and swears.

They gesture at Climber. "Hey! Shut that door, girl!"

Pénko's face is easy to read as he races across the hallway; the grimace of terror is timeless, reaching back to the final glance Climber's brother shot at her; his large fawn eyes that used to change color according to the source of light (gray, sea blue, emerald sometimes) glowing almost violet in the darkness of the well. Pénko is twelve years old, one year younger than her and the same age as Nikólas. The two of them used to hang together. And though he was baptized Pétros and switched his name to the Bulgarian equivalent, Climber was happy to move in the same house with him. He used to crop up out of nowhere whenever his worm of a father tried to trap her.

Pénko cries: "Tásha!"

The guerillas yell, "Shut the fucking door!"

"Fuck off," says Climber.

Pénko opens his eyes wide, then the guerillas do too. One raises his pistol. Climber hauls the door wide open.

••

Climber skitters across the town hall's front yard. The coldness of the pebbles stinging her bare feet registers in her mind only when she halts before the gate. Its door-leaves are half-closed.

"Where's Dad?" Pénko's breath is heavy.

"Fuck him."

Someone shouts: "They're getting away!"

Climber pushes the door open and the two children break into a run that seems to spur the night awake. Dim light fogs the windows of nearby houses; noises from inside their walls ring louder than their footsteps; scream, crashes, a shot. A group of guerillas comes out of a mansion—repurposed as the police station, the largest building in Kotsáki, second only to the one the Mayor commandeered to house the town hall and his family. They've nabbed a couple of bruised Bulgarians in torn uniforms.

Climber swerves into a side-street that leads to the square. At its center towers a long piece of wood parallel to the ground, supported by two poles leaning in acute angles. A dozen guerillas are herding Bulgarians towards the gallows; officers, traitors, comitadjis, the Exarchate's local priest.

Climber's knees and ankles ache—running on unshod feet is hard on joints. They should find somewhere to hide. But where? Pénko is the Mayor's son. And though his father forced her to change her name from Anastasía to Tásha after he took her in, she quickly became Bulgarian to other Greeks.

The guerillas will kill them. Or worse.

Climber slips into another alley. There's only one place she can go. Since she lost her brother, that is. It's as if her feet are answering someone's call. Nikólas' or the paganá's?

There were nights when she used to wake up from her recurring nightmare, feeling an urge to visit her old house, as if she could find Nikólas alive. Mom said the paganá came out when bloodshed was imminent, but she never explained what happened to kidnapped children; and after Nikólas was gone, she would just tell Climber her brother was dead.

Pénko claimed that his father believed the sinkhole was ancient. In the past, those who wanted to call the monsters would spill blood, and those who wanted to keep them under the earth would sacrifice children.

Well, perhaps it's time we find out.

She glances back; Pénko has fallen behind. Could he have figured out where she's leading him? She slows down until he catches up with her.

"Hey, you!"

Under the kiss of two opposite roof ledges topping the alley's entrance, two figures are standing; shapes crowned with berets, their gun barrels pointing forward, erect, and suddenly her throat gets clogged by the odor of mold and brine from the first time the Mayor unbuttoned his trousers and told her to—

"Tasha!"

Pénko's cry pulls her from her nightmare and Climber yanks his wrist and races on when a fountain of stucco as the bullet bursts into a wall; they're being shot at! Threats are shouted at them and doors clang open, spewing guerillas out. Climber's knees and ankles stop aching and her limbs are taken over by a numbness that can keep her moving forever into this labyrinth of graveled paths. *Not forever. I just need to reach the—*

A distant shot, and Pénko falls down. She leans over the boy, groping his clothes in search of blood. He has a fair share of fat under his skin.

"Don't touch me!"

"Oh, fuck yourself, will you?"

It was Climber's brother who used to swear a lot. The Mayor had once told her that he'd shut her foul mouth with his cock.

Then Pénko had barged into his office to ask him if he should prune the rosebush.

A gun rattles, but, thank Panagiá, it's coming from far away. What did Mom use to say when she and Nikólas were hollering at night? *Be quiet or you'll wake the paganá up!*

The memory is a centipede skittering up her spine and into her hair cut short—Climber was begging her mother to do it ever since Nikólas was gone, but Mom had only given in when the Nazis granted the whole valley to the Bulgarians.

Pénko gets up, rubbing gravel off his scratched feet; he's not used to running shoeless, unlike her. "Hear that?" The gun rattles again. "That's a Sten. Fucking English bastards, they've geared the guerillas up to fight us!"

Us are the Bulgarians. As if Climber gives a shit.

They start up the hill of Kotsáki until a forest of tiles spreads below them. Beyond the pitched roofs the expanse of the plains opens up, up to the serrated ridges of mount Tsal Dag, where most of the guerillas dwell. Small lights puncture the veil of darkness, as if the stars have fallen, setting the tobacco fields on fire.

"By the way, thanks." Pénko's breath hasn't slowed down.

"Guess I owe you for the quilts."

"What quilts?"

"When I hid inside that chest?"

"Oh."

"And the rosebush. And the—"

Pénko chuckles. "I thought you didn't notice."

Something rough tickles the back of Climber's palm; Pénko's hand. It's warm and muddy—sweat and soil. "I did."

"Jesus Christ, this your parents' house?"

The crumbled stone fence laden with bristly ivy, the gaping gate, the courtyard overflowing with briars and weeds, and the derelict, roofless building.

"It is."

The wind sweeping the streets carries the distant commotion. Also: voices, footsteps.

"They're coming!" Pénko's grip tightens around her hand. "We need to hide!"

Crossing the gate, Climber feels a pang of guilt, as if she's the Mayor, about to corner a victim. Well, she hasn't trapped Pénko. He's free to leave whenever he wants to.

She wades into the pool of briars scratching her ankles and snagging on her short pants that Pénko had given her. Barbed thorns and caltrops cover the rough ground, and when did the vines grow so much? Less than a year has passed since the Bulgarians' arrival, but Dad had been neglecting the garden before, after Nikólas was gone.

The voices and the crunching of boots are getting louder. Climber skirts around the house which is a toothless skull—the doors and the shutters have been ransacked. A few sickly trees jut out of the briar carpet that's extending to the backyard as well. Once, they were heavy with lemons, oranges and peaches; now they're just husks, their branches twisted like the legs of a cockroach on its back. Only one tree at the center of the backyard stands out, its foliage thriving. Its leaves have the shape of palms stretching gnarled fingers out, and Climber could swear that they sway as if a thousand hags are struggling to escape a deep pit. And the wild fig-tree does shroud a pit of sorts: the entrance to the sealed well.

"We shouldn't be here," hisses Pénko.

I should have come earlier.

A man: "Bring the bitch inside."

"In here? You nuts, comrade? Don't you know about the well?"

"Shit, man; you believe in goblins?"

"They ain't goblins, comrade, they're—"

"Let me go, please!" A woman's cry.

"Tásha! It's Yordánka!" Her past schoolmate. For years the poor girl of Bulgarian descent used to be a popular prey for Greek brats.

"Here," says one of the men and their boots now echo inside the house. Yordánka's pleas for mercy are cut off by a slap.

Pénko's stare hangs on Climber's face, his hand still clutching hers. "We have to save her."

One of the men: "Hey, heard that? Someone's in the backyard."

Climber stifles her curses. She throws off Pénko's hand, drops down and starts crawling away. Inside the house, the men keep talking, but the only thing Climber recognizes is a swooshing sound she has learned recently. The sound of clothes torn apart.

Leaves scratch Climber's back as she slips under the wild fig-tree. She stumbles upon the well's walls—a ring of marble slabs hidden inside the tree's foliage—and fumbles over carved ancient letters that she barely remembers from a time when the wild fig-tree was a small bush sprouting from the boulders shutting the well. Its slabs seem sturdy, but soon she finds a loose rock in the place of one of them. Mom said that Climber's grandparents had put it in, when they sealed this place. *Mom had also said never take it out.* She wedges her fingers in when Pénko bumps on her butt.

"So-sorry."

"Shh!"

The guerillas' grunts are cut off.

"A whisper, comrade. I swear, it came from the well."

"Please, just—"

A slap.

"Fuck, dude, if your dick's idle, let me have her first."

Cries.

Pénko opens his mouth to speak but Climber shuts it with her palm—chilly, dry lips like a toad's skin. She doesn't want to hear anything. They can't face two armed guerillas and yes, they could hide right here.

But that's not what she's here for, right? She pulls the rock out, revealing a gap between the slabs of the well.

"Tásha, what are you doing?"

"The guerillas. They could be here any time." Excuses.

"Tásha, we're not going inside the well."

Climber swallows a glob of saliva, thick and briny like snot. "I am."

The last time Climber was here she could easily pass through the walls of the well. Now, she finds it hard to fit inside the passageway; though during her months she's been working for the Mayor she's shed what little fat she had under her skin. Pénko grunts behind her—*how the hell does he not get stuck?* A tuft of soft roots brush her shoulders like the Mayor's fingertips. *Did the guerillas get that motherfucker? Hopefully.*

The hole opens up and Climber finds herself balancing on a ledge before the well: a barrel-shaped pit that seems to have shrunk. The crackle of gravel landing echoes from its bottom and it doesn't sound as deep as she remembers. Easy to reach. Just a building's story or two below.

This is stupid.

What was once a tower in her eyes, delving deep into the earth, is now merely a long, vertical marble pipe. Above her, the canopy of boulders shutting the well is a pile of rocks held together by the roots of the wild fig-tree. And below, the steps spiraling down the perimeter of the walls, large as shelves in her memory, are tiny, as if built for rats. They're leading into the thick void.

But why are her knees shaking? Panagiá, what is she doing here?

Waiting out the guerillas' uprising.

And what about Nikólas?

Nikólas is gone, you idiot. Forever.

Why did they have to go all the way down, back then?

Because her brother wouldn't let go of Mom's tales. If she only knew what they'd end up doing, she would have stuck to the legends describing paganá as goblins hacking at the Tree of Life. But one night, Mom had told them about the massacre of Old Kotsáki during World War I. Nikólas' jaw had dropped when she told them that though most blamed the Bulgarians, the corpses found the next day had no gun wounds. They were mutilated, butchered. And Climber would swear that her brother's eyes had glowed violet when he heard that some children were missing.

"Shit-shit-shit!"

A whoosh, and Pénko bumps onto Climber's back. She side-steps, groping the passageway's walls for anything to hold onto. Her other hand instinctively grabs Pénko's shirt, but the fabric stretches as he stumbles forward, tilting towards the void.

Pénko is too heavy and she lets go of his shirt. A swishing sound, a gasp, and he falls into the void crying: "Tásha!" the last, stretched syllable cut short by an abrupt thud. Climber stays still, guilt prickling her. She doesn't dare utter a word; could Pénko's fall have awakened the paganá? No, she shouldn't think like that, Pénko might be hurt, he might be—

"Tásha?"

She quiets her voice into a hiss: "Pénko?"

A muffled sob. "I can't see a thing."

"All right, I'm coming to get you. Just keep your mouth shut."

The stairs spiraling down the perimeter of the well are so narrow it seems impossible for a human to step on them without falling. But there's a reason Nikólas used to call her Climber; there was no tree or slope she hadn't defeated. She brushes off dust and gravel from the creases of her soles—shoeless months have turned them leathery. Then she sticks her chest to the wall and pads on the first step.

"I'm so scared, Tásha."

She sighs. Coming in here seems like an awful idea after all, but what will she do after she helps Pénko up the stairs? Search for her brother? Or get out, stumble upon the guerillas, and share Yordánka's fate?

She'll figure that out later. For now, she needs to get to the bottom of the well. She descends like a spider, her chest rubbing against the marble walls.

"Tásha?" Pénko sounds louder. "Tásha, there's a tunnel in here."

A shiver crawls up her spine. "Don't open the—" It wasn't a door but a round marble slab that her brother had once rolled aside. "Just don't touch anything. I'm almost there."

"All right."

Her feet start to hurt.

"But, Tásha, there's no door. I mean, there's just a round rock. And it was already open."

A mellow odor of mold, damp fur, and old rot invades Climber's nostrils. No matter how faint it is, she recognizes immediately the smell. This is the very same scent tunnel exhaled when her brother had—

"Tásha, help!" A rustle, as if Pénko's clawing on the marble walls, struggling to climb up. "Something's in there!"

Climber jumps and drops on soft ground, feet sinking slightly as if it's river silt. A pile of clothes writhes on the floor—Pénko. The round slab is pushed aside and behind it lies a gaping hole.

Her heartbeat is quaking her body, the muddy floor, the walls of the well. This is where she lost Nikólas. Could he still be alive? And behold, as if it's an answer to her thoughts, inside the hole that swallowed him, two embers light up.

"Tásha!"

She elbows Pénko hard, crouches and steps into the tunnel, just like Nikólas did a couple of years ago.

But then, two more embers appear. Two more; four, no, a dozen or more lights puncture the fabric of darkness, as if one of her moth-eaten sheets was spread against a full moon.

Climber squints. The dots are moving in pairs, getting slightly larger.

Closer. They're getting closer.

All of a sudden, her decision to come here seems naïve. She grabs Pénko, whose clothes are wet and warm—*he shed blood inside the well—no, don't think like that.* She jolts him to his feet, tugs him with one hand, gropes for the stairs with the other. She could've grasped Nikólas like this and saved him, had he not sneaked inside the tunnel. But now she has only Pénko left and she starts climbing, chest glued to the walls like a house gecko, holding him whenever he loses his balance, tugging him whenever he halts, until she reaches the opening where they got in.

She crawls out of the well, panting furiously. The wild fig-tree's leaves have turned into claws that graze her back, trying to snare her, but she doesn't stop until she jumps out of their grasp, pulling Pénko along. Then she dashes towards the house and crouches in the corner between the walls and the ground, while Pénko huddles up at her side.

There's no sound coming out of the wild fig-tree. Under their coupled breathing, a faint weeping pours out from inside the house.

Yordánka. Have the guerillas finished with her? Will they leave to join the rest of their gang?

"Tásha?"

"Shh."

Did the Bulgarians arrive to fight the guerillas back? The distant cries and cackle of gunfire don't offer any answers, but Climber would think about anything else just to keep her mind away from the memory of the well and the lights.

"Tásha, this thing inside the tunnel—"

It wasn't alone.

"Shut up!" She doesn't want to hear if Pénko saw the eyes too. She doesn't want him to utter the words; Mom used to say that words are spells, and they could turn uncertainty into truth, a truth where those lights illuminated the contours of faces that bore little resemblance to a human. She won't admit that the first creature lurking inside the tunnel wouldn't charge but was approaching cautiously, as if it wanted to see her up close with its own eyes. Those eyes that glowed—no, she won't even think of it.

"But, Tásha, this thing had violet eyes!"

Footsteps sound from inside the house and Climber feels up the rough stone walls until she finds a gap, a window, to get a glimpse inside.

Two guerillas exit through the front door and amble out to the courtyard. Climber clambers up the ledge and hops inside, then helps Pénko in.

The room bears little resemblance to what she remembers of the house where she spent her childhood years. The walls are ruined and the staircase is hidden under a pile of rocks and broken rafters.

There's a body laying in a pool of blood.

"Yordánka!" Pénko darts across the floor of packed earth.

"I need to take a piss," says one of the guerillas, pulling Climber's gaze outside, to the wild fig-tree coated in silver by the scimitar moon which seems to radiate as if it's full. But it's not, and the paganá appear only on a full moon, right? *No, stupid, it's werewolves that appear on a full moon, Mom said that paganá come out when the moon is a clipped fingernail.*

The wild fig-tree's leaves are stirring while a figure appears out of the corner of the house. The guerilla halts before a withered lemon tree; he's lanky and hunched, with bandoliers criss-crossing his torso and a submachine gun hanging from his back.

A piece of rock spurts out of the fig-tree and Climber almost gasps. It rises sharply before it lands on the guerilla's back. He turns his head—towards the tree, not Climber, thanks to Panagiá. His comrade, a small guy, crops up from the same corner. "The fuck?"

A large rock flies out of the foliage. Then, another. The first guerilla staggers towards the fence, while his comrade strides across the backyard, pistol in hand, aiming at the fig-tree. "Who's there?"

"Tásha, she's alive!" Pénko's squatting on his knees, cradling Yordánka in his lap. Climber gestures at him to shut up.

A couple of gunshots and, then, the wild fig-tree explodes in a cauliflower of broken marble. Climber crouches, shutting her eyes; and when she opens them, both guerillas are on their backs. The cloud sinks, peppering them with dust. The frail trees are caked white as if it has snowed. An eerie silence settles in, and the guerillas raise their heads toward what's left of the wild fig-tree: warped boughs and naked branches, swaying among piles of rubble hemming a gaping sinkhole.

Panagiá. The paganá are coming out!

The taller one glances at his comrade. "What was that?"

The other guy huffs. "The goblins," he hisses.

The taller guerilla brushes dust off his gun nervously.

His friend bursts into a cackle. "Shit man, you should see your face!" He laughs again. "You lapped it up?"

"Whatever." Climber would swear she heard him gulp down.

"Come on, comrade, it's probably some stupid Bulgarians, holed up in there. Had a grenade explode in their hands or something."

Something emerges from the sinkhole. It's a head. Its eyes are two pieces of amber glowing on rat-like fur. It has a stubby muzzle and pitch-black lips stretching wide like a lizard's. Its face is fringed by bristly hair, like the mane of a lion Climber had seen in the Balgárski Yug newspaper.

The first guerilla fires two crackling bursts, stitching the ground with geysers of weeds and soil. *Click-click-click*. Out of bullets. The thing has disappeared but his comrade empties his gun as well.

"Fuck this shit!" The tall guy tosses his submachine gun away and takes off for the gate, only to stumble on his friend and fall down. This time, the head springs up along with two gnarled hands grasping the sinkhole's brink.

The guerillas manage to get on their feet and bolt towards the gate, snaking between broken trees and large marble chunks.

Climber catches herself worrying for them. Indeed, no-one deserves to face this. *Yeah, right. Look what they did to Yordánka.*

Out of the hole, the monster raises its hunched body on two stubby, dog-like legs. It's shorter than Pénko as it leans forward, its two long arms hanging like an ape's—and it's only then that Climber notices it's holding a rusty cleaver.

Its black mane ripples on its hump, raining lumps of soil as it charges on all fours. It covers the last yards separating it from the guerillas in an enormous leap over a withered tree and falls on the taller one. He screeches like Yordánka did as the monster straddles his back and butchers him, its blade bobbing like the pedal of a bicycle riding fast, tearing up clothes, flesh and bones. The shorter guerilla glances back and perhaps the thought that he's armed and facing a creature as tall as a twelve-year old flits across his mind, 'cause he flinches. But then he looks beyond his comrade thrashing prone on the ground, as another creature sprouts out of the sinkhole and another and another.

Head turned back, the guerilla darts for the gate only to slam into the stone fence, and the last thing Climber sees is the paganó coiling for the next leap. Her legs move on their own, shuffling her over to Pénko. She helps him with Yordánka's body. Though the unconscious girl is light, Pénko's limping. They manage to heft their schoolmate up the rubble covering the house's staircase, when someone screeches. The guerilla? They don't pause until they get to what's left of the second floor: a narrow patch of rickety planks and a chunk of masonry with a gaping window. There, they hide.

Climber takes a peek at the backyard. Her skin shivers like the time Pénko got her out of the frozen waters of Aggítis River, into which she had jumped to escape his father. Cold rivulets of sweat trickle down her jawbone and her neck, turning lukewarm as they pool in the socket of her collarbone.

The sinkhole spews paganá by the dozen; one for each hag claw. They trample the weeds and the vines and the frail saplings, a broiling tide of dust-caked fur, bristly manes and grisly bodies carrying the flotsam of rusty blades, its edges flooding over the first guerilla and billowing towards the second. His scream is doused as the swell drowns him in a wave of spattering blood. Then the monsters spill through the gate, well up the fence and pour outside the backyard to the village streets, like a torrent filling up furrows. Climber takes a look below, at the monsters brushing against the walls of the house as they make their way out.

Could Nikólas be among them?

"Panagiá, help us," hisses Pénko and a couple of paganá jerk their heads up. Climber ducks, catching a glimpse of the glint in their eyes; then she hurries to shut Pénko's mouth with her palm. She catches him just in time to ease him down as he faints and his limbs loosen, as if they had been held together by strings that the sight of the paganá has just cut. Then she risks a quick glance below. Could she make out a couple of violet flashes?

Nothing. Is that feeling weighing her down disappointment? She sighs, and it's only now that Climber notices the absence of any vocalization. Sure, there's commotion; the combined skittering of hundreds of legs and bodies nudging each other. But there aren't any growls or howls; no breaths either. She can even get wind of the ruckus from the village; the cries of the guerillas' victims, the gunfire, the explosions lighting up the valley and the foot of mount Tsal Dag. The silence collides with the sight of the monsters, and it feels as if Climber's sinking into a nightmare.

Then, someone howls from somewhere outside the fence; perhaps a house or two away. The first one who saw the paganá? A second scream follows and a third; they multiply, dragging on or being cut short or waning into wails. The sinkhole seems to have drained its grisly load as a few last paganá shuffle towards the gate. The fires glowing in the village flicker. Shots, blasts and bursts of gunfire; screams and cries.

The commotion seems to dwindle as Climber catches sight of the last monster left in the middle of the backyard. Her longing culminates into a last hope, it materializes into a vision she pictures in her head: the paganó halting, turning towards her and piercing her with a violet stare. But the creature hurries through the gate to catch up with the rest of its pack, not sparing a glance at Climber whose eyelids suddenly weigh a ton. Her muscles empty of strength and she collapses on the floor.

• •

Climber opens her eyes to a faint sob. The moon is a silver arc in the gray sky while a dim crimson streak spills over the horizon. Pénko is nestled beside her, hair crusted with earth, layers of dried-up tears smearing his cheeks, his mouth an arched bridge between them. His clothes are stiff with mud and his feet are bloody. She mustn't look any better herself. She opens her mouth to speak, but he places his index finger across his lips to shush her. Yordánka's head is in his lap; the pool of blood below her skirt-worn-backwards has turned sticky. Climber checks Yordánka's neck with trembling fingers; it's marble-cold.

This could be me.

She lets out a sigh and Pénko points towards the wall. Only then does she notice the silence shrouding everything like morning dew. It's the short period when early-risers and late-roosters meet, but there aren't any sparrows or larks chirping, no owls hooting or bats screeching. The dogs and donkeys, all confiscated by the Bulgarians, are quiet. Dead?

Is anyone left alive in Kotsáki?

Below Climber's hideout, the weeds are withered, the trees are broken and the wild fig-tree is a shriveled bush next to the sinkhole that looks small and harmless; a common hollow in the earth, not an entrance to the abyss. Yet there's something nearby. It would look like a shepherd dog sleeping, if it wasn't for its head.

It's facing the gate with the persistence of a statue. Could it be him? Climber gulps, her saliva sour from sleep and hunger. Then she slowly lifts herself up, preparing to punctuate her presence with a cough, when Pénko grabs her arm, pulling her back down. Before she has a chance to scowl him, a second paganó crosses the gate, its rat skin stained with drying blood. It passes by the first monster and hops into the sinkhole.

A third paganó clambers down the fence while two more enter through the gate. One of them carries something in its hairy embrace. It's a baby, sleeping serenely. Climber's heart skips a beat while Pénko's nails dig into her flesh. The paganó climbs down the sinkhole.

Climber nudges Pénko off her. He falls on his knees. New tears wet his cheeks and his shoulders start shaking. He shuts his eyes while his lips recite mute prayers.

More paganá arrive, their fur smudged with red-black spatters, their hands decked in gloves of sticky blood. Some of them are soaked, as if they fell in a barrel of tar. They carry aged, rusty blades, new daggers and kitchen knives, and Climber recognizes the cleaver one of them brandishes as having been the butcher's own. A couple are holding babies, others lug unconscious children on their shoulders. More and more are coming; a rustling throng swarming the backyard.

One of them must be the paganó that had stayed behind, staring at the gate. Climber searches for a blotch of unmarred gray fur standing still against the gory river. And, Panagiá, it's there—and, how strange, her heartbeat eases off a bit. It keeps slowing down as the monstrous tide siphons down the sinkhole, and Climber lifts her gaze away, to the few ribbons of smoke unreeling from the scorched roofs. There are gray plumes smearing the plains too. Then she sees it; and the moment she does, she can hear the distant rumble of engines against the rustle of the paganá that are getting fewer.

A convoy of khaki trucks is filing up the snaking road leading to Kotsáki. Bulgarians. So much for a Greek uprising. What will they find upon their arrival? Will there be anyone left? What will they think? And who gives a fuck?

"Are they gone?" whispers Pénko. Two paganá disappear inside the sinkhole. Only one is left behind. The rumble becomes louder and a few cries are heard.

Pénko's eyes bulge. "The Bulgarians! We're saved!"

He springs up and looks outside only to fall back again.

The lone paganó has raised its head towards them.

The air feels frigid, it wraps Climber like a garment soaked in the Aggítis River. Her vision blurs; Pénko, Yordánka's body, the chunk of masonry hiding them, the dusty planks, the fading slice of the moon, everything starts spinning. And as all colors meld into the gray of the dim morning sky, two dots stand still at the cyclone's center; two eyes the color of violet.

Pénko rummages in his pockets and plucks out a clasp knife, but Climber nods at him to put it back. She stretches up, revealing herself to the monster. Their gazes lock, and as a brush of carmine glows in the horizon, its eyes take an emerald tint—and what is this wet glint damping the fur on its cheek?

"Wha-what are you doing, Tásha?"

It's her turn to bring an index finger across her lips and shush him. Then, she turns her back to the wall, to Pénko and Yordánka's corpse. There's a reason she's called Climber, and she scales down the pile covering the house's staircase nimbly. She crosses the ground floor and stands in a gap in the wall, facing outside. The paganó is waiting for her and if there was a human tear in the fur on its cheek, it is now gone.

Climber steps out of the house.

the hole in the sky

andrew kozma

The hole in the sky is only visible at night. I believe this is why other people don't believe it exists, even my closest friends. There is an angle I can never quite explain, how you have to tilt your head or squint your eyes just right to see it. Even in person, I have trouble. I'll point directly at the hole. I'll hold my phone's camera up so it's visible on the screen, the hole boxed in, and even then, whoever I'm with will stare in frustration, and either end up laughing at my obvious dumb joke or storming off without a word. In neither case do they ever confirm they've seen the hole.

So I stopped talking about the hole in the sky. I stopped going out at night. When darkness comes, I close my blinds tight. Even then, I feel the urge to glance through the slats at the large swath of nothing blotting out familiar stars, so I bought blackout curtains and nailed the edges to the window frame. My girlfriend Elise joked about what would happen if there was a fire: How would we get out? I said I wasn't sure I wanted to, with the hole out there and all.

That was two weeks ago and the last conversation we had, but we're still dating. We never broke it off and, like Newton said, whatever is in motion stays in motion unless something stops it, and nothing stopped us—and if we never talk to confirm what's stopped, then we clearly haven't stopped. I'm afraid of picking up the phone. I'm afraid of calling Elise. I'm afraid whatever is on the other side of that hole reached down to snatch her up on her way home after our "fight" and what person has ever lived who is eager to confirm their own worst fear?

I am not an astronomer. Hell, I even hate astrology. The sky is only ever something the horizon forced on me, like a mother pulling a raincoat over the shoulders of her child when all the child wants is to feel the rain on their skin. Except I don't want to feel the starlight raining down. Everything in the universe is staring and outside, in the open, they're all staring at me. They always have been. But now there is proof.

I am not an astronomer. What I am is an editor of pictures. The government hires me to erase what they don't want seen, and while that sounds sinister, in practice it involves replacing a politician's hangovered bloat with smooth, untroubled skin or removing the photo-bombing protester behind the ribbon-cutting at the opening of the new detention hostel. I am an expert at this: removing what was there so effectively there's no trace of what's missing.

But no matter how perfect my work is, I can always see the ghost of what's been taken. I've won awards for disappearing flaws, all those unwanted elements of our lives. Supermodels with a blemish on their face find that in my touched-up picture they can't even pinpoint where the hideous fault was supposed to be. While in interviews I describe my work as a kind of illusion, Elise explained it as hypnosis. I didn't practice deception, but persuasion.

That's why the hole in the sky bothers me. Even during the day, a person I pass on the street will point up in wonder at a phalanx of geese flying over, and I'll instinctively glance up as well. And my eyes will catch on the void that's not there behind the birds. The hole I can only clearly see at night stands out like a painted-over stain during the day, just like that small imperfection on your living room wall that never goes away no matter how many coats of paint you use, an ineradicable shine to it like a grease spot. There's a sort of radiation from the hole I can feel on my skin, the way you can tell where the sun is with your eyes closed, the way a person across a crowded room is watching you, even though every time you look over at them to confront their rude stare, they're pointedly looking away.

The hole in the sky never looks away.

Elise told me I was imagining it when the flowers turned towards the hole in the sky. Sure, the hole was in the general path of the sun as it skittered overhead, but I could tell the flowers were facing the hole, hungry for what only it could give them. People, too, gradually shifted to face the hole as I talked to them, as they shuffled from foot to foot, hemming and hawing their way through an uncomfortable answer. The neighbor's pack of rescue dogs howled up at the hole on moonless nights. Their eyes reflected something dark. Their bared teeth looked pitted with rot.

One time I saw the waning moon, just a pared fingernail of a moon, pass behind that hole in the sky and, as it did, something else appeared. The part of the moon that was in shadow bubbled black as tar and the sun-touched bit gleamed with the piercing brightness of a plasma torch. The border between the light and the dark blurred like a camera going in and out of focus. And whatever the moon was, whatever it had become, it was too close. A plane flying into George Bush Intercontinental passed behind the moon. What emerged on the other side was not the same. And all the next week, there was a spurt of people dying throughout the city, their bodies rotting before the ambulance even arrived. Instead of spontaneous combustion, spontaneous decomposition.

I was paid to edit those pictures so they'd be palatable on the local news, once the epidemic was too big to be contained. The bodies had collapsed, but the features were still clear, like an ice sculpture at the end of the day. Their skin bubbled, the queasy flow of it evident even as a still image. I returned the skin to smoothness, gave it back shape. I edited the harsh sodium glare from their expressionless eyes. Eventually, they returned to being bodies, to being the quiet dead.

I have not heard from Elise, but I know she is out there living her life. In her apartment or at her job or visiting her mother's condo or in her car. She's in her car, the engine is running and, though she usually has music from her phone piped through the speakers, the only sound is the hiss of hot air pushing hungrily through the vents eager for cold skin to latch onto. Her phone is on the seat beside her and she wants to call me, wants to call desperately, but can't quite bring herself to.

Something taps on the window—the start of a storm or a curious cop—but when she looks over, nothing's there. And in that moment, she thinks of me clearly. A nothing—there. Right there. In the passenger seat where I should be as we fight the urge to make out instead of going to our favorite restaurant to eat dinner on the porch under the night sky.

I open the front door and let the cold air in. There are clouds tonight, lit up by the lights of the city. Around the house, there are enough trees that their spindly limbs act like a sieve for the sky, but I can still see it. I mean, I can feel it, a pocket of gravity up above that draws my eyes to it. I force myself to look away, scanning the street. Just a few cars, their shattered windows gemming the sidewalk. There is a spot where Elise always parked to avoid the thieves, out of the way in the entrance to the park, bathed in bright streetlights. A short five-minute walk. That's all it would be.

My eyes to the ground, I can feel the hole in the sky drawing me out from the house. I should just shut the door and be done with it. But in the glow bouncing off the low-hanging clouds, I'm a shadow of myself, as though there's a second body eager to burst forth from inside me. And when I step out onto the porch, there's a slight resistance holding me back, as if part of me is being left behind. It breaks easily, no more than a momentary hesitation, and soon I'm under the frail arms of the winter-shocked trees.

Elise always made me walk ahead of her when we hiked through the woods. She couldn't stand the feeling of spiderwebs catching against her skin, convinced that it meant the spiders were jumping ship, too, finding new homes in her clothes and hair, and she'd wake in the middle of the night cocooned in silk.

It was a fear not even worth mentioning. I kept it a secret all the times, at home, I'd pick spiders off myself to drown them in the sink. There was no need for her to know.

I walk the path through the trees we always walked together. Originally, it was something the feral cats created, the small path littered with the decomposing corpses of squirrels and birds. Then runners began to take the path since it was safer than the sidewalk, and the path stretched its maw wide, brush bunching up along the sides, and letting us feel safe from that wilderness on either side. Now, the only corpses we saw on the sides of the path were the occasional bodies of starved cats caught in catch-and-release traps someone placed ages ago and then forgot about.

Elise never wanted to get involved with those traps. And I couldn't really blame her. The cats inside were yowling balls of terror. And someone placed the traps, right, so someone would be back to take care of the cats. I never tried to convince her otherwise. There's physical editing—the blacking out of text or the removal of an image—and there's mental editing, learning to unsee what it is you so clearly see and never wanted to. The problem with being an editor is that I've trained my entire life to notice what other people don't, and make sure that other people never do.

The hole in the sky won't let me un-notice it, even if I wanted to. I don't want to, because even if I could stop myself from sensing it up there, that wouldn't stop it from being up there. And I'd prefer to be aware. I'd prefer to know that something is watching me through that hole—or that the hole itself is watching me—and that, on this cold, still night, I can feel it reaching down towards me and I can't help hurrying, like a mouse trying to escape an owl. The hole in the sky grows, becoming heavier above me, maybe not reaching down at all, but lowering itself, getting closer, coming to my level to, finally, say hi.

The path empties into a tiny parking lot of six spaces and four streetlamps, all of them brightly shining on Elise's car. The car is dusted with leaves and debris, rain over the past weeks having pasted the dirt onto the car instead of washing it clean. There's something like steam on the inside of the car windows. One tire is flat, the vehicle canted towards the ground like it's sick. Under the harsh lighting, the red paint looks scabbed over.

I walk over to the driver's side door. The hole in the sky drops before me like a window and I'd have to reach through it to grab the door handle. I can't look away, however much I want to, however much my heart races and my lungs hurt and my ears burn against my phone, waiting for Elise to pick up, to tell me she's safe at home, to say, "Hello?"

ABOUT THE CONTRIBUTORS

Tiffany Meuret is a writer of monsters and twisted fairy tales. When not reading or writing, she is usually binge-watching comfortable sitcoms from her childhood or telling her kids to put on their shoes for the tenth time. She lives in sunny Arizona with her two kids, two chihuahuas, gecko, and tortoise.

Keith Rosson is the author of the novels *The Devil by Name, Fever House, Smoke City, Road Seven,* and *The Mercy of the Tide* as well as the Shirley Jackson Award–winning story collection *Folk Songs for Trauma Surgeons.* His short fiction has appeared in *Southwest Review, Nightmare, Cream City Review, PANK, Redivider, December,* and more. He lives in Portland, Oregon.

Erin Brown is a Black, neurodivergent author of horror, fabulist, and fantasy fiction. She has been published in *Fantasy Magazine, FIYAH Magazine, The Deadlands, Midnight and Indigo,* the *Los Suelos CA Interactive Anthology, 3Elements Literary Revue,* and *Eye to the Telescope.* She also has work in the anthology *It Was All a Dream,* and forthcoming in *Fabulist Magazine* and *Zooscape Magazine.* Erin was shortlisted for Brave New Weird 2022.

A.M. Muffaz is a Malaysian author based in San Francisco. Her first book, *Finches,* came out in 2021 from Vernacular Books and was nominated for a World Fantasy Award in 2022.

P.G. Streeter lives in Maryland, where he teaches high school English and philosophy. He knows the dreams and nightmares his two brilliant sons conjure will someday surpass his own.

Josh Hanson is the author of the novels *Calliope Street* and *King's Hill* and the novella *The Woodcutters*. He is a teacher and a graduate of University of Montana MFA program. His previous work has appeared or is forthcoming in various anthologies as well as *The Deeps, The HorrorZine, Siren's Call, The Chamber, BlackPetals*, and others.

Claire Rudy Foster is a queer, nonbinary trans author who lives in Portland, Oregon. Foster's debut novel *The Rain Artist* was awarded the Gold Medal in Science Fiction by the Foreword INDIES. They are also the author of short story collections *Shine of the Ever* and *I've Never Done This Before*; and bestselling non-fiction books with recovery advocate Ryan Hampton.

Keith LaFountaine is a writer from Vermont and an HWA member. His short fiction has appeared in *The Vanishing Point Magazine, Tales to Terrify*, and *Bewildering Stories*. Other work can be found on his website and his social media pages.

Ethan Warren is the author of *The Cinema of Paul Thomas Anderson: American Apocrypha*, published by Columbia University Press. He is currently working on his second book for the press, to be titled *When I Paint My Masterpiece: Bob Dylan on Film*. Ethan is a member of the Boston Society of Film Critics, and lives on the south shore of Boston with his wife and their children.

Rajiv Moté is a software engineering director and writer (SFWA, Codex Writers) living in Chicago with his wife, daughter, and a tiny dog. His stories can be found in *Beneath Ceaseless Skies, Diabolical Plots, Year's Best Hardcore Horror Vol. 5*, and other publications.

K.M. Parker writes speculative fiction, espectially fantasy, sci-fi and horror. In addition to writing, he loves to travel, and tries to visit some far-off location every year. His other interests include video games, tabletop gaming, and historical fencing. He lives in Florida with his wife and three dogs.

Taylor Dye is the author of five novels, including the most recent fourth book within the world of *The Intermediaries, The Intermediaries: Patriot Day*. Dye is also the author of *Fear Into Darkness*, the first book in the Trustice Jeffries superhero saga, along with numerous short stories, the latest including "Sunrise," "The Lighthouse At Land's Edge," and "Luca's Peaceful Place."

Joey R. Poole is the author of *I Have Always Been Here Before* (Cowboy Jamboree Press 2020) and editor of the cryptid anthology *It Came from the Swamp* (Malarkey Books 2022). "Forever" is an excerpt from *Buried*, a crime fiction/vampire mashup novel-in-progress. Another excerpt was published in *Shotgun Honey*'s *At the Edge of Darkness*, an anthology of stories that blur the lines between horror and crime fiction. He lives and writes in Florence, South Carolina. Follow his SubStack newsletter *Bookmark Planet* for writing news and musings on his quest to read books from all over the globe.

Chloe N. Clark is the author of *Patterns of Orbit, Collective Gravities*, and more.

Kayli Scholz is the author of *Saint Grit* (Ghoulish Books, 2023), *Black Rain Season* (Curious Corvid Publishing, 2024), and *Yeehaw Junction* (Moonstruck Books, 2025). She lives and writes in the wilds of Florida, currently working on a new novel. She loves cryptids, all things horrors, and her cats.

Kate Leone is an author, editor, activist, and teacher who lives with her wife in central Massachusetts.

Kayla Whittle currently works with medical journals. She has published stories in *Luna Station Quarterly* and The Colored Lens. She also has stories in the anthologies *Beyond the Veil* (Ghost Orchid Press), *Eros & Thanatos* (Quill & Crow Publishing House), *Of Fate & Fury* (Silver Wheel Press), and *Of Ink and Paper* (Nightshade Publishing), and has pieces included in *Dangerous Waters: Deadly Women of the Sea, Seers & Sibyls*, and *Daughter of Sarpedon: A Tempered Tales Collection*, all out by Brigids Gate Press. Her work has also been featured on Flash Fiction Podcast. Much of her writing features queer representation, often including ace or sapphic characters. Most often she can be found on Instagram @caughtbetweenthepages or on Twitter @kaylawhitwrites. When not writing, she's usually busy reading or planning her next Disney vacation. She currently resides in New Jersey.

R. Lazarus is a writer and poet. When not writing, R. Lazarus can be found at witching hour, when the moon shines like a flashlight from the pitch black Pittsburgh sky.

Jeremy Horwich lives and writes in Chicago, Illinois.

Antony Paschos lives in Athens, Greece. His fiction appears or is forthcoming in *Interzone*, *Galaxy's Edge*, *ZNB Presents*, *Metaphorosis* and other magazines.

Andrew Kozma is a writer and poet. His fiction has been published in *Escape Pod*, *ergot*, *The Dread Machine*, and *Analog*. His book of poems, *City of Regret* (Zone 3 Press, 2007), won the Zone 3 First Book Award, and his second poetry book, *Orphanotrophia*, was published in 2021 by Cobalt Press.

F.Z. Boda prefers to remain anonymous.